POOF!

BY: M. LEE PRESCOTT

Published by Mt. Hope Press

Copyright 2017, Mt. Hope Press

Cover design by Ashley Lopez, E-book Formatting Fairies

For my dear family, always.

CHAPTER 1

A warm June evening found me sitting on my deck, chatting with my sister, Annie, and my spry, eighty something father. Dad and I are finally on speaking terms after many years' estrangement. My name is Ricky Steele. A year earlier, I fell into a late-life career as a private investigator and have found that the job suits me, except when my fifty something body gets bruised and battered in the line of duty.

The last night of Annie's visit, I'm already dreading her departure. "Please stay till next week. Why do you live so far away? My niece and nephew barely know me and now Hannah's about to make me a great-aunt!"

Her bright green eyes twinkled. "You could come and visit us, sister dear. The last time you came to California was for Hannah's graduation. Flights are cheap. Dad and Rita came out three times last year."

"I work, or haven't you noticed? Even cheap is expensive for me."

Dad tipped his wineglass in my direction. "My darling, a ticket is only a phone call away. My treat."

"Thanks, Dad, but I've got it covered. Maybe in the fall." I sighed. It wasn't the expense. I just hate to leave home.

Dad stood. "Sorry, girls, got to run. Oh, almost forgot. Ricky, Rita would like to speak with you. It's important. She'd like to take you both to lunch both before Annie leaves. The Club, one tomorrow?"

I opened my mouth to protest, but my sainted sister beat me to it. "Dad, we were thinking of a beach day before my flight."

"Aren't you flying in the evening?"

She nodded.

"Then there's plenty of time. Please, Ricky, do this for me."

Annie smiled sweetly. "What about a late breakfast? That way we could still hit the beach in the early afternoon?"

"Let me give her a call."

He pulled out his cell phone and stepped inside the house, closing the door behind him.

I paced the deck, watching the setting sun, crimson and sparkling over the bay. "What the hell does she want?" My stepmother and I were not exactly buddies. Annie shrugged, stepping to the railing and gazing out at boats returning home for the night. "Probably wants to invite herself for a visit. Rita does love the beach and her shopping. She's always trying to spot celebs."

Annie lives in Laguna Beach. Her house has survived fires, earthquakes and mudslides. Dale, her husband, is a skilled carpenter and the house has expanded over the years. It now rambles over much of their hillside property.

The slider opened. "All set. She'll meet you at the Grille at 11. You can choose between the brunch or lunch menu."

After giving us each a hug and kiss, he departed. We sat in companionable silence for a while. Finally, I said, "Do you really want a beach day tomorrow?"

"Not especially."

We laughed, refilled our wine, and settled in to watch the stars come out. "We could call Vinnie, if you want some excitement, this being your last night and all?"

"Anything's fine with me. I'm fine right here, hanging out with my big sister. We've been so busy this trip. How are you really, Ricky?"

"You know me. Never down for long. My Whitley buddies are coming for our annual sleepover week after next. That's always fun. My jaw hurts from laughing by the time they depart. I know they'd love to see you."

"I cannot stay two more weeks. Who's coming?"

"Katie, Lolly and Alice," I said, referring to my three dearest boarding school friends.

"Lucky you. You've managed to maintain so many of your old friendships. I envy that."

"They keep me sane, as a swinging single."

"About that, Ricky. Any new beaus?"

"Uh-oh, just remembered, my cupboards are pretty bare."

"So I've noticed. I also notice you've changed the subject."

"My point is we'll want to venture out for dinner."

"Fine with me. Now, come on, I haven't heard a word about your love life this trip."

I snorted. "What's that?"

"What about the hunky Jay Harp?"

"Yes, and doesn't he know it? We had some spectacular moments, but he's gone. Commitment-phobic. Always trolling, always keeping a few of us stringing along. He did bring Wilda into my life, though. She's saved my ass more than once."

I referred to the six foot-three Amazon who is my associate and bodyguard. When I start a case, I call Wilda and she makes it her business to have my back. Ninety percent of the time, I never know she's there, but she does keep a desk in my office and has been known to hang out from time to time.

"I know. I want to meet her!"

"I'm sorry. Bummer that she's out of town. Gets back tomorrow night, which is yet another reason for you to change your ticket and stay longer."

"I can't. I wish I could. I'll just have to meet Wilda next trip, unless you want to bring her to Laguna?"

I shook my head. "I love the woman, but it's not that kind of relationship. What do you think Rita wants?"

Annie shrugged.

Our stepmother, Rita, is my age. When she married our father nearly twenty-five years ago, she brought along two kids, Cassie and Matthew. Until her offspring went off to college, Rita mostly pretended that Annie and I did not exist. I believe she assumes that she and her offspring will inherit Dad's considerable estate. I have no idea of the terms of Dad's will, and don't care, but if I had to guess, Rita may be disappointed. Philanthropy is very important to our father.

CHAPTER 2

Annie doesn't love the Rainbow like I do, but she agreed to dinner there. We strolled arm in arm, enjoying the warm evening and easy sisterly talk, finishing each other's sentences. As we stepped into the bar, we spied my neighbor Vinnie sitting a table with a stranger. In contrast to Vinnie's dark eyes, wavy black hair and solid build, the other man was leaner, medium build, salt-and-pepper hair, deep blue eyes. Gorgeous in a mechanic, hardhat kind of way. Both men were filthy so I assumed they had just come off a job. Like me, Vinnie works a variety of odd jobs. I suspect some of them are not entirely legal.

Vinnie waved, bedroom eyes beckoning. "Hey, ladies, come join us."

Annie is happily married, but she has always had a huge crush on the dark-haired Adonis who lives next door to me. *Who didn't?*

"Can we?" she whispered.

I gave her a look. "Hold on."

As Vinnie's eyes drew my sister like a magnet, I dragged her to the bar to place our orders. We each ordered salads, chorizo rolls, and Coles River Lagers on draft, then sashayed over to join the guys.

Both men stood as we approached. "Rick, Annie, this is Charlie Bowen. He just moved in up the street. Has a triple lot. Pretty incredible. We've been workin' on his house all day."

Bowen shook our hands, his firm grasp lingering, deep blue eyes locked on mine. "Wonderful to meet your both. Vin tells me this is a great neighborhood."

"None better," I said. The instant attraction to yet another bad boy made my knees wobble. *Get a grip, Steele!* "What house is yours?"

Bowen grinned. "The one that had columns until yesterday."

"You bought the Parthenon?" I said, referring to a huge white monstrosity one street over.

He laughed. "Guilty as charged. I'm transforming it into a seaside cottage."

"Good luck with that. Now that you mention it, we did hear a crash or two yesterday. Was that the fall of the columns?"

"Probably. Please sit."

Vinnie held out a chair for Annie. "Once you're settled, Ricky and I'll have a block party and introduce you around. Our neighbors on the other side are king and queen of cocktails and canapés." He referred to octogenarians, Maddie and Fulty Stockman. Both were deaf as posts, but inveterate party animals.

"Sounds great," Bowen said. He tipped his beer in my direction, giving me a hundred-watt smile as he sat next to Annie.

The interplay between Mr. Gorgeous and me had not been lost on my eagle-eyed sister. "So, do you have a family, Mr. Bowen?" she asked.

"Charlie, please. I have three kids, all grown."

"So, it'll just be you and your wife in that huge house?"

He grinned. "I'm single. How about you ladies?"

Annie actually batted her eyelashes. "Married, two kids. I'm visiting from California, Laguna Beach."

"Ricky's single," Vinnie said, winking at me, then leaning back in his chair, smiling like the Cheshire Cat.

I wanted to strangle them both. *Here we go, headed into yet another discussion of my pathetic love life! Not on my watch!*

I sat up sharply. "So, what do you do, Charlie? Are you a carpenter?"

If Vinnie grinned any wider, his face would break in two. His new buddy was no doubt already knee-deep in one of his nefarious schemes.

"I'm semiretired. How 'bout you?"

"I'm a private investigator, among other things."

His face registered genuine shock. "Wow, I'd never have guessed that. Have you been in business for a long time?"

"A few years. I have a bunch of other part-time jobs. And if you're going to make cracks about me being a bit long in the tooth for this line of work, you can save them. I've heard them all."

"Actually, I was going to say that's fascinating. My youngest daughter, Michaela, thinks she wants a career change and is interested in doing some kind of investigative work. Her college roommate works for Homeland Security and loves her job."

"Well, I'm a far cry from those guys. For one thing, they are highly trained. They're also armed to the teeth at all times and I hate guns."

"But you have one," Annie said coyly.

Jack, the owner, delivered our food and another round of beers. The guys were having the clam boil with chorizo rolls on the side. After Jack's departure, Annie continued, ignoring my glares. "Ricky's had so many career changes, I've lost count. She's a very gifted artist and writer."

"A true Renaissance woman," Bowen said.

"Okay, okay, can we talk about someone else now?"

I directed my full attention to my warm chorizo roll dripping with grease and oh, so delicious. We spent the rest of the meal chatting about home renovations. It sounded like Bowen's would be going on for many months. Nosy Annie made several more attempts to learn about his work, but the blue-eyed grease monkey managed to deflect every inquiry. From whatever occupation he was semiretired, it must have been a lucrative one.

Finally, Annie and I rose to say our goodbyes, both of us slightly tipsy.

"Nice to meet you, Charlie," she said, gazing pointedly at me.

"Yes, welcome to the neighborhood. See you around," I said. "I don't have a card with me, but Vinnie can give you my numbers. Tell your daughter to give me a call."

Bowen stood up. "Count on it. Maybe we could grab a drink or coffee? Lunch or dinner sometime?"

"I'm kind of busy at the moment."

Vinnie grinned, patting his companion on the shoulder. "Ignore her, Charlie. She's never busy and she's not seeing anyone."

I gave him my iciest glare.

"Come on, Rick. You guys'd have fun," Vinnie said.

Bowen stood. "I really would love you to meet Michaela. I know she'd love to talk to you."

"Anytime," I said. "Now, we really have to go." I nodded at him, carefully avoiding direct eye contact, gave Vinnie one final glare, and nudged Annie along.

I was still fuming on the walk home. "I could kill Vinnie. Trust him to reveal the pathetic status of my love life to every Tom, Dick and Harry."

"Maybe it's time to change that, sister dear. Charlie's interested."

"No, he isn't, and besides, I have absolutely no interest in getting involved with a biker, mechanic or whatever. I've had enough heartache."

"How do you know he's s biker?"

"Well, let's see, the grungy clothes and days-old beard?"

"They've been working on his house. Of course they're dirty and grungy! He seemed really smart to me. Cute, too."

"Trust me, I know the type. I'm ready for bed and I do not want to hear another word about Mr. Cute!"

CHAPTER 3

Annie packed her bags and left them by the door for the six-thirty flight to Los Angeles. After a beach walk, we headed to Dad's country club. Lack of traffic and miscalculations on my part meant that we arrived at the Grille at ten thirty. With time to spare, we wandered along the first fairway, staying well out of the line of fire as foursomes teed off and went their merry way. A verdant green oasis, the Club lay at the outskirts of Spindle City and was home to all manner of wildlife. As we strolled along, woodchucks lumbered into the tall grass, birds darted all around us, and several gray foxes skirted the edge of the cart path.

We spent many childhood days here, taking golf and tennis lessons, which, in my case, came to naught. Annie was a decent tennis player and had been an excellent young golfer, but I was hopeless. Soon after our mother's suicide, I put my foot down and that signaled the end of my country club life.

Shortly before eleven, we walked onto the terrace adjacent to the Club's informal dining space, the Grille, where we found Rita waiting. After hugs and air kisses all around, we settled down with our menus. Annie and I had dressed in capris and summer tops, my top a muted Hawaiian, Annie's a mauve, sleeveless linen. Her straight flaxen hair was tied back in a loose ponytail, mine curly and unruly as usual. Slender and fit, Rita wore a sleeveless summer dress with a lime-green and pink floral pattern, matching lime-green sandals and gobs of gold on her wrist and neck. Her shoulder-length auburn hair, expertly dyed, was swept back with a slim tortoise headband, and her perfectly manicured nails were a pale pink.

"What'll you have ladies? My treat, of course."

Annie and I ordered sandwiches, Rita a small cob salad. The waitress poured iced tea for all three of us and departed. We spent a few minutes staring aimlessly around the dining room before she cleared her throat.

"Girls, thank you so much for doing this. I know Annie's last day is precious. Ricky, I have a delicate matter. I thought of calling, but then decided we should speak in person."

"What's wrong? Dad isn't sick, is he?"

Rita waved her hand. "Oh, no, dear, nothing like that! You know your father. He's healthy as a horse."

More silence. I waited, watching her twist her napkin round her index finger. Annie and I exchanged glances, not sure what to say.

"Would it be okay if I jumped right in?"

"Of course, please do," I said, setting down my glass and giving her a reassuring smile.

"It's Cassandra. She would be furious with me for speaking to you, but I feel I have to do something."

I nodded, trying to remember when I'd last seen her daughter, Cassie. Christmas, maybe? In her late twenties now, she was a younger version of her mom, red-haired, slender and lovely.

"She's been with her boyfriend, Josh, for two years now. Josh Peabody. I can't remember, have you met him?"

"Tall, dark, athletic?"

She nodded.

"I think we met around the holidays. A real cutie."

"Well, that cutie has broken my Cassie's heart. Left her place one day last week and has cut off all communication. He left a terse note saying he'd be in touch, but he hasn't called, texted, emailed, nothing. She's frantic. Hasn't the faintest idea what she did or why he's gone. His roommate has nothing to say, or if he does, he's not telling Cassie. "

"Rita, hi." The voice was familiar, the association not a pleasant one.

Jill Carlson, wife of my ex-husband Robbo Carlson popped into view and the two women exchanged air kisses.

"Jill, hello, dear," Rita said, clearly not pleased at the interruption.

Jill then stepped back, arms spread, as if she meant to swoop in for a group hug. Her straight blond hair was tied back and she appeared to have just stepped off the tennis court. Her white tennis skirt and sleeveless aqua singlet showed every curve and sinew of her perfectly sculpted body. "The Steele sisters, what a surprise!"

"Hello," I said, rising to shake her hand. Annie followed suit. "How's life in the fast lane?"

She laughed. "Fast. Brackett and Pearson is growing by leaps and bounds. You probably heard, I made partner five years ago, so the load has shifted a bit. Let the young ones do the drudge work."

One of my stepmother's best friends, Jill worked for a law firm specializing in patent and corporate cases, as well as international trade and acquisitions. I had not heard that she made partner, nor was I terribly impressed. Robbo and I met and married in law school. Less than a year later, we divorced due to his affair with Jill. I dropped out of school and our paths diverged.

"What are you up to these days, Rick? Someone told me you are some kind of investigator."

I nodded. "Private investigator, yes."

"How in the world did you get into that line of work?" Jill gazed from one to another of us, presumably waiting for an invitation to sit down and catch up on the last three decades. Rita had other ideas. "Sweetie, let's have a drink this afternoon. On the terrace, five-ish? Are you free?"

"Should be. I'm tied up for a few hours, but by then I—"

"Terrific. I'll finish my golf lesson, shower and meet you there."

Recognizing dismissal when she saw it, Jill forced a smile. "Ladies, wonderful to see you. Rita, later." Turning heel, she disappeared.

Annie reached over and squeezed my hand. Her green eyes studied me, knowing full well the pain Rob Carlson's betrayal had caused all those years ago. I winked at her. Jill had done me a huge favor. Robbo and I would have made each other miserable.

Oblivious, Rita waved her hand at the waitress, requesting iced tea refills. Full glasses and our meals in front of us, she resumed her tale. "My poor Cassie is frantic and I have to do something."

Annie gave me a glance. "Has she tried to contact him or his family?"

"No…yes…I don't know. She won't talk to me about it except to break down and cry. She can't work. She isn't eating. We've got to do something."

"We?" Reluctantly, I set down my incredibly delicious portabella baguette.

"Yes, we or you, specifically, my dear. I would like to hire you."

"To?"

"To find Josh, of course."

"Rita, I'm happy to help, but this sounds more like a lover's quarrel. Don't you think you should let them work things out?"

"Ordinarily, I would say yes, but something isn't right and your father agrees. Josh and Cassie had been talking about marriage, children, buying a house, the whole bit. They were looking at a real cute place in Freetown, right on the lake. Josh isn't the flibbertigibbet type. He's been completely dependable, until now. In fact, he's been a steadying influence on Cassie. She's almost finished her nursing coursework. She's done so well with his support and encouragement."

"Did they quarrel?" Annie asked.

"No, nothing like that. Ricky, please say you'll help. Just a quick peek around. Maybe you could quietly chat with his roommate? Josh's parents? His coworkers? See if anyone knows where he is?"

"So, Cassie and Josh weren't living together?"

"No, she loves her little condo and he has a roommate. He spends many nights at her place, but they were waiting until they found the right place to move in together. Occasionally, they stay at his apartment, I think, but they're usually her condo."

"The roommate is?"

"Jimmy Chen. He roomed with Josh at Harvard. Jimmy works for Meridian Imports. Not sure what he does for them, but they hired Josh last year to do some teaching for them. Josh teaches English to their employees, I believe. He also teaches GED classes. Both are part-time jobs, but Josh is a trust fund baby so money is not an issue."

I exchanged looks with Annie. "Rita, I don't know how I can help. If he's really missing, maybe you should go to the police?" I could help, but I had a bad feeling about the whole thing and my gut was screaming *no!*

She grasped my wrist. "Please! Just a quick peek. That's all I'm asking. It would mean so much to me, and your father. He's worried sick, too."

I sincerely doubted our father was worried sick, but heard myself agree to do a little poking around, for my usual fee. She immediately pulled out a check already made out for twenty-five hundred dollars, which was a thousand dollars more than my usual retainer. Stranger things had happened, but this was right up there.

After a tearful goodbye at the airport, I left Annie and returned home to whip up a quick salad and take a twenty-minute walk. Afterward, dishes washed and stacked, I went to my computer to see what I could learn about Meridian Imports. I still believed Josh's disappearance was a lovers' spat, but it couldn't hurt to gather a little background before paying a visit to Jimmy Chen, the roommate.

Meridian's website was colorful, but cryptic. The home page displayed a montage of their products—scarves, purses and jewelry. I was no expert, but the stuff looked like designer knockoffs. There were links to "About Us," which was a bland paragraph touting their fair-trade practices and quality imports. Other links brought me to vague descriptions about their employee benefits and the "Contact Us" link, which listed the web address, no names, and no staff directory. Zilch.

I was just about to click back to the home page when I noticed tiny text in the corner, in two-point, microscopic font. Squinting, I read "Represented by Brackett and Pearson" with an address and phone number. Now that was odd. Why put that on a company website? It appeared that I would be speaking to Jill Carlson again in the near future whether I liked it or not.

CHAPTER 4

Monday morning, I walked into the living room and gazed out to find fog lapping at my deck, the river completed obscured. I fed Beaky, my cat, who was meowing piteously by her food bag, then pulled on shorts, sneakers and an old gray tee shirt and headed out. My legs felt great so as soon as I reached the beach, I broke into a slow jog—the only kind I do these days. I decided to go a mile out, then circle around. As I made the turn at the boat landing, the sun was wrestling its way through the clouds. As the fog lifted, I looked up to spy a German-shepherd-type dog, more like a horse dog, headed straight for me. Now, I love dogs, even horse dogs, but how was I to know if the Hound of the Baskervilles meant to rip me to shreds or pass by without a glance? I braced myself as he leapt and we both went down.

"Carter, Carter! Here boy!"

I knew that voice, but could not see beyond the massive head. The friendly beast licked my face, clouding my eyes with slobber.

"Hey, he likes you!"

Charlie Bowen grabbed hold of Carter's collar, pulled him back, then reached out a hand to me. Flabbergasted, I rolled away and righted myself, aware that my tee shirt was scrunched up around my neck, revealing my torn gray sports bra. My hair, a rat's nest, was now caked with sand.

I yanked down the shirt, brushed my legs off and fluffed my hair, endeavoring to pull myself together. "Mr. Bowen, we meet again."

A beautiful, open smile played round his deep blue eyes. "Charlie, please. Good morning. Is this your usual running time?"

"I don't have a usual time."

"Too bad or I'd try to coordinate."

"Besides, you really can't call what I do running."

"Me neither. You *could* just agree to have dinner with me?"

"Is this your usual modus operandi when you move into a neighborhood?"

"Hard to say. I've moved around a lot the past few decades. Have never had a neighborhood."

"I'm kind of busy this week."

He nodded, eyes studying me. He had an unnerving gaze, warm and intimate.

"Okay if I keep asking?"

His question took me aback and I stared dumbly for several minutes before replying. "I guess that'd be okay."

"Great, and thanks. Michaela told me you guys spoke."

I nodded. "She sounds terrific. Happy to have her come see us."

"She's keyed."

"We can always use an extra pair of hands, particularly someone who's organized."

He grinned. "Carter and I are just heading down the beach. Wanna take a second jog or walk?"

"I can't. I have work." I bent down to pet the horse dog, who immediately began licking my hand, arm, leg, any exposed part of me. "This is quite a beast. What kind is he?"

"German shepherd mix. Maybe some Great Dane or Lab. He's a rescue. Found him as a pup when I was traveling."

"He's a sweetheart," I said as Carter's eyes rolled back in ecstasy. "Did you name him?"

"For Jimmy Carter."

"He's my favorite president, at least in my lifetime."

"Mine, too," he said quietly, eyes studying me.

"Well, I've gotta go and I'll bet Carter's eager to get moving."

"I don't know. He seems pretty taken with you."

"Well, see you guys around."

"We'll make sure of it, won't we boy? Have a good day, Ms. Steele."

"Ricky, please."

"Okay, then no Mr. Bowen either, deal?"

"Deal," I said, smiling in spite of the warning bells sounding in my head. There was either a fierce attraction going on here, or I was so sex-deprived I'd lost all reason. "Nice to see you," I added and was rewarded by another wide grin and more slobber from you know who.

CHAPTER 5

Once home, I showered, dressed in jeans and a clean tee shirt, ate a bowl of muesli, then headed out. Rita had given me the address for Josh and Jimmy's apartment. It was in a small restored three-decker in one of the city's neighborhoods currently under siege by wealthy young Boston professionals. The new train made their commute doable and real estate was a tenth of what they'd pay in Boston.

I parked and took the steps to the front door. The outer door was unlocked so I stepped in and found the buzzer labeled Chen. I was about the press the button when a woman in a suit, briefcase in her hand, pushed open the inner door. I nodded and slipped in as if I knew where I was going. They'd done a pretty good job with renovations, and had preserved all the dark trim and crown molding. Someone took good care of this building. The small lobby was clean and well lit. An elevator at the far end stood open, but I decided to take the stairs.

Street sounds were muffled as I climbed. By the time I reached the third floor, I was enveloped in silence. I took a deep breath and knocked. Scuffling from within told me someone was at home. After several minutes the door opened and a short, slender Asian man, mid-thirties, appeared. "Yeah?"

"I'm looking for Josh Peabody. Is he in?"

"Who wants to know?"

"My name's Ricky Steele. I'm a private investigator. Are you Jimmy Chen?"

"Not that it's any of your goddamn business, but yeah, I'm Jimmy."

So friendly. I'm sure to get lots of helpful information from this charmer. It appeared that he had just stepped out of the shower. He wore a purple velour bathrobe trimmed in satin and had a towel wrapped round his neck. His feet were bare.

"Might I come in for a minute? I'm happy to wait if you were in the middle of dressing."

"Suit yourself, but only for a minute. I've gotta get to work."

"Is Josh here?" I asked, following him into an attractive living room finished with buttery leather sofas and what appeared to be antiques or decent reproductions. A thick kilim rug covered the wide pine floor and the off-white window treatments looked expensive.

He plopped down on one of the sofas, waving his hand inviting me to sit on the other. "Nope."

"Do you know where he is?"

"Nope."

"But you live and work together. Isn't that strange?"

"Nope."

"Mr. Chen."

"Jimmy, please."

"Jimmy, when was the last time you saw Josh?"

He paused to do a ridiculous pantomime of thinking. He knew damn well when he'd last seen his roommate, but he sure as hell wasn't telling me. He shrugged. "Maybe a couple of days ago."

"Could you possibly be a little more specific?"

"Aren't you a little old for this line of work? What're you, on the dark side of forty?"

I silently counted to twenty, taking slow deep breaths. "If I had a dime for every time someone has said that to me. Now, about Josh?" I certainly wasn't about to tell him he'd paid me a compliment in underestimating my age.

"He told me he needed to get out of town for a couple of days. Maybe to his parents' house in Windy Harbor or somewhere else?"

"Somewhere else?"

He shrugged. "I'm his roommate, not his babysitter."

"You both work for Meridian Imports, do you not?"

"I work for Meridian. Josh teaches the GED and English classes. There are a bunch of sites around the city. The company sponsors them as a community service."

"Well, if he went away, who's teaching his classes?"

"They have subs."

"So, you don't teach?"

He laughed. "Not my thing."

"Well, what is your thing?"

"I'm in sales."

"What can you tell me about Meridian?"

"Successful import company, very civic-minded. They believe in giving back to the community."

"Is Josh paid for his teaching?"

He nodded. "But don't ask me how much cause that's not my area. Now, I hate to break up this little tête-à-tête, but I've gotta get to work."

"Who owns Meridian?"

"I said, that's enough, lady." He stood and went to the door, opening it wide, and waving his arm. "Out you go. Go play private eye someplace else."

I pulled out one of my cards and handed it to him. "If you see or hear from Josh, please ask him to be in touch." The second he closed the door, my card would be rocketing into the trash.

CHAPTER 6

I headed to my office and met Wilda on the stairs. "Were you following me?" I asked.

"A dodgy neighborhood."

"Yeah, well I'm going to a dodgier one this afternoon," I said, telling her about Meridian and the warehouse that housed the school and who knew what else.

"Okay," she said. "Good to know."

Wilda was a woman of few words. Today she was dressed in her uniform, black skinny jeans, tee shirt that appeared to have been painted on and strappy sandals with five-inch heels. Her long dark hair was pulled back in a braid that reached the middle of her back. A black baseball cap hung from the strap of her giant black leather purse. She followed me into the office and sat at a desk we had recently poached from one of the vacant offices. My office is on the third floor of a cavernous mill building. Outlets shops occupy the first floor, the second floor is mostly vacant, and there are seven tenants including me on the third floor. A few of us are steady tenants, but some of the offices turn over regularly. They often leave good stuff behind. We wait a decent interval to see if someone will collect the remaining items, then assume they are free for the picking.

"We might be getting a part-time employee," I said. "She's actually volunteering to learn about the business. Since Janice ran out on me, this place has gone to wrack and ruin."

Wilda harrumphed, the sound deep, throaty.

"Well, greater wrack and ruin, then. Anyway, if this kid comes, maybe I'll put her to work filing, typing, that kind of stuff. What'dya think?"

"Your business."

"Think we could fit another small desk or table in here?"

"Probably."

"I think there are still a few pieces of furniture in the architect's office. Maybe I'll check later."

Wilda rose. "I'll do it."

Five minutes later she returned carrying an oak desk and chair. The desk was small, but it looked as if it weighed at least a hundred pounds. Wilda was carrying it like a beach chair. I shook my head and pointed to the corner. "That'll be the best place. Did you see any lighting fixtures?"

"No, but I'll take a look."

Five minutes later, she was back, an attractive desk lamp with green glass shade in one hand and a wrought iron floor lamp with a woven shade in the other.

"Wow, classy," I said, taking the items. I placed the lamp on our new desk and the floor lamp beside the table holding the coffeepot and microwave. "All in all, a fine day's scrounge," I said, grinning at my enigmatic associate.

She nodded and I headed into my office, the Inner Sanctum, we called it. It had a bank of windows, my desk and a few filing cabinets. Unlike the outer office, it was a colossal mess. Too discouraged to sit down, I did an about-face. "Hey, Wilda, I'm gonna get some lunch. Want anything?"

"Thanks, I'm good."

That was another thing about Wilda. She ate only healthy food. She never cheated. Ever.

I walked down to Dino's, just around the corner. It's a typical greasy spoon, but his soups are relatively healthy. I ordered a cup of minestrone soup and a chicken salad sandwich and felt healthier already. Dino brought me a huge iced tea without my asking. I guess I'm just that predictable.

"Hey Rick, how's tricks? No Dino Deluxe today?" He referred to the diner's specialty, an enormous burger with lettuce, tomato, onions and mushrooms, smothered in his special sauce. I dreamed about Dino Deluxes.

"Not that hungry, I guess."

"When are you not hungry?"

"When I'm trying to eat healthy, if you must know."

"Oh, boy, who's the lucky guy?" Dino grinned and slipped into the booth opposite me. About my age, maybe a hair older or younger, he had a full head of salt-and-pepper hair and a compact, muscular frame, that belied the twelve-plus hours he worked in the diner surrounded by greasy, artery-clogging food. I suspect Lois, his wife, keeps his eating in check. They make terrific salads, though I seldom order them.

Lois was behind the counter, clearly miffed that her husband had taken a break when the diner was packed. A short, attractive redhead, she also appeared to steer clear of burgers and fries. I waved and she smiled, frowning at Dino.

"There's no guy. I just felt like chicken salad today."

"Yeah, and I'm the Easter Bunny."

"Ha ha. There's no guy, I'm just trying to change my diet a bit."

"Feeling your age, huh?"

"I think that's your cue. Lois is not happy."

He turned and Lois beckoned. "Gotta go, Rick. Bring your guy in soon."

I scowled, taking a bite of my delicious chicken salad. My expression was lost on Dino, who was now behind the counter receiving a tongue-lashing. *Way to go, Lois!*

CHAPTER 7

After lunch, I forced myself to sit in my office and spent an hour or so cleaning and organizing. Wilda had disappeared. Finally, satisfied that I could function at my desk, I did a computer search for the Peabodys in Windy Harbor. I quickly found an address and phone for a Jacob Peabody. They lived at the Bluffs, an exclusive gated community of million-dollar homes just south of the Harbor where my father and Rita have a second home. I dialed the number and a woman answered.

"Mrs. Peabody?"

"Mrs. Peabody is not at home. Can I take a message?"

"How about Mr. Peabody or their son, Josh?"

"To whom am I speaking?"

I took a deep breath and decided honesty might be the best policy. "Ricky Steele. I'm a private investigator looking into Josh's disappearance."

Dead silence.

"Hello, are you still there?"

"To my knowledge, Josh has not disappeared."

"So, you've seen him recently, Ms....?"

"Listen, Ms. Steele, I'm only the housekeeper and I don't feel comfortable answering your questions."

"When will Mrs. Peabody be home?"

"I'm not sure. She's a busy lady. If you leave a message, I'll make sure she gets it."

Yeah, right. I gave the nameless housekeeper my phone number and rang off, reasonably certain I would not be hearing from the busy Mrs. Peabody. Clearly, a trip to the Bluffs would be necessary.

I grabbed my bag and headed out. I had the address of Meridian and decided to cruise by on my way home. Vinnie, Maddie, Fulty and I were having dinner together, and as usual, I had not picked up my contribution—wine and dessert. I stopped at a package store around the corner, then intended to stop at the Creamery for several cartons of ice cream after my drive by the Meridian warehouse.

I turned down Water Street, passing several mill buildings on either side, some renovated, others abandoned, windows broken or boarded up. I checked the address and found the building halfway down the block. A small sign, Meridian Imports, hung over a door at the far end of the building. I pulled over and hopped out. The street was deserted and quiet for a weekday.

I decided the best approach would be to start with the front door. I pushed the buzzer and a woman's voice said, "Meridian, can I help you?"

"Hello, my name is Ricky Steele. I wanted to find out a little about Meridian's products. Is there anyone in who could speak with me?"

She buzzed me in. "Come on up. Turn right at the top of the stairs. We're in the first office."

A short wisp of a woman in cherry-red suit, black stilettos and a crisp white blouse waited at the top of the stairs. She appeared to be in her twenties, maybe early thirties, her dark red hair pulled back in a tight chignon. "Hello, welcome to Meridian. I'm Nancy. follow me."

She led me into a light-filled office with three desks, one of which was occupied by another woman of similar vintage, her wardrobe more subdued. Brown slacks, beige top and flats. Her straight blond shoulder-length hair was tucked behind her large ears. She looked up from her computer screen, gave me a slight nod, then returned to her work.

Nancy waved in her colleague's direction. "That's Betty. She's our computer whiz." I would have liked a long chat with Betty, but instead followed Nancy to her desk and sat as she pulled out several catalogs. "Are you buying for a retail store?"

"Yes," I said, flashing her my best shopkeeper smile. "I own the Driftwood Boutique in Windy Harbor. Do you know it?"

With a glance at Betty, she said, "No, I don't think so. It sounds nice, though." *How could she since it was as phony as my retailer persona?* I had no doubt that Betty was googling the Driftwood Boutique and would soon discover that I was lying. I had to work fast before Nancy booted me out of the building. "Would Mr. Pullman or Mr. Winter be in today?"

"I afraid not."

Betty squinted, studying her computer screen.

"When could I catch them?"

"I'm sorry, I couldn't say. They keep their own appointment books. Perhaps if you leave a message?"

Yeah, right, she looks really sorry. "That's okay. I'll come back on another day." Out of the corner of my eye, I caught Betty's slight nod to her colleague. *I am busted.*

"Ms. Steele, we're very busy today and very selective about our clients. I'm going to have to get back to you about your shop. Would you have a card? I could have someone to call you?"

"Gee, my cards are in my other purse, but here's my cell, if you think we can do business." As I scribbled my number on a slip of paper and handed it to her, I decided to take a chance. "One more question. One of your employees, a family friend, Josh Peabody, recommended Meridian to me. Would Josh be around today?"

"I'm sorry, who?"

Betty turned away and began rustling papers.

"His roommate, Jimmy Chen, who I believe also works for Meridian, thought I might find him here?"

"I'm sorry, Ms. Steele, but I have absolutely no idea who either of those people are. Betty, have you heard of them?"

Betty shook her head.

"What about the school? Is it in session?"

"School? I think you must have us mistaken for some other place. We really are very busy today."

My head was spinning and I felt as if I'd stepped down the Rabbit Hole. "So sorry. I'd better check my facts next time. I apologize for bothering you."

A smile plastered on my face, I said goodbye. Assuming the building had more than one entrance, I decided to circle the block. I found three more doors, all locked. As I completed my circuit, and rounded the mill's north side, I nearly ran into a bicyclist. Looking up, I was shocked to find Charlie Bowen staring down at me.

"Oh, my God! You could have killed me."

"Sorry, you came out of nowhere."

"Are you following me?"

He laughed. "And why would I do that?"

Why indeed? I realized I must look like a deranged idiot. "I don't know. What are you doing riding your bike so far from home?"

"Commuting."

"Oh?"

Charlie cleaned up well. In biking shorts and a tee shirt, he looked smokin' hot. He had shaved and his face wasn't covered with soot and sawdust. His beautiful blue eyes held mine and I found it impossible to look away.

"I volunteer at the clinic around the corner."

"What do you do at the clinic?"

"Oh, you know, whatever they need. Clean up, trash, anything. What are you doing down here?"

I regarded him for a minute, then said, "I'm looking for someone. Don't s'pose you've ever run into a Josh Peabody?"

"Name doesn't sound familiar. Does he live around here?"

"No, but he's gone missing and I've been asked to find him. He works in this building." I pointed to the small sign. "Do you know anything about the company that owns this building? Meridian Imports?"

"Not a thing, but don't forget, I've only been here for a short time. I can ask around if you like."

"That would be really helpful, thanks."

"Wanna grab coffee or something?"

"I can't. I've got plans."

"Yeah, I should probably get going too."

"See ya."

"Still hoping for that dinner," he said, giving me one of his gorgeous smiles.

"You an optimist, aren't you?"

"Always. See you round the neighborhood."

I waved as he hopped on his bike. I knew I should invite him for dinner. Vinnie, Maddie and Fulty would be delighted, but those alarm bells were ringing. He was much too cute. Heartbreak would certainly be right around the corner. *Besides, he can't come to dinner—he's headed to work. The late shift by the looks of it. So, I was right to say nothing.*

Chapter 8

"Remember, Fulty, not much gin and lots of lime." My shouted words fell on deaf ears as our host mixed a second round of gin and tonics. Vinnie and I were manning the grill.

"What's that, doll?" Fulty said as he filled my glass three quarters full of Tanqueray before adding ice cubes and a splash of tonic. Except for his hearing, Fulty was spry and sharp as a tack. Always tanned from May to September, he wore his signature shorts and Hawaiian shirt tonight. Maddie, his wife, was a little wisp of a thing. She had always reminded me of the actress Jessica Tandy. Tonight, she was dressed in a plaid housecoat that she had no doubt purchased in the 1940s.

Vinnie grinned, flipping the bluefish. "Leave him be, Rick. You can pour it over the porch rail and add tonic while he's not looking,"

"But it's such a waste."

"They have cases of the stuff."

Maddie tottered over with a plate of deviled eggs and we both took one. On her second martini, she was already three sheets to the wind.

"Thanks, Mad," I said. "Want me to take those?"

"I'm gonna sit awhile and let you youngsters pass, okay?"

"Perfect," I said, smiling as I took the plate from her. She took a seat in one of their rockers and raised her glass in toast.

"She's a goner," Vinnie whispered, although he could have shouted. They were both deaf as posts. Fulty had perfected the art of the one-sided conversation. Fortunately, he was bright, funny and interesting. A great reader and inveterate consumer of news programs as long as they had closed-captioning, he had strong, well-informed opinions on almost any subject.

"Here you go, kids," Fulty said, handing us our drinks. "I think I'll join my bride if you've got this covered."

"No prob, Fult," Vinnie said, nodding and gesturing to get his point across.

When the Stockmans were settled, I turned back to the grill. "Saw your buddy today."

"Who's that?"

"Charlie Bowen."

"Oh, yeah? You two been out, then? I invited him tonight, but he was busy."

"You what?"

"Charlie's really interested in you, you know."

"No, he isn't. He just wants me to take his daughter on as an apprentice. Can you believe it? After all the money they shelled out for medical school, the kid wants to be a PI."

"Sounds like you and law school."

"Ha ha."

"Well, the daughter thing is bullshit, Rick. He's definitely interested."

"How do you know? You've known him for what, a week?"

"I know people, Rick, and I know chemistry when I see it. If you two aren't hot for each other, then no one is."

"Don't be ridiculous."

"He's a great guy. Much better than the bums you usually drag home."

"Can we please change the subject?"

"Sure thing, babe, but Charlie's good people. Trust me."

"Same subject."

"Just give him a chance, will ya?"

"Thank you, Yenta. Now can we *please* talk about something else?"

"Our hosts are takin' a little catnap, so shoot."

"Have you ever heard of Meridian Imports?"

"Don't think so. Why?"

"I've been asked to locate one of their employees, Josh Peabody. He's my stepsister's boyfriend."

"Lovers' spat?"

"Maybe, but I promised her mother I'd look for him."

"Isn't your stepmother some kind of whack job?"

I chuckled. Vinnie had heard too many stories about Rita and my father. "Sort of…maybe…but she seems genuinely concerned. My stepsister is a basket case, apparently."

"What does she say?"

"Nothing, cause Mommy Dearest doesn't want Cassie to know she hired me."

"What's the guy do at this Meridian place?"

"He teaches English to non-native speakers."

"So, Meridian is a school?"

"Not really. They apparently run the classes as a community service. They're some kind of import company. Their building's on Water Street. I checked out their website and wasn't terribly impressed with their wares."

"If they're importing a bunch of crap, they're probably smuggling something. Most of those places are. Want me to ask around?"

"Would you? That'd be great. Thanks."

"Fish is ready. Should we let sleeping dogs lie?"

"No, they'd be so disappointed. I'll wake 'em while you load up the plates."

CHAPTER 9

I allowed myself a slow start to my day in deference to a pounding headache, no doubt thanks to Fulty's cocktail mixing wizardry. It was close to ten when I hopped in the car for the twenty-minute drive to Windy Harbor. I had not heard from Josh Peabody's mom—no surprise there—so I decided popping in might be best. I called and asked Rita to alert the Bluffs gatekeeper that I was coming. A guest tag awaited me as I arrived and was waved in by the friendly gatekeeper.

Armed with the house and street number, I made a show of heading toward my father's place, which was on the development's north side, then veered south once I was out of sight. After several wrong turns, I found Heron Way and headed down to number twenty-two, which was on the ocean side. I rounded a corner and there it was—the Magic Kingdom. My jaw dropped as I stared up at the massive white castle on the bluff, complete with turrets, about a hundred chimneys and a slate roof that stretched for miles in either direction. I half expected Sleeping Beauty to poke her head out of one of the turret windows.

Fortunately, the gate to the home's twenty-foot-high iron fence stood open. One less hurdle for yours truly. A cherry-red Mercedes coupe was parked in the circular drive, but no one appeared to be about. I parked on the street, walked up the drive to the front door, and rang the bell. After several minutes, the door swung open and a middle-aged woman in a pencil skirt, creamy silk blouse and sensible heels appeared. Her hair was cut short, obviously dyed coppery brown. In my opinion, the hair color and shirt, bunched up around at her ample waist, were not becoming, but what I know about fashion could be written on the head of a pin.

"Can I help you?"

I recognized her voice—the housekeeper.

"Is Mrs. Peabody at home?"

"You're that private investigator, aren't you? How did you get in? The gateman didn't ring."

"No, I was in the neighborhood visiting so I thought I'd stop by."

"Well, people don't just stop by at the Bluffs. Residents pay a great deal of money to protect their privacy. I'll have to ask you to leave, now."

"Just five minutes. I'd think Mrs. Peabody would want to know that her son is safe."

"How do you know she doesn't? Now, please, Ms. Steele, if you go now, I won't call the guard to escort you out."

A door opened at the far end of the vestibule. "Isabel, is everything alright?"

"Yes, Madam, someone asking for directions."

I recognized that it was now or never. "Mrs. Peabody, please. Just five minutes of your time. It's about Josh!"

"Why, of all the nerve," Isabel said, moving to close the door. I put my foot out, stopping her.

"How dare you! I'm calling the gatehouse," she said, eyes blazing.

"That's enough, Izzie. Let her in."

The housekeeper opened the door and stepped back. A tall, slender ash blonde in sage-green linen slacks and a sleeveless blouse stood regarding me, one hand on her hip, the other holding a stack of papers. She appeared to be in her mid-fifties, hair and makeup understated and elegant. "Come through, Ms. Steele."

She led the way into a small sitting room with an attached greenhouse, beyond which a large expanse of lawn stretched to the bluffs and the ocean beyond. "Sit, please."

She took one of two armchairs covered in muted floral silk and I its match.

"I'm sorry to barge in, but I've been asked to look into Josh's disappearance and I would assume that you'd want to know his whereabouts as well."

She gave me a quizzical look. "Who says Josh is missing?"

"His girlfriend, Cassie."

"Well, that's absurd. Maybe they've had a spat. She's a little high strung. Do you know her?"

"She's my stepsister," I said.

"Oh?"

"My stepmother, Rita Steele, asked me to try to locate Josh. Cassie's been worried sick."

"You're Ralston's daughter?"

"Yes."

"I knew your mother. She nannied for my family one summer. My siblings and I loved her."

"Are you a Wallace?" I asked.

"Yes, Lillian Wallace. I was so sorry to hear about her death."

"That was a very long time ago."

"Yes, "she said, nodding.

"What can you tell me about Josh? Has he been in touch?"

"Yesterday, as a matter of fact."

"Is he home?"

"No, he called. He didn't say where he was, just asked a favor. We didn't speak long."

"What was the favor, if you don't mind my asking?"

"I do," she said, lips pursed.

"Did he seem agitated or upset?"

"Not in the slightest."

"Did the favor have anything to do with his teaching at the Meridian school?"

"No."

"Was he trying to relocate?"

She sighed, perhaps weary of the block and parry. "Not that he said. I guess it won't hurt for me to tell you that he wanted money transferred from his trust account."

"Is that unusual?"

"Actually, yes. Josh is very frugal and his monthly living allowance more than covers his expenses. I had no problem arranging the transfer. It's his money. He said he'd lost the folder where he keeps all his pass codes so he asked me to go to the bank and make the transfer for him."

"Was it a large sum?" I asked.

"Not for us, but you'd probably think so."

I waited, taking deep breaths.

"He wanted fifty thousand dollars," she said.

"And you weren't concerned?"

"No, he said he was buying a car and some furnishings for his apartment."

Can the woman really be as cool, calm and collected as she sounds? I glanced down at her hands. She had a lacy handkerchief between her fingers and had wound it into a tight knot. Hmm…

"Does Josh ever talk with you about his work at Meridian Imports?"

"Never heard of it. Josh has been teaching English to little Asian children, I believe."

"Yes, but the school is funded by Meridian and it operates out of their building. Do you know what days Josh works?"

"No, but we don't talk that often. He hasn't been home for a while, maybe since he brought Cassandra down to have dinner at the Club. We wanted to meet her and nagged so much that he finally gave in. This was before he started teaching. I believe his friend Jimmy got him the job."

"Jimmy Chen?"

"Yes. My husband and I were not pleased."

"About the apartment or Jimmy Chen?"

"Both. It was a dark, dismal place and Jimmy has always been very cocky and full of himself."

I couldn't disagree with that. "Well, thank you, Mrs. Peabody. I apologize again for barging in."

She walked me out. As I opened the door, she grabbed hold of my arm, green eyes pleading. "Please let us know if he's in some kind of trouble." The mask had fallen and she looked scared to death.

"Do you think he's in trouble, then?"

"No, of course not. We just never liked Jimmy, that's all."

There was more to this story, but I wasn't going to hear it from Lillian Peabody. "Well, thanks again. I'll be in touch if anything comes up."

When I drove by the gatehouse, dropping the pass into a wooden box, I half expected the guard to leap out and grab me by the collar. Instead, he waved and pushed the button to open the gate.

As I drove back to the city, my cell phone rang. "Hey, girlfriend, you ready?" I recognized the voice. It was my childhood friend, Bunny Stark, now a successful realtor and travel agent.

"Hey, Bun, what's up?"

"Tonight?"

"What about it?"

"Geez, Ricky, you didn't forget, did you? The clambake?"

"Oh, my God, Bun, it's Tuesday, isn't it?"

"Yes, and don't tell me you've forgotten."

"Just kidding. I'm looking forward to it. You know how I love clambakes and your company!"

"Humph, I'll pick you up at five sharp."

"Casual dress, right?"

"Well, some of us might glam up a little, but the way you eat, I'd suggest old jeans and a bib."

"Ha ha. See you then."

CHAPTER 10

The clambake was at Francis Farm, home of the best clambakes in the world. A benefit for a local dog shelter, this event always drew a large crowd. An animal lover who doted on her three French bulldogs, Bunny was on their board, and our attendance at the bake was an annual ritual.

True to her promise to glam up, Bunny sported midnight-blue, satiny capris and a matching floral top that hugged every curve. Her blond hair was swept up in a chignon and sparkling, dangly turquoise earrings completed the ensemble. Bunny was at least three inches shorter than me, but you'd never know it. Her white platform sandals added a good five inches. I wore a nicer pair of jeans and a beaded jersey top. While not up to Bunny's standards, the outfit made me feel wanton and sexy, though God knows why I cared. I'd be covered with butter and clam juice by the end of the night. I eschewed my usual sneakers for espadrilles and wore silver dangly earrings of which Bunny approved.

"You look hot tonight, Rick. Maybe we'll spot some prospects."

Bunny was between men at the moment, not a happy place for her. As soon as we arrived, she flew off to say hello to her board buddies. She asked me to come along, but I declined and headed to the bar instead. A Dos Equis in hand, I was strolling across the grass towards one of the dining tents when a voice called from behind me.

"Ricky, hey!"

I turned to spy Robbo Carlson, my ex-husband, hurrying up, waving a Miller Light.

"Hello, Bob."

"You here alone?"

"I'm with Bunny. I've never seen you at this before."

"My new boss is on the board and made it clear to all of us that we should purchase tickets."

"Where's Jill?"

"She has a business dinner so I'm flying solo tonight."

I hate that expression, "flying solo," but forced a smile. "So how are things?"

"Great, never better. Kids doing well, work hectic. How 'bout you?"

"Same ole, same ole."

"You look terrific, as always, Ricky. Not a day over forty."

"Thanks, you too." In truth, he looked about seventy. His complexion pallid, sandy hair thinning with a comb-over that was not fooling anyone.

"Hey, look, that's my boss now," he said. "Want to meet him?"

"Thanks, maybe later. You go, I'm good. Gotta find Bunny."

As he hurried off to kowtow, my eyes scanned the crowd. I had not yet spotted Bunny when a familiar face popped into my line of vision. Charlie Bowen stood under the tent, chatting with a small group, a young woman at his side. *Hmm, Mr. Gorgeous does get around.* As I ogled, he looked away from his companions and caught my eye, nodded, then turned back to the conversation.

"Hello, my long-lost friend! I was hoping you'd be here."

Her voice behind me was accompanied by a hug and I turned to embrace my dear friend, Karen Spencer Harp. "Hey, Karrie, what a surprise!"

"Are you with someone?"

"Bunny."

"Wonderful, I'd love to see her." Another childhood friend, Karrie, along with Bunny and me were founding members of the Maple Tree Club. This was when city neighborhoods were still safe for children to roam freely and erect make-shift clubhouses in backyards and vacant lots.

"How 'bout you?"

She blushed, eyeing me coyly. "Actually, I have someone I'd like you to meet."

"A man?"

Her eyes lit up.

"You didn't tell me you were seeing someone!"

"Well, since we haven't spoken for what, six months, that could be why."

"Is it serious?"

"Kind of," she said, flashing a shit-eater grin.

"Oh, Karrie, I'm so happy for you! I'd love to meet him."

"Ted's over there with his golf buddies. Do you believe it, I'm dating a golfer? My mom's in heaven and Ron's probably rolling in his grave." Her ultra-liberal, activist husband had been murdered the previous year. Among his many crusades in their small town had been land conversation and preserving farmland from development, including golf courses.

"Is he from the Harbor?"

She nodded. "He moved there eight months ago. He's retired."

"Is he cute?"

"I think so, but I'll let you be the judge."

"Is he good to you?"

"Very."

"Oh, Karrie, I'm so pleased."

"And what about you, my friend? I understand from Jay that you guys aren't seeing each other anymore?"

"You know your brother-in-law."

"Yes, I'm afraid I do. I was hoping he'd found his home with you. It's time for Jay to get off the swinging singles train."

"Jay Harp? Never." I laughed, but truth be told, our breakup had been devastating. I had opened up and allowed Jay Harp to break my heart for the second time. *Never again.*

"He's always asking if I've heard from you."

As we stood talking, arm in arm, I kept my eye on Charlie Bowen. From time to time, he glanced in my direction, but for the most part, he seemed engrossed in conversation.

"Karrie, before we meet your sweetheart, see that guy over there in the blue shirt, with his arm around the young woman?"

"Dr. Bowen, you mean?"

"Charlie Bowen. I don't think he's a doctor."

"If you're talking about the drop-dead gorgeous man next to the tent pole, that's Dr. Charlie Bowen. Ted and I met him at a benefit last month. Do you know him?"

"He just moved into my neighborhood."

"Lucky you. He's the most eligible bachelor you're gonna find here or anywhere else, for that matter. Uh-oh, isn't that Bunny bearing down on him?"

As we watched, Bunny practically threw herself at Charlie. Unfazed, his expression remained open and friendly as they began chatting.

"Let's go meet your golfer, shall we?"

"I want to know about Charlie Bowen," she said as we began strolling toward the far end of the tent.

"There's nothing to tell. He moved into the neighborhood. Vinnie's been helping him renovate his house and he introduced us."

"And?"

"And nothing. He asked me out, but I've managed to deflect him so far."

"Are you crazy?"

"No, just cautious. I'm still healing from Jay."

"Jay's a jerk. This guy's solid as a rock. He's pretty major, Rick. Been all over the world on humanitarian missions. He's some kind of infectious disease specialist. One of the top in his field, as I understand it."

"That doesn't necessarily make him a reliable partner, boyfriend, whatever."

"Well, I'd certainly give him a test drive. Ah, here's my Ted," she said, touching the arm of a tall, slender man with snowy-white hair and a chiseled, handsome face. As he gazed at Karrie, his eyes filled with obvious affection. He wore a green golf shirt and khakis, a navy sweater draped around his shoulders.

"Ted, I'd like you to meet my dear friend, Ricky Steele. Ricky, this is Ted Foster."

He shook my hand, grip firm. "Hello, Ricky. Karen's told me so much about you."

And yet I've just learned about you, I thought, smiling up at him. "Ted, so glad to meet you."

He drew Karen closer, arm circling her shoulder. "Can you sit with Karrie and me?"

"I fear my friend Bunny has us at the other end of the tent, but we can rendezvous at the bar from time to time."

We chatted for a few minutes until the bell sounded, signaling that chowder and clam fritters were being served. "Well, I'd better find Bunny. I'll look for you two later. So nice to meet you, Ted. Karrie, let's get together soon, okay?"

"Definitely. We'll make a plan."

I hurried off to find Bunny. As I reached the tent, I spied her seated beside a younger guy, the chair on her other side empty. I was just making my way through the crowd when he grabbed hold of my arm.

"Ricky, hi."

"Well, Dr. Bowen, you do get around," I said, a trifle more flippantly than I should have.

If he heard my "Dr. Bowen" comment, he didn't acknowledge it. "You look sensational."

"Thanks. You don't look so bad yourself."

He touched my arm again, sending warmth from my head to my toes. "Listen, I know you're heading to eat, but can I bring Michaela over at some point?"

"Of course. I'm sitting over there," I said, pointing to Bunny.

"Yes, I met Ms. Stark. She's a force of nature."

"That's putting it mildly. Feel free to pop over anytime. I guarantee Bunny's wooing the gentleman on her right so I'll have plenty of time to chat."

He smiled and let me go. It took every fiber of my being not to fling myself at him. *Get a grip, Steele!*

As I reached the table, Bunny patted the empty seat beside her. "Well, well, Ms. Mysterious. I met your Dr. Bowen. He's hot."

"He is not my Dr. Bowen. I hardly know him and didn't even know he *was* a doctor till tonight."

"Who cares. He's single, gorgeous and he's interested. Why the minute I mentioned I was here with you, I could tell by his baby blues that he's hot for *you.*"

"Is not!"

At that moment, our chowder and clam cakes arrived and I decided to put Dr. Bowen and his hotness aside to enjoy my very favorite meal in the world. An hour later, the remnants of the clambake lay all around us. An embarrassing mountain of clam shells sat in front of me, three times as many as anyone else's at the table. Several people had commented on how much I must like clams, but I was too busy wolfing them down to reply. Just as my lobster was set before me, Bunny elbowed me and I turned to spy Charlie approaching, a dark-haired young woman at his side.

"Hi again. Is this a good time?" he said, grinning as he surveyed the carnage on the table.

"Of course," I said, grabbing several packets of moist towelettes, tearing them open and vainly attempting to clean my hands as I stood.

"Ricky, this is my daughter Michaela."

The short, dark-haired woman with a pixie haircut and turned-up nose extended her hand. "Hello, Ms. Steele, so glad to meet you in person. Everyone calls me Mike."

"And everyone calls me Ricky," I said, taking her hand. "My associate and I have cleared a space for you when you'd like to come in. Are you *sure* you're interested in investigative work?"

"Absolutely, really interested."

I watched her father beaming proudly and felt the loss of never having children, one of my few regrets in life. "Well, you're welcome to come see what we're about anytime. I was thinking about it yesterday and we actually could use a little clerical help while you learn about the business. I'm 'fraid that might seem too boring and certainly way beneath your pay grade. After all, you're a doctor like your dad."

"Not at all. I'm craving a change."

"I forgot to ask on the phone. Do you live close by?"

"I have an apartment in the Highlands."

"That's great. We didn't set a start date. Do you have a day in mind?"

"Tomorrow?"

"How does ten thirty sound?"

"Perfect," she said. She had the same hundred-kilowatt smile as her dad. He mouthed "thank you" to me as I gave Mike directions to the office.

"Well, we'll let you dig into your lobster," he said. "That is, if you have any room left."

Bunny snorted. "You cannot imagine the depths of this woman's stomach!"

I rolled my eyes.

"Oh, Ricky," he said, "I almost forgot. I checked with people at the clinic. No one knew much about Meridian. Course I only talked to people on duty. Want me to keep poking?"

"Thanks, that'd be great. I'll see *you* in the morning," I said to Mike, waving as father and daughter headed off.

I sat back down and gave Bunny a jab. "Thanks for your flattering comment about my eating."

"It's one of your most loveable qualities, dearie. Besides, your mountain of clam shells and the mess you've made of that pretty top told them everything they needed to know. I warned you to wear your bib."

I peered down aghast to find my chest dotted with grease. "Oh, shit! This'll never come out and it's one of my favorite shirts!" I blushed crimson, thinking how I must have looked to father and daughter. *Sensational, indeed!* With a shrug, I tore into my lobster.

As we drove home, Bunny peppered me with questions about Charlie. Where had we met? How long had we been seeing each other? Blah, blah, blah.

"I mean, Ricky, I'd have gone after him myself but he's decades too old for me."

"I hate to break it to you, Ms. Cougar, but he's probably our age."

"My point exactly." Bunny only dated *much* younger men. "Although, sweetie, I'll bet Dr. Bowen has got us by a few years. He's not my type, but he's perfect for you. Nice-looking, a little rough around the edges, doctor, gorgeous blue eyes. And he's clearly into you, which makes him even more perfect."

"Can we stop this, please?"

"Okay, but I want regular updates on your Dr. Bowen," she said, pulling up in front of my house.

"For the hundredth time, he's not *my* Dr. Bowen and there will be no updates."

I hopped out and came around to say good-night. "Thanks, Bun. Good to see you. We didn't even talk about your latest beaus."

"Oh, you know," she said coyly. "I have a few prospects. I'll keep you posted. Tootle-loo, sweetheart. Let's do dinner at the Club soon. I have to use up my minimum."

"I prefer the Rainbow."

"Yuck. Stay away from that place, Rick. The grease'll kill you!" She waved and drove off.

CHAPTER 11

When I stepped into the office shortly after ten, two pairs of eyes looked up. "Hey, Mike, welcome. I'm sorry, I thought we said ten thirty."

"You did, but I wasn't sure I'd find it so I left early. I was having my coffee in the hall when Wilda came and let me in. We've been getting acquainted."

"I see that." I nodded to Wilda, who gave me an ironic smile.

"Can I do anything for you?" Mike said.

Unaccustomed to all this morning chitchat, I stood staring at my two coworkers, in a bit of a daze. My mornings are usually spent in quiet solitude, allowing me time to make lists, collect my thoughts and make plans for the day. Managing employees' workload had not been on any list since Janice, my former, very part-time assistant flew the coop. Wilda managed herself.

Rousing myself, I said, "Well, let's see. Let me head in and check my schedule. Then we can chat, okay?"

I resisted the strong urge to shut my office door while endeavoring to get on with my usual routines—bill paying, checking messages, and shuffling papers. This lasted about ten minutes.

"Mike, got a minute?"

She instantly appeared at the door. I waved her in and she sat in one of the two empty chairs in front of my desk. I came around and took the other.

"Wilda stepped out," she said.

"She does that."

"She's an interesting person."

"One of a kind. She's paid to be invisible, but now and then she likes to hang out here."

She regarded me quizzically, but said nothing.

"The thing is, I haven't had people in the office for a while. I'm kind of a loner so I probably won't be a very good host."

"No problem. I want to help if I can, but I promise to stay out of your way."

A lovely young woman, Mike was petite, with an athletic build and bright chestnut eyes as arresting as her father's baby blues. She had worn the uniform today—jeans, a tee shirt, and running shoes.

I smiled. "Well, if you're willing, I am. As I think I told you, my very part-time office assistant, Janice, moved to Antigua with her boyfriend. Since she left, the office has been in shambles. Paperwork is not my thing and the desktop on my computer is so crowded I can't find anything."

"Well, I'm willing to dive in, if you point me in the right direction."

I decided to let her tackle the paper nightmare first. We chatted a while and I set her to work on the file cabinets and the boxes and piles on my desk. I retreated to the outer office to make phone calls.

My first one was to my friend Bud, a former tenant in the building who moved his insurance business to fancier downtown offices. I do a lot of work for him and was way behind. He had left a number of voice mails, each one a little more peevish than the last. I braced myself, expecting a tirade, but he was in a great mood. We spent some time prioritizing the jobs, including one that had to be completed "today, Rick, no if's, and's or but's." I promised results by five and rang off.

The next call was to the law offices of Brackett and Pearson. I asked for Jill Carlson and was transferred to her assistant, Tina.

"Oh, I'm sorry. Ms. Carlson is all booked up today. Is it urgent?"

"Kind of. What about tomorrow?"

"Well, let's see. She has an opening at eleven."

"Perfect. Please put me in." I asked for directions, then rang off, hoping that my contacting Meridian's attorneys would not set off any alarms. I was getting a bad vibe about the entire organization, despite their do-gooder school.

I rang Jimmy Chen, but his phone went straight to voice mail. I really wanted to poke around that apartment again. I grabbed my bag and peeked around the door to the Inner Sanctum. Papers were everywhere, but Mike seemed to be making headway.

She looked up at me. "I think I'm getting the hang of it. I'm making a pile that may be recyclable, but you probably ought to take a look before I shred and chuck."

"Poor thing, and this is why you went to medical school?"

She blanched and her bright open expression vanished.

"You okay?"

"Sure, yes," she said, gazing downward. When she finally met my eyes, hands on hips, she appeared to have shaken off whatever demons had grabbed hold of her.

"You hungry?"

"Starved."

"Great. Let's grab lunch and then you can come along on a drive-by, if you want."

"But what about this?"

"It's been like that for over a year. A few more days won't hurt."

Chapter 12

We settled into a booth at Dino's.

"Hey, Rick," Dino said, filling our water glasses. "Who's your beautiful young friend?"

"Mike, this is Dino, and that's his wife, Lois, behind the counter." I waved and Lois winked.

We both ordered the soup and half a sandwich, mine a BLT and Mike's a grilled cheese and mushrooms.

"Can I get you something besides water, ladies?"

"Iced tea for me," I said.

"Me, too. Thanks, Dino," Mike said, smiling up at him.

Unlike my sometimes prickly self, Charlie's daughter was open and warm, comfortable in anyone's company. *Too bad this is only temporary*, I thought. *She'd be a great addition to the team, not that I could afford her.* Wilda takes a percentage of every job and works several other jobs when I don't need her.

"Sorry about my freak-out earlier," she said, shuffling her silverware from side to side.

I said nothing, waiting for her to continue.

"Being a doctor is amazing, especially working with my dad. It's just really intense and I needed a break."

"I can imagine."

"Thanks for understanding and thanks for allowing me to be here. Sorting someone else's paperwork is a perfect occupation for me right now."

"Happy to have you. And you're doing *me* a huge favor."

Dino soon appeared, serving our meals with a flourish. "I added some curly fries and coleslaw, dolls."

"Thanks, Dino," I said. "This looks great."

We ate in silence for several minutes, enjoying every bite of Lois's kale soup and our luscious sandwich halves. Finally I asked, "So, how long have you and Dad been living in this area?"

"He's been here about a year, me six months. Once he decided to buy his house, I knew he'd be sticking around. We've been together so long, growing up and then work. I missed him."

"So, how have you found life in this broken-down mill city?"

"Okay, actually. There's lots going on down on the waterfront and I've joined a church with a terrific young minister. She rocks. She's brought a lot of people my age into the congregation and we have a great time."

"Boyfriend, or significant other?"

"Not yet. I dated a guy when I first moved here, but it didn't work out. How about you? Do you have a partner?"

"Nope. Failed relationships are kind of the story of my life. I'm not very good at them, apparently."

"Maybe you haven't met the right guy?" I looked up to find her smiling, a twinkle in her eye.

"Maybe, but I had a tough breakup recently so I'm on the bench right now."

"Good. You and Dad can be friends. He's looking for buddies."

"Oh?"

"He's spent so many years traveling that he never seems to have time to meet women."

"What about your mom?"

"They split up years ago. She got fed up with his constant traveling and went looking for love somewhere else. She's remarried, a cardiologist. They live in Providence. We're not close. She pretty much made our childhood a horror show."

"I'm sorry. That's too bad."

"What about you? Do you have family around here?"

"My sister Annie lives in California. Our mom died when we were young. My dad's still going strong. He lives in the city with my stepmother, Rita. She's the one who hired me for this job."

"I'm sorry about your mom. Was she sick?"

"In a way, I guess. She committed suicide."

Mike blanched as she clapped a hand over her mouth. "Oh, Ricky, that's terrible. I'm so sorry."

"It was a long time ago." I turned away and waved at Dino for the check.

"On me, dolls. Lois insists," he said as he swished by the table. Dino does this about once a month. I repay him by doing small jobs like rewriting his blurbs when they change the menu.

We spent several hours researching for Bud's insurance fraud case. This involved a visit to the Registry of Deeds and a trip to the Main Library, where I pulled out my laptop and wrote up the report, then paid five dollars to the reference librarian to print two copies. I swung by Bud's office and told Mike to deliver the report "into Mr. Dixon's hands only," then waited idling at the curb. Before she'd exited the building, my cell phone rang.

"You have an assistant now. Good. There'll be no excuses for work to be late."

"I love you, too, Bud. Give my best to Mary." I clicked off as Mike hopped into the jeep.

"He's a nice guy," she said. "Seemed shocked to see me."

I laughed. "Good, serves him right."

I turned the jeep onto Main and headed for Prospect. I managed to find a spot a half a block from Jimmy and Josh's apartment. I parked and killed the engine.

I turned to my new assistant. "Much as I'd love to have you with me, it's probably safer for you to stay in the car."

Her face fell. "You're the boss."

"It's just, I don't want to answer to your father if anything should go wrong."

"I've spent the better part of my adult life in countries at war. I'm sure I'll be safe on this quiet little street, but it's your call." She gazed downward, no doubt holding her breath.

"Oh, what the hell. Come on, let's go."

We started up the sidewalk just as a tall young man hopped out of a battered truck and headed our way. He looked familiar. Tousled brown hair, jeans and faded Battleship Cove tee shirt. As he gazed up, I was pretty certain it was Josh Peabody. He paused and I thought he might bolt, but then he spied Mike and interest flickered in the hazel eyes.

"Josh?" I said, trying not to spook him.

"Guess you found me," he said, throwing up his arms in mock surrender.

"Do you remember me?"

He nodded. "We met last year at your dad's. You're the PI who spoke to Jimmy and my mother."

"Guilty as charged."

"How you get by the gatehouse gauntlet at the Bluffs?"

"I have my ways."

"I was expecting someone younger, like her," he said, gesturing at Mike.

"Sorry to disappoint you. This is my associate, Mike."

He came forward, hand outstretched, and shook her hand. He made no move to shake mine.

"So, what'd you want?"

"Cassie's worried."

"She hired you?"

"No, and she'd be furious if she knew I was here. Her mother hired me."

"Figures. Well, you've found me. Your job is done."

"Can I tell Cassie you'll be in touch?"

"It's complicated."

"Oh?"

"Do you want to come in? I've got to grab some stuff."

I said a prayer of thanks for Mike's presence. No way he'd have invited me in had I been alone.

"Sure, we have a few minutes," I said. *What am I going to tell Rita?*

We followed him in and up the stairs. As he unlocked the door, I was never so grateful for our light lunch given what awaited within.

CHAPTER 13

Jimmy Chen, or what was left of him, lay on the kilim rug. He was almost unrecognizable, his face a swollen mess of black and blue. Some of his fingers had been broken and blood was everywhere. A straight-backed wooden chair lay on its side to the left of the body, strips of duct tape dangling from it.

"I should check for a pulse," Mike said, grabbing latex gloves from her bag as she knelt beside him, hand to his neck.

Josh turned green, rushed into the kitchen, and vomited into the sink. As I called 911, Mike stood, shaking her head, then stepped back to stand beside me. I'd seen dead bodies, but nothing like this. From the ugly crimson line circling his neck, it appeared he'd been strangled, but the poor man had suffered before death.

I skirted the body and stepped into the kitchen. "Josh, listen to me. I need you to pull yourself together. We have about five minutes before this place'll be crawling with cops. Are you listening?"

He nodded, wiping his mouth with a dirty dish towel.

"This apartment has been turned upside down. I need for you to check around your room and Jimmy's and see if anything's missing. Can you do that?"

He nodded.

"Good. Just steer clear of the body, okay?"

Josh disappeared into the bedroom and I joined Mike, who was ashen-faced, staring at the remains of Jimmy Chen.

"Mike, are you okay? Do you want to wait in the jeep?"

"No, I'm fine. This isn't…I mean, I was trying to…" Tears rimmed her eyes and she listed to one side.

Fearing she might keel over, I grabbed hold of her arm. "It's okay."

Clearly it was not okay, especially for Jimmy Chen, but I patted her back. I was glad to comfort her but at the same time frustrated at the missed opportunity to snoop around. Then I remembered, I had found Josh Peabody. My job was done.

I had requested Douglas Roberts. Ten years my senior, he spent most days at a desk, but occasionally accompanied a homicide team into the field. I breathed a sigh of relief when the tall and slender man himself walked through the apartment door.

"Jesus Christ, what a mess. Steele, what the hell are you doin' in the middle of this? No bullshitting."

As his men fanned out and began processing the scene, I gave him a quick rundown of the situation, ending with the chance meeting with Josh Peabody on the street.

"That doesn't explain why his roommate here is dead. What'd we know about him?"

"He works for Meridian Imports. In locating Josh, I've been trying to speak to the people who work there, but they're an elusive bunch."

"We'll see about that. Is that guy with the green face the roommate?"

"Yup, that's Josh."

"Mr. Peabody, I wonder if you might accompany Ms. Steele downstairs? I'd like to talk with you both in a few minutes?"

Josh nodded and started for the door, holding a box. "Whoa, kid. What's that you've got there?" Roberts stepped forward to peer into the box.

"Just a few clothes and stuff."

"Everything stays for now. Once we've gone over things, we can bring you back to collect your clothes, okay? Now, wait outside and I'll be down directly."

Josh dropped the box to the floor and followed Mike and me out of the apartment, where the three of us sat on the front steps. Josh started to speak, but then fell silent. He was trembling.

Mike and I exchanged glances. "Josh," she said, patting his arm. "You're in shock. Can I get you some water?"

He shook his head and I gave her the eye. She hopped up and headed for a convenience store on the corner.

I placed my hand on his shoulder. "Can I call someone for you?"

"No, thanks."

"Did you find anything missing?"

He nodded. "All my school stuff. The kids' papers, my plans, everything. Jimmy's stuff is gone too. No briefcase, no computer. At least I had my computer with me. He also had a small portable safe. That's gone as well as the cash he keeps in his closet. At least, I think it's gone. I was just checking the closet when I heard the cops' voices. After the weird thing that happened to my phone and computer, I'm sure his phone is gone, too."

"Weird thing?"

"The school has a rule—cell phones and laptops go in a box just outside the classroom door. After class yesterday, I picked my phone and it was off, which was weird 'cause I usually just mute it. When I turned it on, it was scrubbed clean, every app gone. My emails, texts, photos, everything."

"Can I see it?"

He pulled an iPhone out of his back pocket and handed it to me. Sure enough, except for settings, the weather, a calculator and his internet, text, and mail connections, the screen was blank. When I clicked on the message icon, there were no contacts, no messages, nothing. Same with email and internet.

"Did you try recovering things?"

He nodded. "I spent hours at the Apple store yesterday, but no luck."

"What about iCloud? Are you on that?"

"We tried that. iCloud storage had been wiped clean, too. How would someone know all my passwords?"

"Tech-savvy people can get past a password in the blink of an eye. How long are you in class?"

"Three hours or so."

"More than enough time. What about your computer?"

"I lock that in the school office. It's been scrubbed too. Email, internet history, cookies, all that stuff. My school files are missing, too."

Mike returned with three bottles of water and handed one to Josh and one to me. I stood. "Just on the off chance that the evil ones missed something, I'd like you to lock up your computer."

"It's in the jeep. Would you take it?" he asked, gazing at me with sad puppy-dog eyes.

"Of course." No sooner had we transferred the laptop from his jeep to mine than Roberts appeared.

After eyeing us, he knelt in front of Josh and patted his knee. "I know this is a shock, Mr. Peabody, but do you feel up to answering a few questions?"

Josh nodded.

"Good. Let's have you come downtown, to the station. My men or Ms. Steele can drive you. Your choice."

Josh looked at me, eyes pleading.

"I'll drive him. Mike can follow in his truck."

"Fine," Douglas said, grabbing me by the elbow and pulling me aside. "And when we get there, I want every scrap of information you have about this mess, comprende?" I opened my mouth to speak. "Save it, Steele."

As I led Josh to the jeep, I realized I'd never seen Roberts so angry or so scared. *What the hell have we gotten ourselves mixed up in?*

CHAPTER 14

We spent the afternoon at the police station, answering the same questions over and over. Although I offered Mike my car to take a break after they were through with her, she declined and stayed with us until the end, mostly glued to Josh's side. At about five, Roberts ushered Josh out of his office and pointed at yours truly. "You, in here, now."

"Wait here," I said to Josh and Mike. They nodded, now holding hands.

"Close the door," he said, sitting behind his desk. It looked very much like mine, several mountains of paper and various takeout boxes and empty coffee cups littered across the top.

I moved a box of papers and sat on a metal chair. "I thought we were done."

"We are and you are, do you understand?"

"Douglas, as I told you, my job is over. I was hired to locate Josh Peabody and I did."

"By pure dumb luck."

"By being in the right place at the right time. Don't you think it's fortunate that Mike and I were there with Josh when he found Jimmy?"

"And what if you'd decided to pay Mr. Chen a visit last night?"

"Is that when he died?"

He raised his hand. "Shush, I'll do the talking. What if you'd walked in while those guys were making mincemeat out of Jimmy Chen? Do you think they'd have thought twice about whacking you, too?"

He had a point. "Well, I wasn't, so they didn't." *Best to keep the conversation light and breezy.*

"Don't get cute with me, Steele. You are to stay away from anything to do with this, do you understand? Go home, catch up on your knitting or get busy with one of the hundred other odd jobs you do."

"I don't knit."

"I mean it. These guys are nasty."

"Don't you think I know that?"

"Then stay out of it, please," he said, eyes softening.

"You don't have to worry about me, Douglas. I saw the body, remember? I'm done, kaput."

"Good. Now, take that kid home and give him a shot of brandy. He looks like shit."

"Will do. Thanks for coming this afternoon."

"Get outta here."

I found Mike and Josh gazing out the hall window. "We can go. Anyone hungry?"

"Believe it or not, yes," he said. "I haven't eaten since yesterday."

"Then let's eat. We'll leave your truck here and pick it up after."

I drove to Lizzy's, praying the dinner crowd would be light so early on a Wednesday night. It was. We took a table in the back and studied our menus for several minutes.

Judy, one of the regular waitresses, brought three waters with lemon. "Hey, Rick, long time no see."

"Hey, Judy, you're lookin' good."

"Lost thirty pounds. Been jogging with my new boyfriend and working out with his trainer."

"Well, it shows."

"Thanks. Can I get you folks something to drink besides water?"

Josh and Mike ordered beers and I asked for a Chianti. She rattled off the specials, disappeared and returned almost immediately with the drinks. "So, what'll it be?"

I ordered the special, baked cod, Mike, the fish stew, and Josh, pork chops. We all ordered salads and he got quahog chowder as well. Lizzy's has a to-die-for quahog chowder.

Judy headed to the kitchen.

"You don't see hair like that every day," Mike said, smiling at Josh. Judy's short spiked hair was pink this week with dark green streaks.

"Feeling any better?" I asked.

He took a long sip of beer. "Starting to, but I'm still freaked out."

"As well you should be," I said. "Have you got somewhere to stay tonight?"

"I spent the last four nights in a motel in Somerset. I checked out this morning, but I guess I could go back. Not like they're full."

"You can stay at my place," Mike said. "My roommate won't mind. We have a very comfy couch."

"Thanks, let me think about it."

"There's my place, too," I heard myself saying. *Blurring the lines, as usual.*

"I know!" Mike said, clapping her hands. "My dad's place! He'd love to have you and God knows he's got the room."

"Whoa, whoa," I said. "How do you know he be glad to have a houseguest with his house torn apart?"

"'Cause I know my dad. He's spent most of the past thirty years sleeping on dirt floors crawling with maggots, snakes and spiders. He won't care in the slightest."

Yuck! I actually don't mind snakes, but spiders and maggots—*double yuck!* "Okay, call him and ask, if that's what Josh wants."

Mike excused herself and stepped out onto Lizzy's terrace to make her call. Josh appeared to be in la-la land after three swigs of beer. I decided food was in order so I waved Judy over and asked for peanuts, popcorn, anything the bar could give us quickly. She returned with a basket of popcorn and bowl of mixed nuts, which Josh inhaled. As he ate the last of the nuts, he seemed to perk up and color returned to his cheeks.

"Better?" I asked.

"Much."

"Do you have a plan for what's next?" I asked.

He shrugged. "Nope. You know, I'll miss the teaching. I really liked it and the kids."

"You're not to go near Meridian."

"But what about the kids?"

"I'm sure the police are checking it out right now."

"I hope so. I'm so worried about Lin."

"One of your students?"

"Yes, she's a sweetheart. Her older sister, Joy disappeared a week ago. Poof! Lin hasn't seen or heard from her since. I asked in the office and they said she'd moved to a new school."

"Excuse me?"

"That happens pretty often. Meridian apparently has a network of schools in different parts of the country. They're always relocating kids, to join family members or move to a school that's better suited to their needs."

"Is that so. What do you know about these other schools?"

"Zip. I tried to get information, but there's nothing online about them. I've been trying every kind of search I can think of this past week."

Nothing, indeed. There was something going on here and I didn't think it involved school transfers. "How old are your students?"

"They range in age from five to twelve. They come to Meridian to learn basic English before they can enter a regular school."

"And do they master English before they leave?"

"In my opinion, no. They usually relocate them too soon. I've only been working there for a few months, but most of the kids that move away would have a really difficult time in a regular school. It's weird because we're billed as a GED program, but no one is old enough or skilled enough to even start that track. Although I've heard that Meridian sponsors GED classes around the city, I've never seen one."

"How many classrooms at the Water Street site?"

"Just the one. I work on English—speaking, reading and writing—in the mornings, and another teacher comes in and does math and a bunch of other stuff in the afternoon."

"What's her name?"

"Kim Smith. She calls herself a social worker. Looks like she belongs on sales floor of Nordstrom. Wear fancy designer suits and high heels. Says she wants the kids to know she respects them so she dresses her best for school."

"Do you know anything about this Ms. Smith?"

"No, and I've only talked to her a couple of times in the office. There's break room with coffee machine next to the classroom and I've seen her in there. When I ask the kids about her, they shake their heads and say nothing. It's my impression that they're not fond of her."

Mike returned and gave us a thumbs-up just as our salads and Josh's chowder arrived. "Dad's cool. Happy to have Josh as long as he wants to stay."

I took several bites of my spinach salad, then set down my fork. "How many kids are we talking about?"

"As I said, they come and go, but usually between fifteen to twenty. We had eighteen this past week before Joy disappeared."

"So, do they live with their families?"

He shook his head. "Meridian's pretty vague about that. I've asked a bunch of times cause I wanted to teach them some basic family words, but never got a straight answer. Apparently Meridian runs a group home somewhere in one of those massive houses in the Highlands. Jimmy's seen it. He knows, I mean, he knew where it was. A bunch of the kids live there, not just ours."

"Where did they come from?" Mike asked, popping her last crouton into her mouth.

"Most are from mainland China and the rest from India."

"This isn't making sense," Mike said as Judy brought our entries.

"My thoughts exactly," I said, smiling at Judy as she cleared the salad plates and Josh's empty soup bowl.

We enjoyed our meals in relative silence. Josh picked up the check amid mild protests from us ladies. I wanted to ask him about the fifty thousand dollars his mother had mentioned, but decided that could wait. Besides, this whole affair, while tragic, was no longer my business. I would, of course, beg Douglas to look into the children's plight, but I suspected we might already be too late.

Mike drove Josh's truck and he rode with her. I followed. When we arrived, Charlie was sitting on his front porch drinking a beer and reading *The New York Times*. "Hey," he called, coming down to meet us, shaking Josh's hand. "Good to meet you, Josh. Come on in. Want something to eat?"

Mike hugged her father. "Oh, Dad, I'm sorry, we should have brought takeout for you."

"No problem. I'm having some of Jack's wonderful kale soup and a couple of his chorizo rolls, to which I'm now officially addicted. Drink anyone?"

"Thanks, I'll pass," I said, looking around us. The place was still rough and nowhere near completion, but it was going to be amazing. It appeared that he had knocked down walls and opened up the entire downstairs, which was bisected by a massive stone two-sided fireplace. "This is incredible," I said.

Charlie smiled. "It will be, someday."

The young people disappeared upstairs, Mike giving Josh the grand tour. "Are you sure about this?"

"Absolutely. Sounds like the kid's in shock."

"A bit. Did Mike tell you?"

"Gruesome."

"It was," I said, leaning against the kitchen counter, gazing out at his spectacular view of the river.

He placed his hand over mine. "Are you okay?"

Startled, I stood up straight, withdrawing my hand. "I'm fine, but what a way for Mike to begin her first day."

"She's seen worse. She was upset about the murder, but I haven't seen her this excited in a long time."

"I suspect the cute Mr. Peabody may have something to do with that."

He laughed. "I suspect you're right. Thanks for doing this, Ricky. It means a lot to me."

"Happy to. She's terrific. I predict that she'll have my office whipped into shape in a couple of days. And she was a huge help with Josh today."

His eyes held mine and the knee wobble started up. I cleared my throat. "Well, thanks for this. I'd better get going."

"Sure you don't want a drink?"

"Thanks, but no. Do you think Mike needs a ride?"

"I'll take her if she does, or she can borrow my car. She appears in no hurry to depart."

I smiled at him. Charlie Bowen was a nice man.

"You have lovely eyes," he said, reaching out to touch my cheek, just as Mike and Josh came into the room.

I stepped back, flustered. "I'm gonna take off. Mike, let me know if you need a ride to the office tomorrow morning, okay?"

"I can take her," Josh said. "Ricky, can I talk to you on the porch for a minute?"

"Sure," I said, nodding to Charlie and Mike and following Josh out.

He closed the door. "I want to hire you."

"Excuse me?"

"I want to hire you to find Joy and make sure Lin's okay. If I can't go back to Meridian tomorrow, I still want to know they're safe."

"This is out of my league," I said, remembering Douglas's warning.

"Please. I have money. I'll pay whatever you say. Name your price."

"Is that what the fifty thousand dollars was for?"

He nodded. "I asked Jimmy how to find Joy and he said I'd need lots of money. He's the one who suggested the fifty grand. He was gonna get things started last night. See if we could find the girls."

"Jesus Christ."

"Please, Ricky. I need to know they're safe."

"Let me think about it overnight, okay? You can stop by the office in the morning and I'll give you my answer."

He nodded. "Okay, well, good night."

"Josh?"

"Yeah?"

"What about Cassie? What should I tell her?"

"I love Cassie as a friend, but it's over. We've known it for months, but she hasn't wanted to accept it. I broke off communication for a few days to think. I was actually going to call her tonight. I'll phone her tomorrow. You don't have to do anything, thanks."

I waved and walked to my car.

CHAPTER 15

I was already at my desk when Josh and Mike walked in, Wilda two steps behind them. We all grabbed coffee or tea and sat in the outer office, bringing Wilda up to speed. As was her wont, she said little, but listened attentively, nodding occasionally. Finally, Josh looked at me. "Have you decided to help me?"

I had thought of nothing else since the previous evening. I swallowed, pushing thoughts of broken fingers out of my mind. "I have." I glanced at Wilda, who was shaking her head.

"While I'd rather not get involved after seeing what they did to Jimmy Chen, I'm also pissed." I gave Wilda a look. "There are children's lives at stake. I just can't walk away."

Josh let out his breath. "Oh, God, Ricky, thank you."

"There is a caveat here and I'm not just saying this because I know you're wealthy. After seeing Jimmy, I would say this is very dangerous work. I'm also going against strict instructions from the police. If I'm going to put Wilda and myself in potential danger, I'm going to request hazardous duty pay."

"What's your usual retainer?"

"I charge a thousand a day with a retainer of fifteen hundred."

Without blinking, Josh pulled out a check and made it out, handing it to me. "Twenty thousand enough for the first week?"

"That's probably a tad too much," I said, picking my mouth up off the floor.

"No, it isn't," Wilda said quietly.

"Deal, then," I said, shaking his hand. "Now, I'm late for an appointment. Not a dangerous one. I think I'll be fine at the law offices of Brackett and Pearson."

"Want me to ride along?" Mike said, popping up.

"No, thanks. You get back to your filing. Wilda, you gonna hang around today?" She nodded. "Good. I don't think anyone should be working here alone right now. What are your plans, Josh?"

"Much as I'd rather not, I'm headed to the Harbor, to my parents' to pick up some clothes and a few things. Dr. Bowen says I can stay until the police are through with the apartment, but I'm never living there again. I'll start looking for a new place soon."

"Okay, then," I said with cheerfulness I didn't feel. I grabbed my bag and started out. Wilda followed me into the hallway and closed the office door behind her. "Boss, got a minute?"

"Sure."

"You know I have your back, but I think we need more muscle."

"You got someone in mind?"

She nodded.

"Good, call 'me. Twenty thousand will buy plenty of protection."

"Maybe," she said, turning away.

*****

The law offices of Brackett and Pearson were located on North Main Street on the second floor of what had once been a lovely old bank. The woodwork gleamed and the carpet muffled even the heaviest steps. I took the stairs and was greeted immediately by a raven-haired receptionist. "Hello, I'm Tina. Can I help you?"

"Hello, we spoke on the phone yesterday, Tina. I'm Ricky Steele. I have an appointment with Ms. Carlson."

"Oh, of course. Let me ring and see if she's free."

Tina had just picked up the phone when the lady herself swished in. "Ricky, hello! I was so surprised to see you on my schedule. Come in, come in. Can Tina get you anything? Coffee? Tea? Water?"

"Thanks, I'm fine." I smiled at Tina and followed her boss into a large office, furnished in muted greens and blues. A series of bird watercolors hung on cream-colored walls, their hues perfectly coordinated with the furnishings. There were two upholstered chairs and a love seat, their silken fabrics swirls of color and light. I'm not expert, but I would guess that cost of decorating Jill's office exceeded the value of my home.

"Sit, please."

I took one of the two armchairs and my hostess settled herself on the love seat, stretching out like she was the queen of Sheba. Her grey silk suit had been expertly tailored, a far cry from the tennis duds she'd worn last time we met.

"Thanks for seeing me, Jill."

"My pleasure. Is your sister still in town?"

"No, she's back home."

"You're close, aren't you?"

"Yes."

"Robbo always says he's never seen siblings closer than the Steele girls. He was jealous, I think."

"I doubt that. He's close to his brothers."

"Yes…" Her voice trailed off. "He still carries a torch for you, you know."

"That's absurd."

She shrugged. "We have an open marriage so I get plenty of attention. I'm happy. No problem there."

Why don't I believe you? "Listen, Jill, I know you're busy so I'll be brief. I came to ask you about one of your clients, Meridian Imports?"

She feigned thinking for a minute or so. "Hmm, sounds familiar. I think Phil takes care of that account."

"Phil?"

"Phillip Brackett? He's one of the senior partners. He's out at the moment, but due back soon. Shall I ask him about it and get back to you?"

"That would be great. In the meantime, is there anything you might be able to learn from your digital records about Meridian? I'm particularly interested in the school they run for young non-native speakers."

"Let me see." She stood and went to her computer, clicking and searching, a frown creasing her brow. "Hmm, not much here. No mention of a school in these records."

"It's run out of their building on Water Street."

"Not according to this. All I see is storage and office space. They'd surely let us know if there was a school on the premises. There's all kinds of insurance and liability issues with that sort of thing."

That sort of thing, indeed. I could see I would get nothing from Jill and I doubted Phil would give me the time of day. I decided a hasty departure was in order. I wanted to take a second peek at the Meridian building before Phil got back and alerted them.

"Well, thanks, Jill."

"What's your interest anyway?"

"Some of the pupils have gone missing. In fact, it's kind of a revolving door over there. Someone who cares about one of the missing children asked me to try to locate her."

"That's horrible! I hope you find them. Please let me know if I can help in any way."

We exchanged air kisses and I was on my way. I called Wilda to let her know where I was headed and made certain my Smith & Wesson was handy and loaded. I hate it, but this was one of the rare times when I was glad to take it along.

Chapter 16

I parked two blocks away and walked along Water Street, peering up at the second floor of Meridian's building. The first floor of the building was unbroken granite walls, which made sense if the building was used for storage. I assumed the classroom space was upstairs where there was a bank of windows. I walked around to the rear of the building and tried each door, surprised to discover the middle one unlocked. Its entryway was tidier than the others and had a fancy doormat that had not been there on my previous walk around the building.

I ignored the brass doorbell and knocker and quietly pushed open the door, stepping into a small ornate vestibule with soft, mauve carpet, chandelier, and carpeted stairs leading to the second floor. I could hear voices, a man and woman talking somewhere above. Taking a deep breath, I began creeping upward, stopping at each stair to listen. A shaft of light from above lit my way. As I reached the landing, I spied a couple disappearing down a corridor at the other end of a light-filled room.

After listening for several minutes, I heard only silence and peeked around the door frame. The room, some kind of lounge, was empty, bathed in soft light from several lamps, its furnishings exquisite. I don't know what I was expecting, but it wasn't this. I gazed around the antiques-filled space furnished with sumptuous chairs and sofas. Perhaps this was Meridian's entertaining space, or perhaps I was looking at inventory from the import business?

There appeared to be only two doors, the one I'd come in and the one the two people had used. Along the left wall was long buffet table covered with china and a large floral arrangement. On the wall to my right hung an enormous gilded mirror, at least twelve feet long and six feet high. I stepped closer to have a better look and was startled to see that it was a window, or two-way mirror, that afforded a view of a long, empty room. The room had wooden floors and ten-foot windows lining the west wall. It was completely bare, not a paper, box or speck of dust. It appeared to have been recently swept and several large pictures had been removed from the walls, leaving their outlines behind. *Chalkboards? Classroom chalkboards?*

Just as I leaned in for a better look, something sharp stabbed my shoulder and everything went black.

*****

When I woke my first thought was to wiggle my fingers, all intact, though my hands were tied behind my back. My feet were similarly bound. Something was stuffed in my mouth with what felt like duct tape over it. A tight blindfold over my eyes was giving me an eyeball ache. *At least I'm alive*, I thought as hands lifted me, then dropped me into what felt like a wooden box. Realization dawned. I moaned and wiggled as the coffin was nailed shut.

Did I mention I hate small spaces? Between the dust, the gag over my mouth, and my certainty that I was about to be buried alive, I panicked, gasping for breath, certain that I would pass out at any minute. I took slow deep breaths, listening. Their footsteps retreated and I heard scraping and a loud creaking sound like a rusty hinge. *Where the hell was I?*

Time passed, I'm not sure how much. I tried to remain calm, but I was having difficulty breathing and mindfulness was losing the battle with claustrophobia. As I began to slip into unconsciousness, I heard scuffling, then several loud crashes, scratching from above and then air! As I breathed in, my blindfold was ripped off.

"You okay, boss?" Wilda peered into the box, Mike beside her. Beside them stood a mini Arnold Schwarzenegger.

"This is Frank," Wilda said, as if that explained all. Mike reached in and untied my hands, helping me to sit up.

I ripped off the duct tape along with half my face and pulled the filthy rag from my mouth. "Where are they? Did you…?"

"They'd gone," Wilda said. "We waited till they left."

"Where are we?" I asked, looking around at a stone-walled chamber.

"Oak Grove Cemetery, the Bodington crypt."

I untied my legs and gripped the sides of the coffin. "Whoa," I said, sitting back down, the walls spinning.

"Frank." Wilda said, titling her head toward me.

Frank hoisted me on his shoulders like a sack of potatoes.

"That's really not necessary," I said as he carried me out. All three of them ignored me.

After being dumped into the back seat of Wilda's Land Rover, I leaned back and passed out.

CHAPTER 17

The next thing I remember was lying on my couch, Charlie Bowen leaning over me, his beautiful blue eyes full of concern. "Not sure what they gave her? How long's she been out?"

"A couple of hours," Mike said. "Her pulse is really low."

"Probably sodium pentothal or something similar. Let her sleep it off and I'll come back later."

"I don't need to sleep it off," I said, attempting to rise on my elbows. "Oh…"

"Yes, you do," he said, gently pushing me down. "You're to stay put. Vinnie and Wilda will look after you. Mike, with me."

It was dark outside when I woke again. Amazing aromas filling my senses. No sooner had I inched into a semi-sitting position, than my bedroom door opened and Douglas Roberts stepped in.

I stared at him, wondering if I was hallucinating. "Douglas, how did you—"

"Save it. When you recover, I'm seriously thinking of throwing your senior citizen ass in jail."

I sniffed. "I'm not technically a senior citizen yet. Who called you?"

"No one friggin' called me, although they damn well should have," he said in a loud voice intended for whoever was in the next room.

"Don't blame Wilda. She was too busy following me."

"Thank God. Were it not for her and her sidekicks, you'd be resting for all eternity with Fred Bodington."

"Ha ha. So how did you know?"

"Never mind how I knew. Did I not tell you to stay the hell away from this?"

"There are children involved."

"I don't care. You call me, and we take care of it. Jesus Christ, you came this close," he said, making a two-inch bracket with his fingers. "My only consolation is that you won't be going anywhere for a few days at least."

"And why is that? Josh Peabody has hired me to find two missing sisters, and I intend to keep looking."

"Gonna take the bus or ride your bike around town?"

"What're you talking about?"

He reached into his pocket, pulled out his iPhone, and pulled up a photo, which he flashed in my face.

"Oh, my God," I said, grabbing my reading glasses as I took the camera from him. "Is this what I think it is?"

"Check the plate. It's one of the few things they left behind."

I stared at my jeep, or what was left of it, resting on the street where I'd parked it. No tires, no rims, windows all smashed, hood opened and bashed in, doors hanging at odd angles.

"Engine's gone, seats were slashed, dashboard ripped out. We found it when we got to the Meridian building."

"Oh, my God, Douglas."

"We got a call about that mess. I figured they'd done a Jimmy Chen on you and you were already dead and buried." As he spoke, his eyes got misty and he looked down at the floor.

"Douglas, I'm sorry, but as you can see, I'm fine."

"Save it. You not fine. You had enough Seconal in your system to fell a horse, and you were probably an hour or two from death when your buddies found you."

"But that's my point exactly. They found me because I took precautions and phoned Wilda."

"Look, I know you think Amazon woman is invincible, but I can tell you, even she was shaken up when we got here."

"Where is she? I want to talk to her."

"She and your little pixie friend went around the corner to the dad's for dinner. Vinnie and the hulk are watching over you."

"Well, good, then I'm all set." I swung my legs over the side of the bed, noticing that I wore sweats and a different tee shirt than I'd had on earlier. I hoped Mike or Wilda had done the honors. "What'd you find in the warehouse?"

"Get back to bed."

"I'm great, fine," I said as my bedroom walls began spinning.

"Yeah, right, and I'm fuckin' Santa Claus. You shouldn't hear a peep, but after your ordeal, I'll give a few highlights. Get back in bed or I'm not sayin' a thing."

"Can I go to the bathroom, please?"

He shrugged. "Can you make it on your own?"

I rose, holding on to the wall as I made my way to my bathroom and shut the door. *Yikes, don't let me fall flat on my face or pass out on the toilet!*

When I was safely back in bed, sitting up straight, willing my eyes to focus, I crossed my arms and stared at him. "Okay, so what happened?"

"Building's empty except for a couple of offices used by the import business. We executed the search warrant and talked with several people in the office. Secretaries mostly and the office manager, Ms. Smith. The big honchos were out, but I've got an appointment with one of the owners tomorrow, Wade Pullman."

"Good luck with that." I made a mental note to ask Josh about Pullman. "What about that fancy room upstairs with antiques and the two-way mirror?"

"There's nothing like that. Aside from the offices, the rest of the building is either empty or filled with boxes."

Incredulous, I shook my head. "Did you look everywhere? Up and down all the staircases? Go in every entrance?"

"Yup."

"So, what about the fancy entryway in the back, with the chandelier and carpet leading upstairs?"

"Babe, I think you're hallucinating. There was nothing like that."

I sat up, waving my arms. "Douglas, I swear to you, I'm not hallucinating! I saw it—the fancy room, the empty classroom space and the enormous two-way mirror that looked into the schoolroom."

"Steele, there is no schoolroom, no mirror, no antiques, no nothing."

"But they were there. Have you talked to Josh Peabody? He's been teaching in that space."

"According the people in the office, there's never been a school there."

"Well, that's ridiculous. Jimmy Chen hired Josh a few months ago. He and Kim Smith, who claimed she was a social worker, were the instructors."

"Well, I don't know if my Ms. Smith is *the* Ms. Smith, but she never mentioned this mythical school."

"It's not mythical, Douglas!"

"Well according to Ms. Smith and the office people, Meridian uses the building for office space and storage, period."

"What about Meridian's civic-minded claims?"

"She did mention that they support a couple of summer camps, but not at the Water Street site."

"This is craziness."

"No, what's craziness is you barging in there after what happened to Chen. He was a young guy and you're what? On the far side of fifty?"

"Never mind. I'm younger than you and that's all that matters."

"Well, you're to stay away from Meridian, hear me? We'll reinterview Peabody and get his two cents on the kids and the school, but you are barred from going anywhere near that warehouse, comprende?"

I sniffed.

"And, if I find out you have, I'll throw you in a cell. Now, get some rest. I imagine your neighbor's ready to serve you dinner."

CHAPTER 18

I had just sopped up the last remnants of Vinnie's incredible cioppino, groaning with pleasure at the garlicky bread soaked with broth, when Charlie Bowen walked in. Clearly my bedroom had become Grand Central Station and everyone felt free to walk right in.

"Hey, Charlie," Vinnie said, rising from a chair by the bed and removing my tray. "Want seconds, babe?"

"No thanks, Vin. Couldn't fit another bite."

"How bout some of Maddie's molasses cookies?"

He had me there. Maddie's molasses cookies were to die for. "Well, maybe a couple. Bring a plate, in case Charlie wants one." I turned to him. "Trust me, you will."

When Vinnie disappeared, leaving the door wide open, no doubt to facilitate eavesdropping, Charlie turned to me. "So, how are you feeling?"

"Like I've been hit by a bus."

"I took a blood sample. They injected you with Seconal."

"So I heard."

"Oh?"

"The police were here."

"Good." His beautiful, kind eyes gazed down at me, a smile on his face.

"Listen, Charlie, I am so incredibly sorry that Mike's become involved in this. Wilda never should have brought her along."

He raised his hand. "Mike's a big girl. She can take care of herself and as I told you before, she's seen worse, *and* been in worse danger."

"Still, she thought she was in for some light filing and maybe a chance to shadow a bumbling idiot of a PI. Suddenly she's examining mutilated bodies and rescuing people who've been buried alive. I'm furious with Wilda, by the way."

He laughed. "Don't blame her. Mike says she begged and since Wilda thought it was just a routine tail, she didn't worry. When they saw several guys destroying your car and you being dragged out of the building, there was no time to drop Mike off."

"Still, I feel awful."

"Well, don't. Or, if you must feel guilty, have dinner with me tomorrow night. By then, your head should have cleared. Think of it as penitence."

"Ha ha."

"Come on, Ricky. It's just dinner, not a marriage proposal."

"Fine."

"Good, pick you up at seven?"

"Where are we going, fancy or casual?"

"Casual. I thought we'd go to Sagres."

"One of my favorites," I said, referring to the city's best Portuguese restaurant, recently rebuilt after a fire."

"I know." He gave me another of his killer smiles, then rose and disappeared before I could ask how he knew about my fondness for Sagres. It didn't take a genius private eye to know that nosy Parker in the kitchen had spilled the beans along with who knows what else. *Have I no secrets? No mystery? Humph!*

*****

Although fuzzy-headed, I did feel better in the morning. Not good enough to jog, but I meditated, did some yoga stretches and took a short walk. When I returned, I had some tea and one of Fulty's muffins. Between Vinnie's soup and the Stockmans' baking, I had enough food to keep me going for a week. As I sat at my small dining table in the living room, gazing out at the river, it suddenly dawned on me that I would not be going anywhere without a car. Now I'd have to spend the day car shopping, one of my least favorite activities. How would I even get to a dealership?

I have a small rainy day fund that would certainly cover the cost of a decent but older used car, or the down payment on something newer. With the way New England winters were going, I decided that I'd seek something that was good in the snow. I phoned Vinnie for recommendations on where to look. He was at the gym, but rattled off several venues, ending with, "Lou's the best so I'd try him first. Tell him I sent you and don't make a deal till I've spoken to him."

I rang off and called Mike.

"Good morning. How're feeling?" she said, chipper as can be.

"Better, thanks. Where are you?"

"At the office, knee deep in paperwork. Wilda let me in."

"Great. Ask Wilda to make you an office key."

"Okay."

"Even though I forbid you to work in there alone."

"Of course. Is there something you needed?"

"Yes, sorry. As useful as the filing is, I need you to come pick me up and drive me around looking for cars."

"Okay, should I tell Wilda?"

"Yes, and what's happened to Frank?"

"Last I heard, he was guarding you."

I stood and went into the kitchen, drawing back the shade on the window overlooking the street. An unfamiliar truck was parked on the opposite corner. "Ask Wilda what Frank drives."

"A black Tacoma," she replied without hesitation. "He followed us yesterday."

"Thanks, Mike. See you soon." I hung up and realized I'd forgotten to ask her about Josh. *Ah, well, all in good time.*

I showered and changed, throwing the laundry Vinnie had started into the dryer. Beaky was meowing frantically so I gave her extra treats and a fresh bowl of water. She pays no attention to her regular food until she's wheedled several handfuls of Tasty Treats out of me. I was just sorting through the enormous satchel I use as a purse when I heard the doorbell.

At least someone respects my privacy, I thought, as I went to the door, checking the side window first and spying Mike.

She was in sleeveless jersey, capris and flip-flops in deference to the warmth of the day. I considered changing when I felt a blast of hot air from outside, but then I shrugged and followed her to her bright red Subaru Crosstrek.

"Do you like this car?" I asked as we headed to the first dealership.

"Love it. I had to wait a while because I wanted a hybrid, but it was worth it."

"How 'bout in the snow?"

"Well, I bought it last February so just caught the tail end of winter. Seemed good."

"Your dad drives a hybrid, doesn't he?"

"Range Rover, megabucks. Much too expensive for me. He loves it. It's his one big extravagance."

"If you don't count the mega mansion he's creating around the corner?"

"Well, there is that, but look where it is. No offense, I love the Grove, but in relation to what he could afford, it's pretty modest."

"I guess so. Look, here's Lou's."

Lou had nothing but Cadillacs, Lincolns and a particularly garish gold Grand Marquis. When I mentioned Vinnie, then asked him about Subarus, he scribbled a note on a piece of paper and handed it to me. "Give this to Sharky Nadeau at Spindle City Subaru. He's give you a good price."

The name Sharky did not sound promising, but I gave Mike the directions and we headed off. Sharky took one look at me and declared, "Sweetheart, the Outback was meant for you," which I took to mean, "Let me show you our best little old lady car."

Much as I hate to admit it, Sharky was right. From the moment I sat in the very comfortable beige driver's seat, I was sold. The exterior was teal blue and it ran like a dream, smooth over the bumps and quiet as a mouse compared to my old jeep. It was two years old, but only had eighteen thousand miles and appeared to be in great condition.

Sharky handed me the keys. "Give a spin, dolls. I'll be here when you get back."

I drove out of the lot and took the highway on-ramp. As we toodled down the highway, I turned to Mike. "Have you heard from Josh?"

"He stayed at my dad's last night. He's doing great."

"I need to talk to him. What were his plans today?"

"I think he's apartment hunting."

"He shouldn't be. I wish he'd stay with his parents until this calms down. He could be in serious danger, and he'll put your dad and you in danger, too."

"My dad can take care of himself, and so can I. Want me to call Josh?"

"No, let's wait till this ordeal is over, okay?"

She nodded and we rode in silence, leaving the highway at the next exit and circling back. "What do you think?" I asked as we rounded the corner and the dealership came into view.

"It's great."

"Now, for the negotiations."

I pulled over and called Vinnie, alerting him to where we were. Two hours later I had a new car at a price much lower than I'd expected. I believe several conversations between Sharky, Lou, and Vinnie took place behind the scenes. Since the car would not be ready to go until the following morning, I asked Mike to call Josh and we met him for a late lunch at Dino's. Mindful of my impending dinner engagement, I ordered a cup of soup and a small house salad. They both got Dino burgers with curly fries.

Once Dino had disappeared, I leaned forward, gazing at my companions across the booth. "Josh, you are the only person who insists there was a school at Meridian."

"That's bullshit. I've worked there for almost five months. Ask Kim Smith or any of the office staff. Did you check with Nancy and Betty?"

"The police did. Smith denies knowing anything about a school, children, anything. Nancy and Betty concurred."

"That's insane. I spent every minute I could in that classroom. Did they check the whole building?"

"Yup."

"And they didn't find it? Maybe the room was locked and they thought it was a closet. The windows look out on the river, huge windows, and there were desks, chalkboards, all kinds of stuff."

"Gone."

"Are you sure?"

"I saw the room. It was empty, nothing on the walls, no furniture, not even a speck of chalk."

"So, the kids are gone?"

I nodded.

"Oh, Jesus, that means they've taken Lin, too. Ricky, you've got to believe me. The

school was real. Joy and Lin are real, the rest of the kids, some as small as five are real and—"

"Whoa, you don't have to convince me. I saw the classroom and I have a good idea of where the children go."

"Where?"

He sat on the edge of his seat, eyes full of concern. I didn't have the heart to tell him my suspicions. Not until I was certain. "I'm not sure, but you are not to go near Meridian. Don't contact them, don't let them know where you are, nothing. And I'd ditch your cell phone and get a new one immediately."

"Why?"

"'Cause if they have the capability to erase all your data, I'd bet they can find your location in the blink of an eye."

We ate our lunch in silence. Then Josh drove away, claiming he was going grocery shopping for Dr. Bowen. Mike and I headed to the office and Frank followed close behind.

CHAPTER 19

I knew I could wear jeans and be comfortable at Sagres, but I pulled out gray linen slacks and a soft cream top, its V-neck showing just a hint of cleavage. It was an outfit that made me feel comfortable and sexy. Unfortunately, when I gazed in the mirror, I realized my wild, untamed hair spoiled the sexy effect. In vain I tried to tamp it down, but without much success. I added silver earrings and necklace, and my prized Navaho bracelet. I then refrained from consulting a mirror until I heard Charlie's knock. When I opened the door, his look buoyed my spirits.

"Hey, you look sensational."

"Thanks, so do you." And he did, in khakis and a blue sports shirt that matched his eyes. "Want to come in for a drink?"

"The reservations are for seven. Maybe after?"

"Of course, let's go." I grabbed a gray sweater and my bag.

"That's quite a purse you have there."

"Doubles as a weapon when needed."

"I can see that."

We were quiet on the drive over aside from some idle chitchat about his house progress. He parked in the side lot. As we made our way in, his hand touched the small of my back, sending ripples of electricity through my already sex-starved body.

"Bowen," he said, smiling at the maître d'.

We settled in at a back table, removed from the rest of the dining room. I wondered if Charlie had requested it. When the waiter appeared with the wine list, Charlie asked, "Have any idea what you'll be having?"

"Some kind of seafood."

"Do you like Vinho Verde?"

"Love it."

"Okay if I order a bottle?"

"Absolutely."

As he conferred with the waiter, asking for recommendations, I marveled at his warm, easy way. There was a calm about him to which people responded. Finally, after a long, friendly conversation, the waiter rattled off the evening's specials, then disappeared.

"What?" Charlie asked, noticing me staring.

"Mike's so much like you."

"I'll take that as a huge compliment and say I hope I'm like her. We've spent a lot of time together over the years."

"Tell me about them. Where did you grow up? Where have you lived? Travels? Anything."

"I was going to ask you the same thing, but since you beat me to it, okay. Grew up in Concord, New Hampshire. Always thought I'd go back, but never did."

"What about schools?"

"Went to St. Paul's through high school, then Dartmouth. Came this way for medical school at Brown." I smiled. As if reading my mind, he said, "I'm a bit older than you so I doubt our paths crossed, although I did teach in the med school for a while. In fact, that's where I met my second wife."

"What didn't Vinnie the blabbermouth tell you about me?"

He grinned as the waiter appeared. After Charlie tasted and approved the wine, the waiter poured, then set it in an ice bucket on the table. "Have you decided on dinner?"

Charlie looked at me.

"I'm easy. I always have the mariscada, but take your time if you haven't decided."

"I will take a few minutes," he said, looking up at the waiter. "But, in the meantime, could we order appetizers?" He gazed over at me. "You hungry?"

"Starved."

"Okay if I choose?"

"Of course."

"We'll have an order of quijo de cabra and an order of amejois bulhao de pato, please," he said. To my ears, his Portuguese sounded flawless.

"Very good choices," said the waiter, who bowed and disappeared.

"So, I ordered—"

"Littlenecks and goat cheese. You forget I've eaten here before, and I followed along with my menu. Where did you learn to speak Portuguese?"

"I took a crash course when I moved here. So many people who come to the clinic don't speak English. It wasn't too difficult as I have a little background, and I speak Spanish."

"And?"

He shrugged. "A smattering of others."

Hmm. I made a note to ask Mike. *Probably fluent in about twenty.* "So, you've been married twice?"

"Yes. I met and married my first wife in college. Layla and I married in the Dartmouth Chapel our sophomore spring."

"So, she wasn't Mike's mom?"

"No, we didn't have time for children. She was killed by a drunk driver the first week of junior year. She was pregnant."

"That must have been terrible. I'm so sorry."

"It was a long time ago. Almost forty-four years. She was a blithe spirit."

"So, your second wife is Mike's mom?"

"Yes, Patty. She was my student. Brilliant. She's a general surgeon in Providence, specializes in pediatric cases. She also teaches at Brown. We divorced in our early forties. She was fed up with me being gone three quarters of the year. Don't blame her. She married again, one of the city's top cardiologists, Lyman West. They're happy, I understand."

"I've heard of him. So, Mike isn't your only child?"

"No, my son Charles—we call him Bow—is thirty-four, married to a terrific woman, Katie, two young children. He's an attorney and she's a school teacher, but she's home with the kids now."

"Do they live nearby?"

"Derry, Connecticut. Mike and I go down to see them pretty often and they like to come up. We're talking about renting a beach house in Windy Harbor next year. You have any connections down there?"

"No, but my father and stepmother, Rita, do. They live at the Bluffs. It's at the north end of the harbor."

"Pricey, huh?"

"Most of the Bluffs is McMansions."

"Well, if it was just a week, a big place would be great and we could all stay."

"I could check with them, if you like?"

"That's be terrific, thanks." Another kilowatt smile.

"Is Mike your youngest?"

"No, my son Will is twenty-eight. He and his partner, Colin, are artists. They live a collaborative in Providence."

"Wow, are they making a living with their art?"

He grinned, tasting a sip of the delicious wine. "There may be some subsidizing, but they both work in galleries downtown."

The waiter came with the appetizers and took our dinner orders. Charlie ordered cadeirda a Portuguese, which sounded very similar to my mariscada. When he disappeared, Charlie said, "Your turn. Let's hear the Ricky Steele story."

"Not nearly as glamorous as yours. And you didn't tell me a thing about your work in Africa and other parts of the world."

"Another time. I want to hear about you."

"You mean the few scraps of information Vinnie left out?"

"Come on, out with it."

I gave him the short version, mentioning my mom's suicide and hurrying forward to cover boarding school, my two-minute marriage and my years trying to find myself and my career. He got a huge kick out of how I became a private investigator after impersonating one at my boarding school reunion.

"So, have you found yourself as a PI?" he asked, holding my eyes with his intense gaze.

"Maybe. Believe it or not, despite the obvious pitfalls of being in this profession at my age, I actually enjoy it. It suits my devious mind."

He laughed. "How come a beautiful, smart, talented person like you isn't in a relationship?"

"I could ask the same of you?"

"I asked first."

"Truth is, I'm not very good at relationships. Men seem to wander away after a few months."

"Maybe you haven't found the right man?"

"Maybe, but at this point, I've kind of given up. Not sure the heartache's worth it."

"No kids along the way?"

"No, and that does make me sad. I'd probably have been a lousy mother, but it's still a loss."

He reached over and squeezed my hand just as Tony, our waiter, delivered our entrées. The food was out of this world and we chatted idly as we ate, about his work at the clinic, my various jobs and the neighborhood. We shared a creamy, aromatic Portuguese flan for dessert, and then Charlie insisted on paying. We waddled out after sharing the last sips of Vinho Verde. I'm embarrassed to say that I fell fast asleep on the drive home and he had to help me inside.

"I'm sorry," I said, arms circling his shoulders. "The wine really hit me."

"No problem. We'll have that drink another night. You need to get to bed. Do you need help?"

"Absolutely not," I said, straightening up.

"I had a really good time," he said, hands holding my waist, propping me up.

I gazed groggily into his eyes. "Me, too."

He drew me close for a soft kiss, and I almost collapsed. "Sure you don't need help? I'm a doctor, after all."

"I'm fine, really." I stepped back, grabbing the kitchen counter to steady myself.

"Well, then, good night." He kissed my forehead. "Remember to lock up behind me."

"Always do," I said, already missing him.

I peeked out my kitchen window in time to see Charlie's rover disappear around the corner. Frank's Tacoma was parked in its usual spot.

I breathed a long, deep sigh. "Bed," I said aloud. "Now."

CHAPTER 20

I woke Saturday morning fuzzy-headed. I jog-walked the beach, secretly hoping to meet Charlie, but he and Carter were nowhere in sight. I'd had a really good time the previous evening and was embarrassed about falling asleep in the car. *Some date!* After a shower and cereal, I cleared my dining table and spread out all my notes on Meridian Imports, Jimmy Chen and Josh Peabody. It was a dismal sight, since I'd learned almost nothing. I decided to concentrate on outstanding projects for Bud's insurance cases since I'd done all the legwork weeks ago, but procrastinated about typing up the reports. After several hours at my computer, the reports were written and proofed so I sent them off, feeling satisfied until I remembered two terrified little girls who were out there somewhere.

I phoned Josh, but his phone went right to voice mail. Frustrated, I grabbed my bag and headed out to where Frank was sitting, drinking coffee, two bagel sandwiches by his side.

"Morning," I said brightly.

Noticing my ravenous gaze, he said, "My buddy brought 'em."

"Lucky you. Listen, Frank, would you mind giving me a ride to the car place? They left a message. My car's ready."

Reluctantly bagging his sandwiches, he said, "Hop in," and we were off.

"Sorry to disturb your breakfast."

"No problem."

"How long have you been doing this kind of work?"

"'Bout five years."

"It's been reassuring to have you here."

He smiled a crooked half smile, eyes on the road ahead.

"Where's Wilda today?"

"She's around. Keepin' an eye on the kids."

"You mean both of them?"

He shrugged.

"This is it."

I pointed to the car lot and Frank swung in. I hopped out and headed in to complete a mercifully quick transaction. The salesman came out to give me a brief introduction to what he called "the cockpit." Then, with a wave to Frank, I was off. I had nothing to do at the office and had told Mike to take the weekend off. She claimed she and her roommate were going to the beach. I wondered if that included Josh. I drove into the Highlands and parked near Belmont House, praying Ruth Channing was in. If anyone would know about children's whereabouts in the city, it was Ruth.

An old family friend, Ruth has run Belmont House for decades. In her early eighties, she had supposedly retired, but still oversaw much of the work of the city's Child Services. Belmont was a halfway house for juvenile offenders, but it was not unusual to see kids of all ages staying in the three-story refuge, one of the city's stopgap measures due to the critical shortage of foster homes. While the Highlands is the wealthy section of the city, a few enterprising souls, Ruth Channing among them, had managed, despite neighbors' objections, to convert some of the grandest residences into facilities to serve the community. Belmont House, once the showplace of a wealthy mill owner, now provided temporary shelter to a steady stream of kids.

"Well, well, what a lovely surprise," my father's former schoolmate said, opening the door. "And perfect timing. I'm just about to make lunch. Will you join me?"

"What do you think?" I said, hugging her.

Stooped, but still robust and active, Ruth returned the hug and then patted my back. "Good to see you dear. Come on back."

While she made two tuna salad sandwiches, I looked around the huge kitchen, imagining the cook and understaff scurrying around, preparing meals during the city's golden age. Bells connected to each room and the dining room still hung on the kitchen wall.

"Chips?"

I nodded and she grabbed a huge handful of potato chips and plunked them on both our plates.

"Why don't you grab two glasses and ice and pour us some iced tea. We'll eat on the back porch. Come on."

We settled down at wrought iron table. "This is nice. I don't remember this table and chairs."

"A recent donation. Don't think the donors had used the set more than once when the lady of the house changed her mind."

"It's quiet here today," I said, leaning back, marveling at the lush gardens. Ruth enlisted the kids' help in planting her gardens whether they liked it or not.

"Yes, we only have three residents. Two are out, one sleeping. We're expecting a crowd Monday and Tuesday."

"Gardens look great," I said, biting into my delicious sandwich.

"They're comin' along."

We ate in silence for several minutes. Finally, she said, "How's your father?"

"Annie was in town last week so we got together a few times."

"I'm glad."

During the many years I was estranged from Dad, Ruth never stopped encouraging me to mend the rift. They had been dear friends for many years until Rita came along. In her tired, moth-eaten sweaters and lumpy skirts, Ruth was not exactly "smart" or stylish and Rita had never warmed to her.

"You know they're letting us hold our annual fund-raiser at the cottage this year."

Cottage—there's a misnomer if there ever was one. Dad and Rita's beach house was eight thousand square feet with six bedrooms, movie theater, pool and fully equipped outdoor kitchen looking out on a huge lawn leading down to the sea. "No, I didn't."

"I hope you'll come. It's a clambake, your favorite."

"Hmm, tempting. When is it and how much are the tickets?"

She laughed. "It's next weekend and it's sold out."

"Just as well. I have my three Whitley school buddies coming for our annual sleepover."

"Bring them. I have a small bundle of tickets in the house. It's Saturday night, six thirty. I'll expect your check that evening."

"Well, we all love a clambake. I went to one with Bunny last week and stuffed myself silly."

"Come. It would mean a lot to me and your father."

"Okay, deal. They're coming in Friday afternoon and we eating at the Rainbow. I've been charged with finding a good restaurant for Saturday."

She smiled, twirling a chip on her plate. "What could be more perfect?"

"So, finding a good restaurant next Saturday is not why I came to see you, Ruthie."

"I thought not. Let me get some dessert and more tea and then you can tell me all about it." She rose on creaky knees and went into the house, leaving me with my thoughts as I admired her lush, fragrant peonies.

When she returned with a plate of cookies and pitcher of iced tea, I said. "Peonies were my mom's favorite flowers."

"Mine too. You know, he absolutely adored her."

"Yes."

"He was devastated when she died. I was afraid we'd lose him."

"Yes."

Before our mother's death, Dad was a different person, affectionate, the casual tousle of our hair as he passed, a loving husband and father. All that changed the day he came home to find his two young daughters covered in blood vainly trying to shake life back into their mother, screaming because they could no longer find the face she had blown away with her father's old service revolver.

"It was a long time ago."

"'Twas," she said, pouring our tea. "Now why don't you tell me how I can help, dear."

"I've been asked to look into the disappearance of two young Chinese girls. The person who hired me was their teacher, at a school run by a company called Meridian Imports."

Ruth's eyes clouded over and her normally open, placid demeanor gave way to a brittle hardness. I wondered if she had suddenly taken ill. "Ruth, are you okay?"

"I know Meridian," she said in a voice just over a whisper. "We've been quietly watching them."

"I thought the kids you oversee are mostly older?"

"Yes, but we couldn't ignore Meridian once news of what they were doing came across our radar."

"And?"

"Ricky, I'm not sure I should say more. It's too dangerous."

"Please, Ruth, we believe these girls' lives are in danger."

"They are."

"If you know something, please help me."

She gazed up at the second floor windows, then stood. "Let's sit in the shade," she said, leading the way to a stone bench in the corner of the yard, overlooking a small pond filled with koi.

"You understand that nothing I tell you can go further?"

"You have my word."

"We've been aware of Meridian and the school for over a year. We've been to the police numerous times, but every time they go out there, they find no trace of children or the classroom. We've been trying grab the children, but so far, we've only rescued one boy. He had just arrived when we waylaid him so he spoke no English."

"What do you mean, just arrived?"

"As far as we've been able to learn, almost every child who passes through Meridian has come from mainland China. Maybe a few from India. They're either kidnapped or sold to Meridian and brought here illegally in containers. Some die in transit. Others are barely alive when they arrive. They feed them, get them moderately healthy, then send them to school."

"For how long?"

"Some a few months, others sometimes a year. It depends on the work for which the child is being groomed."

"What kind of work?" I asked.

"The lucky ones go into domestic service, others to factories, where they are virtual slaves. However, Meridian is one of many operations across the country that specializes in something more vile and horrifying than child labor. Many of their children, boys and girls, are sold to wealthy buyers, who—" She paused, tears rimming her soft gray eyes.

"Sexually exploit them."

"Yes."

"Child pornography?"

"Some, but Meridian specializes in grooming personal sex slaves, some as young as five."

"Oh, my God," I said, remembering the two-way mirror. "When I broke into Meridian, there was a lavishly furnished lounge area with a two-way mirror that looked over the classroom."

"We've heard about that. Prospective buyers are brought in to observe the children and make their selections. They give instructions about how they want a child trained, language and so forth. It's unspeakable. We've also heard that some children are auctioned off, but not in that building. One of our people got close, but now they've vanished again. They always seem to be one step head of us, and the police."

"So, you have people in Child Services investigating?"

"Not exactly. We recruited outsiders for this. They work with a few of my most trusted people."

"Could I speak to them?"

"I'm not sure it's safe, my dear. I heard about your abduction, which means that Meridian already has you in their sights. I can't risk my people, especially after this week."

"What happened?" I asked, realizing with sickening clarity what she was about to say.

"One of our inside people was murdered."

"Jimmy Chen," I whispered.

"Yes," she said quietly. "He was one of our best and very brave. The poor man was brutally tortured before he was killed. I doubt he told them anything, but we have had to pull back and lie low."

"You said 'one of our inside people.' Does that mean you still have someone of the inside, working for Meridian?"

"Yes, one, but I cannot say more."

"Is there any way I could speak to one of your people safely?"

"Let me do some checking and I'll get back to you."

"Do you know police officers who've been working this?"

"No, but Sergeant Roberts would know. He's overseeing things."

Is he indeed? No wonder he didn't want me involved.

"What about you? Are you in danger?"

"My dear, I'm eighty-two. If something happens to me, I've lived a full life. Jimmy's had just begun."

"Oh, Ruthie," I said, hugging her. "Do be careful. I have a bodyguard I could lend you."

"Not right now, but I'll think about it." She reached into her apron pocket and pulled out four tickets. "The clambake, a hundred dollars each, good cause."

"We'll be there."

CHAPTER 21

After a power nap, I called Josh. He was staying the weekend at his parents' home at the Bluffs. He sounded upbeat until he heard I had learned nothing.

"I can't sit here imagining what might be happening to them," he said, whispering.

"Do your parents know about all this?"

"No and I don't intend to tell them. Dad would freak out and try to throw money at the situation and probably hire a bodyguard for me, like that goon that's following you."

"Frank is not a goon and his presence is quite reassuring." I refrained from telling him that Wilda was keeping an eye on him already.

"Well, I'm not a senior citizen and I don't need a babysitter," he said.

"Neither am I, thank you very much. Look, I have a couple of things leads I want to follow on, so lay low."

"Can't. Just found out about an apartment that's available. I may be moving in this week."

"It would be much safer for you to stay put in your gated community."

"No way."

"Why haven't you changed your cell number yet?"

"It's on my list."

"Even a burner phone is better."

"Look, I gotta go. I'm meeting Mike at the beach."

Mike indeed. At least someone is having fun. I wondered what kind of bathing suit Wilda favored. Probably black and sleek like a seal's skin. Assuming his cell was tapped, I refrained from asking which beach. I was just writing up a tentative schedule for the week ahead when Charlie called.

"Hey, how're you doing? Back to normal?"

I was already in love with his deep, resonant voice. "Whatever that is."

"Carter and I are heading out for a walk in a while. Wondered if you'd like to join us?"

"Love to," I heard myself say, despite my resolutions about getting involved.

"We'll be over in an hour or so."

I rang off and continued my paperwork. I would to need pay another visit to Brackett and Pearson, but this time I intended to speak to Phillip Brackett, the person who handled the Meridian account. No telling what the aftermath of that tête-à-tête would bring, but at least Frank would have my back. I also intended to gently beg Ruth again, hoping she would put me in touch of one of her people who was looking into Meridian's activities.

I called my dad and asked if he and Rita would be around sometime the next day. Turned out they had just returned from a quick trip to Bermuda, where they'd stayed with friends from the Bluffs, Tom and Ginny Brown. The Browns had the Bermuda house, a ski chalet, a villa in Malaga, Spain, and, of course, the McMansion at the Bluffs. To say "different world" would be a ridiculous understatement. Their jaunt explained why my stepmother hadn't been nagging me day and night to see how the case was progressing. Dad invited me to lunch. I accepted and rang off.

I changed out of my torn, stained tee shirt in favor of a clean, intact one and was just tying my sneaker laces when Charlie knocked at the door. Like me, he wore shorts and sneakers.

"Ready?"

With Herculean effort, he restrained Carter, who was scratching my hall floor, straining at the leash. No doubt he had caught Beaky's scent. She was nowhere to be seen and would likely remain invisible for several days after hearing the whining and growling of the horse dog.

We waved to Frank as we passed the Tacoma. *When did the poor man sleep?* An afternoon breeze tempered the sun's heat as we set off, talking and throwing a tennis ball for Carter. When we reached the boat ramp at the far end of the spit, we sat on an edge of old pier and gazed out at the river.

"Beautiful, isn't it?" I said.

"Yes." I turned to find that he was not looking at the river. He brushed an errant strand of hair from my face, fingers lingering.

I took hold of his hand, gently laying it at his side. "Listen, Charlie—"

"There's an attraction here. You feel it too. Don't you?"

"Yes, but I'm trying very hard to ignore it."

"Why?"

"Self preservation." I gazed into his blue eyes.

"I shouldn't say this, but Vinnie's told me a bit about your past relationships."

"I'm sure he has," I said, looking away, reminding myself that I would have to kill Vinnie very soon.

"Don't blame him. I asked. Then I asked and asked and asked some more. I wore him down."

"Why?"

"Because it's been a long time since I've met anyone I'm even remotely interested in, and I'm really interested in *you.*"

"As I told you, I'm not very good at relationships."

"And who says I am?" He turned and took both my hands in his. "Don't you think we owe it to ourselves to see where this might lead?"

"I'm also sick of having my heart broken."

"Sounds like you've been with jerks."

"Maybe."

"Okay, listen, can we at least agree to be friends?"

"We already are."

"Friends who see a lot of each other?"

I laughed. "We do live in the same neighborhood. I've managed it with Vinnie so it could work."

His face fell.

"Well, maybe not quite like Vinnie," I added and leaned forward to kiss him.

In seconds, my friendly kiss morphed into a deep, sensuous one with lots of tongue and heavy breathing. Fortunately, Carter spied a small dog and went berserk, or no telling where the kiss would have led. Charlie did a nosedive into the sand as I stood and stepped on the leash.

Face beet red, he scrambled to his feet. "Carter, sit!"

The command fell on deaf ears. Carter was in the zone. I spied the owner of a tiny white fluffy dog hightailing it in the opposite direction, Fifi clutched to her breast.

"Pain in the ass," Charlie muttered, brushing sand from his face and clothes. When he looked up and saw me smiling, he said, "What do you say we ditch this wretched, untrained beast and have an early at the Rainbow?"

"Good plan," I said as we headed back down the beach, veering off to his house, which was actually closer to the Rainbow than mine.

We both opted for slightly healthier choices, salads and chowder, but did break down and share one chorizo roll between us. When we got back to my house, I said, "Want to come in?"

"I'd love to, more than you know, but I'm catching a plane at three in the morning and I haven't packed a thing. Rain check?"

"Where are you off to?"

"Conference in Washington."

"For?"

"For the World Health Organization."

"How long will you be gone?"

"Till Thursday. I'm spending a couple of days with my sister Ellie. She lives in Alexandria."

"Will you miss me?" I said flippantly.

"Yes, I will," he said, eyes serious. "Take care of yourself."

Before I knew what was happening, he had pulled me close. This kiss threatened to send me into a swoon.

What will Frank think? I wondered as Charlie released me, a huge shiteater grin on his face.

He caressed my jaw with gentle fingers. "Something to look forward to. Until Thursday, then. How about dinner Friday night? My place?"

"Can't. My high school friends are coming for the weekend. Our annual summer sleepover."

"Okay, then how about Thursday night?"

"Won't you be too tired?"

"Never. I get in at noon. What do you say, six thirty?" I nodded as he leaned forward and kissed me on the forehead. I love it when he does that.

CHAPTER 22

Though huge, Rita and Dad's place was modest compared to many of its neighbors. Even so, it was pretty spectacular. Not sure how they'll fare in a hurricane, but on a warm summer day their back terrace was a beautiful spot. The lawn was perfect in sharp contrast to my crabgrass patch and the blue green ocean was calm, waves lapping at the sea wall.

"I'm sorry I don't have better news, Rita," I said, sipping my iced tea.

"Poor Cassie will be devastated. She's crazy about him and they were so happy together."

I decided it was not my place to tell her Josh's version of their deteriorating relationship. "These things happen, I guess," I said.

Dad plunked a plate full of sandwiches on the table. "Help yourself, darling. There are plenty."

I selected two cucumber triangles and two that appeared to be avocado and bacon. "Rita, my work for you is completed and I really didn't use the full retainer, so I'd like to give you a refund."

She gave a listless wave of her hand. "I wouldn't dream of it, especially when you had to go through the terrible ordeal of finding that roommate murdered. How horrible for you."

"Rita's right," Dad said. "You more than earned your advance. Please keep it."

"Thanks," I said. "Is there anything else I can do? Did Cassie have things at the apartment? I could probably get them after the police release it to Josh."

"No, I don't think so and even if she did, I'm sure she wouldn't want them now. I'll ask, though."

My stepmother looked ready to launch into a full swoon, so I turned to Dad. "I saw Ruth Channing yesterday. She was asking about you."

"How did you find her? Well, I hope?"

"Same old Ruth, saving one child at a time."

"Poor dear," Rita said. "I cannot believe she hasn't retired yet."

"She is semiretired," I said, "but her heart can't give it up."

My stepmother frowned. "It's beyond me why she wants to fill that magnificent house with prostitutes and juvenile delinquents."

"Someone has to help them," I said.

"Darling, they've chosen this life," she said, waving a cucumber sandwich.

"Not in most cases," Dad said. "There's a real lack of knowledge and many misperceptions in society about this." Surprised, I listened as he went on. "According to Ruth, it's much easier for people to think of them as delinquents and prostitutes rather than the enslaved, trafficked human beings they are."

Rita shrugged. "I'm sure you're right, darling."

"Ruth sold me four tickets to this weekend's clambake," I said. "That was nice of you guys to host it."

Rita rolled her eyes. "All your father's doing. Can't say no to his old school chum. A truckload of those dreadful Porta Johns arrive Friday along with two tents and all the rest. They'll probably tear up the lawn and we'll need to have it completely resodded."

Dad laughed. "I doubt it, darling. Besides, it's for a good cause. Ricky, you said four tickets? Who's coming with you?"

"This is my annual sleepover weekend with the Whitley crew."

He clapped his hands. "Oh, how delightful!" Dad loved my Whitley buddies, especially Katie Briarwood. Everyone loved Katie.

"Well, at least someone will be having fun," Rita said, nibbling on her sandwich.

After lunch, Dad and I took a short walk on the beach while Rita napped. Then, he walked me to my car.

"Now this is better," he said, admiring the Subaru. "When did you buy it?"

"Last week."

"The old jeep finally gave out, then?"

"In a manner of speaking."

"Well, I'm glad you have safer transportation. Everything okay? You seem a bit off."

I leaned again the car, thinking for a minute, before deciding I could trust him. "I didn't want to tell Rita, but there's more to the Josh story. He's hired me now."

"What for?"

"To look into the disappearance of two young girls who were students at the school where he and Jimmy worked, a school that has now vanished without a trace. Josh is the only one who insists there was a school in the building Meridian Imports owns downtown."

"Meridian Imports?"

"That's the company that supposedly funded the school, but it's gone. Poof!"

"Seems very odd. I feel like I've heard of Meridian, but I can't remember where or from whom."

"Well, if you hear anything about it, don't ask questions."

"Why?"

"It could be dangerous. I can't say why or how right now, but they're a nasty bunch."

"Does Ruth know something about them?"

I nodded.

"What did she say?"

"Not much. She's scared."

"Then please stay out of this, darling."

"Don't worry. I'm okay. The police are all over it and I have people watching out for me."

"Still, this isn't like doing insurance claims for Bud or helping poor Mrs. Petty with some harmless boarding school pranks."

"I'll be fine, Dad," I said, hugging him. "Gotta go."

He stood in the driveway, waving as I drove away. After all the years of estrangement, it was *almost* as if I had the father of my childhood back again.

*****

I spent the rest of the day doing housework, grocery shopping and yard work. Vinnie stopped by, leaning on the fence to watch me trimming my bushes, offering suggestions. Fortunately, he had a date so couldn't linger long. As I wound up the extension cord for my hedge clippers, he gazed at me, grinning. "Guess you'll miss Charlie this week. I hear you two are getting on really well."

"When we have more time, I will be discussing the concept of privacy and how good friends should respect one another's."

"Rick, you kill me," he said, laughing as he disappeared.

I'll kill you if you don't watch out, Buster, I thought, hanging the extension cord and clippers in my small back shed.

CHAPTER 23

Tuesday morning phone's ringing woke me at six fifteen and I squinted as I grabbed it, wondering who would be calling so early.

"Good morning, dear," she said. "Sorry to call so early."

I sat up, rubbing my eyes. "Ruth?"

"I wanted to catch you before you headed off to work. Last night, I spoke to one of our people who has been looking into Meridian's children and he would like to speak with you."

"Of course," I said, jotting down the name and phone number. "Did he say when would be a good time?"

"No, but if you call and leave a message, I feel sure he'll phone you as soon as he can."

"Thanks, Ruth."

"It's with great trepidation that I share this information. Please keep this confidential and be very careful, my dear."

I put the number aside, deciding that Danny Leonardo would prefer a call at a more civilized hour. After meditating and some yoga stretching, I took a long jog-walk, first on the beach, then around the neighboring streets. As I headed home, I loped past Charlie's. The driveway was empty, no Land Rover, and no sign of Josh's clunker truck. Mike had taken Carter to her apartment and the place looked deserted. I sighed, missing him.

Showered and dressed, I poured a bowl of muesli, then grabbed my cell phone and punched in Danny's number.

"Hey," a gravely voice said.

"Danny Leonardo?"

"Yup."

"This is Ricky Steele, Ruth Channing's friend. She told me you'd like to meet."

"Yup."

"How does this morning sound? My office is in the Sagamore Mill Building, number three oh one, or I can come to you."

"Be there around noon."

He clicked off and I was left staring at my phone.

*****

Wilda was at her desk when I walked in, Mike in my office, surrounded by mountains of paper. Since there was no spot for me in the Inner Sanctum, I grabbed several smaller mountains that included current projects and parked myself at Mike's desk.

"What's new?" I asked Wilda.

"Gave Frank the morning off."

"Good. Poor man never sleeps."

"He has people who spell him. He'll be back on the job by noon."

I had barely started on the paperwork when the outer door opened and Rollo Duffy and two of his goons waltzed in.

"Hey, Rick, long time no see."

Rollo is a midlevel crook, drugs, petty theft, numbers, loan sharking, whatever he can get his grubby hands on. He and I went to elementary school together. Overweight, greasy, thinning hair, always dressed in bright shiny clothes, Rollo talks like he has a mouth full of marbles.

"Rollo, how delightful. To what do we owe this pleasure?"

"Miss me?"

"Yeah, right."

"Gotta a minute?"

"Just."

"In private."

Wilda rose and stepped into my office.

"What's with the Amazon woman?"

"That's what you came to see me about?"

"You blue-haired PIs need babysitters now, do you?"

"What'd you want Rollo? I'm kinda busy at the moment."

"Yeah, I can see that. Who's that other Bobbsey Twin in there?"

"None of your goddamn business."

"You makin' enough to hire two employees? Maybe I outta go into the PI business."

"Knock yourself out," I said, shuffling papers, pretending to ignore him. Rollo didn't make frivolous visits. Someone had sent him and not to say howdy-do.

"Look, Rick, I'm semi-retired now and you oughta think about it too."

"Oh, and why's that?"

"Cause you're too goddamned old and if you don't watch out, you're gonna get yourself killed."

"Why would you think that?" I asked, staring into his watery eyes.

"Can't say."

"Well, thanks for the advice. Now, if you don't mind, I have work to do."

Like lightening he crossed the room and took hold of my arm. I glanced to my left and saw Wilda's shadow move to the door, which she had left open a crack. For a pudgy little guy, Rollo could move. "Listen to me," he hissed, sweat dripping from his pasty brow. "That cemetery stunt was nothing. Next time, you won't be so lucky."

"Let go of me."

I stood and attempted to shake loose. He held tight so I stomped hard on one of his shiny leather shoes. He cried out and let me go. One of his goons stepped forward, but he waved him back.

Keeping my distance, I glared at him. "What do you know about Meridian Imports? Do you work for them?"

"Fuck you, Steele. Done my job—you've been warned. You're on your own, honey."

He turned to go, goons following. As he closed the door, the sickening scent of his aftershave lingered.

The door to the Inner Sanctum flew open. "Who was that?" Mike asked, eyes as wide as saucers.

"One of Meridian's temps, I'm guessing," I said, rubbing my arm.

Rollo Duffy was clearly not the brains of the operation, but probably had a small piece of it. While I didn't think he'd harm me, he most certainly knew people who would.

CHAPTER 24

Shortly after noon, someone knocked at the outer door. On high alert after Rollo's visit, Wilda stood and moved to stand behind the door as I called, "Come in." I was still working at Mike's desk, or should I say my new desk.

The door opened and a stranger stepped in, medium height, sandy hair, jeans and a Red Sox tee shirt. In his early thirties by the look of him with a day-old beard, his face was wrinkled for someone so young.

"Hey!" he said, calling in to Mike.

She turned and gave him a smile and a coy wave.

"Can I help you?" I said.

"I'm looking for Ms. Steele."

"You must be Danny."

"You're Ms. Steele, not her?" he asked, pointing at Mike as Wilda emerged from behind the door.

"That would be correct," I said.

To his credit, he caught himself before allowing disappointment to register on his handsome face. "I wasn't expecting a crowd."

"No, of course. These are my employees, Wilda and Mike. I trust them implicitly."

He nodded to each in turn.

Wilda grunted and sat down while Mike returned to work.

"Come on," I said. "There's a quiet place we can talk down the hall." I led him to one of the empty offices that still had furniture and we sat on matching swivel chairs in a space that had been occupied by an interior decorator until a month earlier.

"What the hell is this place?" he asked, looking around.

I shrugged. "It's a work in progress. Cheap office space that businesses usually vacate as soon as they make it big."

"Not you?"

"Let's just say we have our ups and downs." After going it alone for most of my life, saying "we" felt good. "Thanks for seeing me, Danny."

"I'd do anything for Ruth and the kids. Besides, we may be able to help each other."

"I sure hope so. How long have you been looking into Meridian?"

"'Bout six months."

"Have you seen any of the children?"

"Only the one little guy that got away."

"Where is he now?"

"With his new family. They officially adopted him last month."

"How old?"

"Just shy of five, but he looks like a toddler. Poor diet."

"Was he able to tell you anything?"

Leonardo shook his head. "Poor little guy was so traumatized. He wasn't speaking then. No English at all, and only a few words in Cantonese."

"How did he get away?"

"We think he was headed for a placement. With the little ones, especially the boys, they don't care about their speaking abilities, or much training."

I shuddered, clapping my hand over my mouth. "Oh, my God."

He nodded. "These people are worse than evil. Anyway, a cop in the North End found him hiding behind a dumpster. The kid had just crawled out with a stash of food when the cop grabbed him. It was late so he brought him to Ruth for the night. He would have gone straight into the system, but Jimmy, Jimmy Chen, identified him from a photo sent through a cell phone."After that, Ruth made sure that the child disappeared behind a wall of paperwork until she could get legal approval for his adoption. You know Ruth. She doesn't let anyone go until she has just the right place for 'em. The city's had so many problems with group homes that she won't release kids to them anymore. Anyway, his status is still pending, but we'll probably never know where he came from. They estimate a hundred thousand kids, maybe more, disappear in mainland China every year."

I described what I'd seen at Meridian, the lounge, mirrors, empty classroom, and he nodded. "That's all gone now. We don't know where they've taken them, but they'll never bring the kids back to the Water Street site. Your visit and police crawling all over broke that place up. You've pissed off some very bad people, Ms. Steele."

"Ricky, please. Yes, I had a visit from one of their lackeys this morning."

"What?" His eyes registered fear.

"Rollo Duffy. Do you know him?"

"Chump change. If Duffy's involved, it's low-level stuff. He may be a shit, but he's not in the same class as Meridian's gang of thugs. I doubt he was involved with Jimmy Chen's death."

"That's what I think. So, what is it that you do, Mr. Leonardo? You're not with the police. Are you a private investigator?"

He laughed, shaking his head. "Not a PI, no. Let's just say I've been trained to stay in the shadows."

Mercenary. "Are you from this area?"

"Here and there."

"Who pays you? Surely the city wouldn't okay this kind of thing?"

"Let's stick to Meridian, shall we? Who hired me and how I'm compensated is not relevant."

"Not unless it's going to get me killed."

"Sounds like you're already doin' a bang-up job of that yourself."

"Ha ha."

"Tell me about Josh Peabody. Jimmy wouldn't let us go near him."

"Probably trying to protect him, as I am. He's safe. Obviously his teaching responsibilities are over."

"But he's hired you?"

"To find two of the missing children. Sisters. The older one vanished a couple of weeks ago, and now the little one, with all the others. Have you been able to find out where they house the kids?"

"Nope. We've tried to tail them at the end of the day, when they leave school, but they're *really* successful evading a tail. Kids are transported back and forth in several crappy cars, which change constantly. Easier to conceal than vans."

"What about Brackett and Pearson, the attorneys? Have any of you questioned them?"

"Jimmy went to see them a few times, but he got nothing. I'm not sure how much they really know. Meridian does a pretty busy lively import business and that's pretty much all their attorneys know about."

Bullshit. "Well, I'm planning to have a go at them, Phillip Brackett."

"Good luck with that. Be very careful."

"What about your person on the inside? Could I talk to him or her?"

"Too dangerous, especially after Jimmy."

My heart sank and I felt sick. "Do you think he was killed because of my visit?"

"Who knows. Jimmy had been pushing the envelope recently. They were watching him. We were actually gonna pull him out the day he was killed."

"Why?"

"Our other person at Meridian had overheard a conversation and was worried."

"Poor man."

"As I said, pure evil. Listen, I gotta go. You have my number. Call if you find out anything. Our concern is getting the kids out, period."

"Thanks, Danny. I'll be in touch."

He went to use the men's room on his way out and did not take the front stairs.

As I stepped back into the office, I felt an icy draft that sent chills up my spine. "Anyone want to grab lunch?"

"I'm good," Wilda said.

"I'm starved," Mike called, setting down a box. She was filthy after several hours in the Inner Sanctum.

"Are you sure?" I said to Wilda.

She nodded.

"But we agreed that no one should be here alone, right?"

"I'll be around," she said, meaning, "I'll be right behind you, ladies."

After lunch at Dino's, I decided a visit to the police station was in order. Unfortunately, Sergeant Roberts was out. "So, what'dya want to do?" I asked Mike. "I'm thinking of cruising by Meridian, then stopping in at Brackett and Pearson. You wanta get back to your filing? Wilda can stay with you."

"What about you?"

"Frank's Tacoma is two blocks behind us."

"Well, I'd rather come with you."

"Not to Brackett and Pearson. No telling who's watching them. I'd rather they not see you."

In full pout, she stared at me. "I can take care of myself."

"I know, but what you're doing at the office is a huge help. Once you restore order in there, I can get down to work and you can set up your space. Sound good?"

Her face brightened a bit. "Okay."

I pulled up at the side of my building. "Have you heard from Josh today?"

"No. I'm surprised, too, 'cause we were thinking about doing something tonight."

"If you hear from him, tell him to call, okay?"

"Will do." As Mike hopped out, I saw Wilda slip inside. *How does she do it? I move like a herd of buffalos.*

CHAPTER 25

I had just made my second pass down Water Street, Frank right behind me, when the phone rang. "Hey," I said.

"Ricky, it's me," Josh said, voice low. "Can you talk?"

"I'm actually in a dicey place right now. Can I call you back in five minutes?"

"Yeah, sure."

We hung up and I headed downtown. I had not seen anyone as I drove past Meridian, but had no wish to pause long enough for abduction, torture or worse, nor did I want my new car destroyed. When I found a parking space a block from Brackett and Pearson, I pulled in. Frank parked a half a block behind in a questionable space.

I grabbed my phone and called Josh. "Hey, what's up?"

"Ricky, someone's tracking my phone."

"What's that mean?"

"They call constantly and hang up."

"What's caller ID say?"

"Either private caller or an unfamiliar number."

They're trying to find out where you are. "Where are you?"

"Still at my parents', which is not where I want to be."

"Can you square it with the gatekeeper so I can pick you up? I've gotta a quick stop, and then I'll come get you. I have Frank so they won't bother us. Didn't I tell you to get a new phone?"

"This is the new one. 'Member, I gave you the new number yesterday?"

"Well, call and cancel immediately. Then take a hammer to that phone or throw it in the ocean. We'll grab some burner phones later."

"When'll you be here?"

"'Bout an hour, maybe less if I can't find anyone at Brackett and Pearson. See you soon."

Phillip Brackett was in court, as was his partner and Jill Carlson. I asked the receptionist, Tina, for an estimate as to when they'd be back and she was vague. "Might be soon, or they've been known to head out to Aquinessett for a few hours, then pop back later in the day. I haven't heard from them. Sorry."

She didn't sound a bit sorry. "Well, thanks. I'll stop in again."

"Best thing to do is make an appointment, like you did with Ms. Carlson."

I nodded and headed down the stairs. *Appointment, indeed. Give the thugs plenty of time to get into position.*

On the off chance that court had ended several hours ago and billable hours were now ticking off on the fairways of the Aquinessett Country Club, I decided to swing by. I was not dressed for the Club, but could probably slip into the pro shop, where most golfers had a drink after a round. The pink shirts would no doubt frown at my jeans and collarless shirt, but too bad. I wasn't hopping into a golf cart and heading out to the links.

As I rounded a hedge of rhododendrons badly in need of pruning, I spied the porch, crowded with men, shooting the breeze. A worker was raking near the path and I stopped him. "Hi. You wouldn't happen to know Phillip Brackett, would you?"

"Yes, miss."

"Is he here?"

"On the porch."

"Can you point him out?"

His eyes registered suspicion. "Do you know him?"

"Of course! It's just hard to tell who's who in those hats." I batted my eyelashes, which probably scared him.

"Yeah, right." He studied me for a few seconds, then said, "What the hell. Striped shirt, on the end."

"Thanks," I said, and scooted off before he decided to raise the alarm. As I planned my strategy, I remembered the pro, Don Something, my friend Mark Fallon's buddy. Don had helped on a previous case, but only through Mark, and I didn't remember his last name. Then I got lucky. As I approached the porch, a teenager called, "Hey, Don," and a lanky guy in golf shoes, chinos and one of those vests golfers wear came down the steps. I waited until he finished his chat then called to him. He turned, brown eyes studying me.

"Can I help you?" he said, his tone clearly asking, "Can I help you off the premises?"

"Hi, I'm Ricky Steele, Mark Fallon's friend."

Hand on hip, he nodded. "Ms. Steele, what's up?"

"Sorry to bother you. You look busy, but I could use a favor." "Please tell me it's not gonna turn up another body in the woods."

"No, nothing like that. I'd just like to speak with Phillip Brackett and I'm not really dressed for the porch. Could you perhaps ask him to step round back, say someone wants a word?"

"I can, but there's no guarantee he'll come."

"Just say it's a woman asking for him, no name. Please, I promise it'll only take a minute. Then I'll be out of your hair."

"I'll try only cause Mark's good people and I like your dad. Haven't seen him recently."

I smiled. "Thanks, I'll wait back here."

Brackett appeared almost immediately, no doubt expecting some chicky-poo. When he spied me, he made no attempt to hide his disappointment. Early forties, thick auburn hair, shiny face and blue eyes, he had the look of a player who got what he wanted despite a paunch and that shiny face. "Who are you?"

"Ricky Steele. I spoke with your associate, Jill Carlson, a few days ago."

"Lots of people speak to Jill. She's a busy lady. What's this about?"

I was certain beyond a shadow of a doubt that he knew exactly what this was about, but played along. "Meridian Imports."

"What about them?"

"You represent the company, I believe?"

"We represent a lot of companies."

"Do they all employ thugs and kidnappers?"

"Lady, I don't know what you're on, but Meridian is a legitimate and successful business."

"Funny, I don't know any legitimate business where a visitor would be drugged, tied up and buried alive. Nor one where employees are tortured and killed."

"Now I know you're high on something. I've known Wade Pullman and Oscar Winter for years. Meridian's one of their most successful ventures."

"Oh, what are the others—prostitution, pornography and slave trading?"

"This conversation is over."

"Do you have kids, Mr. Brackett?"

"None of your goddamn business."

"I'll take that as a yes. So, how do you sleep at night knowing you represent people who exploit young children in such despicable ways?"

"I haven't a clue what you're talking about."

"The school?"

"The what?"

"Jill didn't know about it, but I bet you do. Have you been involved in legal issues related to Meridian's real estate holdings in the city aside from the Water Street building?"

"You know I can't tell you that. Now, we're done. I'll have you thrown out on your ass if you don't leave immediately."

"Nice bluff. I have as much right to be here as you do. I grew up on this course so don't try to threaten me."

His expression shifted slightly and I expected him to bring up my father, but instead, he remained silent.

"Look, Mr. Brackett, I'm not interested in messing you up. I'm just trying to find two missing kids, tiny kids, who are destined for unspeakable horrors unless we find them."

"I take care of Meridian's legal matters concerning trade and commerce. I know nothing about any kids."

I was sure he was lying. "Please, Mr. Brackett. Please help me."

"Wade and Oscar belong here. They usually have a Friday game, ends around three."

"Thank you," I said.

"Leave it alone, Ms. Steele. That's my advice to you."

He turned and walked away, but instead of rejoining his buddies on the porch, he headed across the practice green toward the men's locker room. As he reached the doorway, he pulled out his cell phone.

Time for me to hightail it!

CHAPTER 26

After I swung by the Bluffs to grab Josh, we went to get him a new phone. We spent over an hour chatting with Chipper, the salesman, about the wizardry that had enabled someone to wipe Josh's phone clean.

"To be honest, it's a little above my pay grade," Chipper said, scratching his head. "Amy might know, but she doesn't work today. You know, if they've got this kind of expertise and technology, you might be better with burner phones?"

"Maybe, but we'll start with this." We thanked him and headed out. Pay grade or not, Chipper had managed to put up all kinds of firewalls and Josh had taken out the contract under a different name. I suspected that this would be plan B with plan C, a bag full of burner phones, not far behind.

As we drove out of the parking lot, I said, "They're probably looking for you. I think I should take you back to the Bluffs."

"Yeah, it sucks, but I don't want to put Mike or Charlie in danger. Can I come to the office and say hi before I go back?"

I gazed over at him with raised eyebrow.

"She called the house."

"Lucky you."

"Look, we're friends. That's all. I had to get away from my parents for a few hours or I'd go nuts."

"I'm sure they're concerned."

"Maybe, but I can take care of myself."

"Just like Jimmy?"

"I've got protection."

"Excuse me?"

"My dad loaned me his gun."

"Which I presume *he* is licensed to carry, *not* you."

He shrugged, gazing out the window.

"Have you ever fired a gun?"

"I was on the Harvard Rifle Team."

"I see. It's not the same, you know, shooting at a paper target. Firing a round into a human being coming straight at you is a very different experience."

We drove the rest of the way in silence. I let him off at the entrance to my building and headed to the back of the lot to park. By the time I got up to the office, the door to the Inner Sanctum was closed and Wilda sat alone, feet on her desk, reading a novel.

"Hey, boss."

"Guess *my* office is occupied."

Wilda shrugged and went back to her book.

I plunked myself down at Mike's desk and spent the next half hour on the phone with Lolly, Katie and Alice, advising them about the potential danger and suggesting that we postpone our get-together. This would mean I'd have to spend four hundred dollars on Ruth's clambake tickets, but it was a small price to pay when friends' lives were at stake. All three of them refused to reconsider, although Lolly did waver. Katie assured me that she be fully armed with pepper spray, pistol, stun gun, and handcuffs. "I've got extras, Rick. We should all be fully equipped." Alice said that after missing our last caper, there was no way she was missing this one.

Finally, I threw up my hands and said, "Can't wait!"

I attempted to reach Doug Roberts, but he was out. I suspected he wouldn't tell me about his meeting with Wade Pullman, even if it had happened. I would have intercept Wade and Oscar at Aquinessett, provided they hadn't gone underground. I googled Wade Pullman and Oscar Winter and came up with zip. All roads led back to Meridian Imports and their stupid website was completely useless unless I was in the market for a tacky scarf or cheap jewelry. I decided to run background checks on both owners. The service I use can take up to twenty-four hours so I set things in motion, then knocked on my office door.

Mike opened it, red-faced, her clothes slightly askew. *Friends, indeed.*

"Hey, Josh. Let's get you back to the Bluffs. I've got a bunch of errands to run."

"Mike can take me."

She nodded.

"Only if Wilda's got your back." I turned and Wilda gave me a thumbs-up. "Okay, well, I'm heading out. Don't stay too late and be careful."

I did a bunch of quick errands, Frank on my tail, then headed home. After organizing my purchases, I decided I needed company, so I strolled out to the Tacoma. "Hey, Frank, I'm heading to the Rainbow for dinner. Wanta come along?"

"Thanks, but I'll hang back." He lifted a large bag of fast food that had no doubt been delivered by one of his associates.

I shrugged, left a note on Vinnie's door in case he wanted to join me, and walked the two blocks alone. The place was deserted except for a couple of regulars at the bar, but it was early. I ordered kale soup, salad and a chorizo roll. When Jack asked what I wanted to drink, I said, "Just water," and headed for a table in the back. I missed Charlie and wondered what he was up to. *Already in too deep.* I sighed, sipping my water, gazing around.

Just as my food arrived, Vinnie walked in, nodding at me, then going to the bar to order. He brought a beer and bowl of peanuts to the table. "Hey, Rick."

"Hey, Vin, I would have banged on your door, but I didn't see the truck."

"Just got back. Been at Charlie's all week."

"That'll be a full-time job for you for the next six months."

"Maybe. He's got a bunch of people in and outta there. 'Sides, I've got other projects."

"And you're commitment-phobic. Can't stay with anything more than a minute."

"Pot callin' the kettle black."

"I suppose." I took a bite of my chorizo roll and sighed again. *How could I miss someone I'd met a minute ago?*

"Heard you guys have been dating."

"We're friends. We had dinner. End of story."

"That's not what I heard." He winked at two young women sitting at the bar.

"And, about that," I said, leaning forward to block his view of the bimbettes. "When did I give you permission to blab about my private life to complete strangers?"

"Charlie's not a stranger. As I told you, he's good people and he's hot for you."

"Is not."

"Is too. Can't stop talkin' about you, babe. Get used to it—you've got a boyfriend."

"Can we please change the subject?"

"Sure, what's new?"

"This case, the missing kids. It's going nowhere. Did you ask around about Meridian?

"I left you a message. Didn't you get it?"

"Where?"

"Your home line."

"Well, it's not there now." My paranoid barometer jumped sky high. Had Meridian's thugs tapped into my phone, too? "When did you leave it?"

"Last night."

"But I was home."

"Not when I called."

"This is what I'm talking about. These people are so far ahead of us. They seem to be able to tap phones and locate us at will."

"Well, they would."

"Oh?"

"They're serious bad guys, Rick. Want my advice? Step back, get out and throw your phone away. If they've hacked into your land line, they probably have your cell too."

"How can I back out when they've got all these little kids? I can't just abandon them."

"What're the cops doin'?"

"Not much, or if they are, they aren't telling me about it. Their Water Street site is empty except for a small suite of offices where they conduct their import business. So, what did you find out?"

"The owners are sleazebags, but they're slippery sleazebags. They're also in bed with very bad people."

"Who?"

"A group wackos called Javelin. They're a mix of white supremacists and neo-Nazi types. Some have military training. According to my guy they've got a bunch of meth labs scattered around the city. About a year ago, they got interested in the child trade and somehow hooked up with Meridian. My guy thinks one of the owners, Wade Pullman, owed them money. I'd bet the ranch one of them killed your guy and probably grabbed you."

"Lovely. Where can we find them?"

"*You* don't find them. That's an order. The cops have them on their radar. That's all you need to know."

"So you do know something!"

"I'm tellin' you, Rick. Leave it alone. Next time Wilda and company may not get there in time and you'll disappear without a trace."

"They must have a headquarters somewhere."

"People like that don't have headquarters. They move in the shadows. Oh, and they employ a couple of tech geeks, Silicon Valley dropouts. One's supposed to be in a class all by himself, mega genius with an ax to grind."

I propped my head on my hands, suddenly bone-tired.

"Walk away, Rick. Get new phones, have someone debug your house and car and go back to trailing cheaters."

"I can't."

"Look, you've got a new guy in your life, great neighbors and friends and despite all odds, you make a decent living as a PI. Leave Javelin to the cops."

I stood. "I gotta go."

"Sit. I'll be finished in five and I'll walk you home."

"Not necessary. If I know Frank, he's waiting outside."

Before Vinnie could protest, I patted his shoulder and walked toward the door. The night was hot and muggy, the air thick as pea soup. I stood on the Rainbow stoop and eyed the street. No Tacoma, no Frank, no nothing. Except for a few cars in the lot, the street was deserted. *Should I wait or be stupid?* Stupid won out as I started walking. I went less than a half a block and knew something was wrong. Since I had no wish to disappear without a trace, I turned back. Something rustled in the bushes alongside one of the few vacant lots and I ran full tilt until safely inside the bar.

Vinnie had moved to the bar and was chatting up the two women. He spied me and nodded. Breathless and shaking, I had no wish to disturb his little tête-à-tête so I headed for the seldom used pay phone and called Wilda. She answered on the first ring.

"Yup."

"Wilda, it's me."

"Yup."

"Is Frank still on duty?"

"Nope."

"So, no one's watching me?"

"Spike's out there."

"What's he drive?"

"You won't see him. That's not how he works."

"What about Frank?"

"Night off. He'll be back in the morning."

"My cell phone's been tapped and I've probably got bugs in my house."

"We using the Peabody kid's retainer?"

"Yes."

"I'll get a guy out there first thing. Throw your phone in the river, now. I'll have my guy bring a couple of burners out with him."

"Be careful, Wilda. I've been hearing horrible stories about Meridian's partners. And before you say 'I told you so,' I've heard it all from Vinnie."

"He's right." She clicked off and I was left holding the receiver. *Spike indeed!*

I made a beeline for the door, but not quick enough. Casanova was at my side as I pushed it open. "I've got protection, you know."

"Yes, you do. Me."

"Let's walk along the beach. I've gotta get rid of my phone."

"Give it to me."

He held out his hand and I gave it over. He threw it to the ground and crushed it with his work boot. "Can't be too careful. Now you can throw it in the river."

CHAPTER 27

After showing Stan, the debugger, around, I left the house with four burner phones and his promise to meet me at the office in an hour. Still no sign of Spike or Frank, but I headed into the city and arrived at the office at eight forty-five. Wilda and Mike were already in, Wilda with a new novel and Mike still battling the mess in the Inner sanctum. Since my laptop was now on my new desk in the outer office, I sat down and got to work. I called Bud and a couple of my regular clients on one of the new cell phones to give them my number in case they needed me. *What a gigantic pain in the neck this is going to be!*

My background checks on the Meridian owners turned up little. Wade Pullman, age seventy-two, had gone to Yale, then got his MBA from Harvard Business School. Oscar Winter, age sixty-eight, had gone to U Mass on the GI bill after four years in Vietnam. I wondered how they had gotten together and what Yale, Harvard and U Mass would think of their alums' post-graduation activities. They had both been married and divorced, Winter three times. He did not appear to have a wife at present. Pullman did. He was married to the former Lesley Granger, thirty years his junior. I ran a few more checks on Lesley Granger and the other ex-wives.

Pullman and Winter had owned Meridian for over twenty years and before that several manufacturing companies with overseas factories in Mexico, China and India. So far, they had managed to operate mostly under the radar. The records revealed a bunch of misdemeanors involving Oscar during his teens—petty theft, breaking and entering, etc. Pullman had been arrested for underage drinking and causing a public nuisance by the New Haven police during his freshman year at Yale, but otherwise he was clean. Both had a number of speeding tickets over the years. *Who didn't?* Winter had an incident after he got out of the service involving a firearm. He was subsequently treated for PTSD but no record since.

Quick checks on the wives came back an hour later. Libby Pullman, Wade's first wife, was an interior designer living in Providence. She had remarried, to a Thomas Waldron, a real estate developer. Lesley Granger Pullman had worked for Meridian until she married Wade. Before that she had worked for Eileen Sloan Modeling Agency and various sales jobs. Winter exes were flung far and wide. Wendy, his first wife, lived in Malibu, California, and was currently a theatrical agent. Joan, his second wife was an artist living in New York City. When not creating gigantic metal sculptures, she taught metal working part-time for various city colleges. Carolyn, his third wife, was the only local one. She lived in New Bedford and was a ER nurse at St. Luke's Hospital. I noted phone numbers for all of them, but thought I might pop in on Carolyn and also Lesley when their husbands weren't around. I spent the rest of the day researching Meridian's trade history and various holdings. I also called Doug Roberts and suggested he get a search warrant for Brackett and Pearson. He told me to mind my own business and stay out of it, then slammed down the phone.

CHAPTER 28

I spent the early hours of Thursday morning at home with my occasional cleaning person, Jeanie Vickers, wrestling my house into shape for "the girls." Tidying the chaos was always a challenge, but my current cases had buried me and I needed reinforcements. Like Wilda, Jeanie had come to me via Jay Harp. I cannot afford a full-time cleaning person, but when I'm desperate, I call "help" and Jeanie never says no.

Katie and Lolly were sharing my guest room and Alice had volunteered to take the pullout couch in my sun porch, which was actually quite comfortable. The sleeping arrangements for us oldsters had been decided upon after a lively email exchange. I had offered to sleep in the sun porch, but Alice insisted. She had traveled the world with her husband, Daniel, a biologist whose area of expertise was water quality, so she was used to roughing it.

Finally, it was time for me to head out. I grabbed my things and found Jeanie in the sun porch, wiping an inch of dust off most surfaces. "I'm sorry to abandon you, Jeanie, but duty calls. I left your check on the kitchen counter."

"Thanks, Ricky. Great to see you. Another hour should do it."

"Remember, don't bother with my room. I'll tackle that later."

"What about a load or two of laundry?"

"I won't say no."

At that moment, my cell rang so I waved goodbye, mouthing another thanks, as I headed off.

"Ricky, is that you?" As I struggled to place the voice, she said, "It's me, Jill Carlson?"

"Hi, Jill, what's up?"

"It's Phil. Phillip Brackett, my colleague? He's dead, Ricky! They found him this morning in his office."

"How?"

"Shot. They say it looks like suicide."

Bullshit. "So, the police are there?"

"Ricky, I'm scared. What have you gotten me into?"

"Excuse me?"

"I talk to you, you talk to Phil and now he's dead." Her voice was shrill, near its breaking point.

"Jill, slow down. Your company has lots of clients. What does your other boss say, Pearson?"

"He's left. Taken his entire family abroad."

"Planned trip?"

"No, we found out by email last night."

"Maybe he's responsible?"

"No, no, no…his whereabouts and all that are accounted for since early yesterday."

"Can anyone reach him?"

"No and he's asked to be left alone."

"Well, surely the police will want to speak with him?"

"Good luck with that. When he wants to disappear, Gary cannot be found. He's always like that on vacation."

"Well, this is a bit different, don't you think?"

"It's bizarre and scary. Robbo thought I should call you."

"Jill, I don't know how I can help, but if you'd like to talk, I'll be in my office most of today."

"Yes, yes, I would. Would two suit you?"

I told her the address and was preparing to ring off when I suddenly remembered I was using one of the burner phones. "Jill, how did you get this number?"

"I called your office and a young woman gave it to me."

With sinking heart, I wondered how we'd ever plug up the dam. Clearly, Jill's phone and all at Brackett and Pearson were bugged. Someone was probably listening to our every word. "Okay, change of plans. Ask the police if you can accompany them to the station and stay there. I'll swing by around two."

"But...?"

"Just do it, Jill. See you then." I clicked off and grabbed the bag of burner phones. I then grabbed a hammer from the back hall closet and smashed the one I'd been talking on to bits on the edge of my front stoop. Instantly I felt foolish, recognizing how long it would take to pick up all the glass shards.

I went back inside and printed a number of copies of a list of my burner phone numbers. I gave one to Frank, then went next door and slipped a copy under Vinnie's door. On my way into the city, I stopped at Ruth's and gave her the numbers, then made a quick stop at the office, where I found Mike hard at work under Wilda's protective eye. I gave them both a list, then asked Mike to share with her dad and Josh. Before they could ask any questions, I ran out, promising to return after my visit to the police station.

When I arrived, Tim Cottrell waved from behind the desk. "Hey, Rick, you lookin' for Roberts?"

I nodded.

"He's not back yet, but there's a woman waiting for you in the conference room."

"Thanks, Tim," I said, hurrying back. I opened the door, surprised to find Tina, Brackett and Pearson's receptionist, waiting for me.

"Hey, Ms. Steele."

"Tina, where's Jill?"

"She asked me to come in her place. She's gone home."

"Bad idea."

I grabbed the conference room phone and dialed Jill's cell. It went straight to voice mail. "Dammit. Tina, do you have Mr. Carlson's number?"

"Of course." She rattled off Robbo's cell number and I punched in the numbers. He answered on the first ring.

"Hello?"

"Bob, it's Ricky."

"Oh, call waiting showed the police."

"That's where I am and your wife is supposed to be with me. Do you know where she is?"

"She's here beside me, in my office," he said, voice low. "She's scared to death, Ricky. What's going on?"

I willed my voice to calmness. "Her bosses are involved with some very bad people and they appear to be cleaning house. I told Jill to meet me here, where she'd be safe."

"I'll drive her over now." He hung up before I could say another word.

I turned to Tina. "It's probably nothing, but do you have somewhere you can go besides the office or home? Maybe a family member's house, preferably out of the city?"

"I can go to my brother's. He lives in Assonet."

"That's great. I'm sure you're okay, but I'd feel better if you took a couple of days off. That goes for anyone who works for Brackett and Pearson. Are there others who—"

"Steele, what the hell is this?" Doug Roberts stepped into the conference room. "This is not your private office. What's going on?" He nodded to Tina, whom he had met earlier when the team was searching the law offices.

"I was just suggesting to Tina that she take a few days off from work. Jill Carlson is on her way over. I thought she's be safer here."

"That's probably true, but this is a police station, not a church. I spoke to Ms. Carlson earlier and she did not seem alarmed."

"Well, she is now. One of her bosses is dead and the other has left on a hastily arranged vacation."

He smiled at Tina. "Ms. Faria, you're free to go. You, in my office, now!" he said, pointing at yours truly.

"Did you learn anything about Brackett's death?" I asked once he'd closed the office door.

"Shot at close range, back of the head. Professional hit."

"This is Meridian's work, Douglas."

"Maybe, but that law firm represents a lot of sleazebags."

"But, it's—"

"Hold your horses. I'm with you on this one. You've poked the bear and he's pissed."

Tim Cottrell knocked, then poked his head in. "Sorry to disturb, Sarge,but there are some people here to see Ricky."

Roberts threw up his hands. 'Of course there are. Send 'em back here and grab two folding chairs from the closet, will ya?"

"Hey, Ricky," Bob said, nodding, as he ushered his wife in.

"This is Sergeant Roberts," I said. "I know you've already met," I said, gazing over at Jill, who looked like she'd aged thirty years. She was trembling as she held Bob's hand in a vise grip. She appeared to be cutting off circulation to his fingertips, which were now ghostly white. When we were all seated, I waited for Roberts to speak, but he sat back in his chair, arms crossed over his chest, and waved at me. "This is your show, Steele. Why did you drag these people down here?"

"For safety, I told you."

He looked over at Jill, his gaze much softer. "Ms. Carlson, is there anything else you can tell me about Mr. Brackett or the firm's relationship with Meridian Imports?"

"I don't know a thing," she wailed, on the verge of tears. "I'd never heard about them until Ricky came to see me. Now they must know I've been talking to her!"

"Did you ask your bosses about Meridian after Ms. Steele's visit?"

"Well, yes, I did mention that she'd been to see me."

"And?"

"And they said Meridian was none of my business, or hers. Gary was furious, as was Phillip. Said I wasn't to talk to Ricky again."

"Is that all?"

"They said she was an incompetent snooper and called her a few names that I will not repeat."

"Pricks," I muttered, receiving a glare from Roberts.

"Did you then take it upon yourself to snoop into company records about Meridian?"

"Absolutely not!"

"So, you know nothing and have nothing to add to this investigation?"

"Yes, but *they* don't know that!"

"That's true. I'm thinking the offices should remain closed until we get to the bottom of this. Is there anywhere you could go, maybe to a family member's, preferably out of town?"

"What about our kids?" Bob said. "They're in school and— "

"I'd go pick them up, pack a bag and head right off. I'll have two officers go with you," Douglas said.

"But what about our work?" Bob said, his eyes darting from Roberts to me.

Jill stood up, grabbing his sleeve. "Bob, focus! Did you hear the man! Oh, God, what if we're too late?"

"School?" Roberts said.

"Yes, they're still at school. Oh, God, oh God!"

Douglas picked up the phone. "Cottrell, get in here." He looked up at Jill. "You misunderstand. I meant, what school?"

"The high school," Bob said, rising to stand beside his wife. "They're in tenth and twelfth grades. Emily and Bobby."

Douglas gazed up as Tim Cottrell appeared at the door. "Call over to the high school. Tell the officer to pull Emily and Bobby Carlson and bring them to the office. You and Sunderland go with the Carlsons here to pick up the kids."

Without a word, Jill and Bob followed Tim out. I stood, hoping to escape in their wake.

"Steele, sit." His tone was neither welcoming or inviting.

"Now, I know what you're gonna say, but—"

"Did I ask you to speak?"

"But Douglas, I can explain. I wasn't even near—"

"What did I say? Did I not specifically tell you to stay out of this?"

"Yes, and I have. I'm just quietly looking for the kids."

"So, you call ambushing Phil Brackett at his country club and making all kinds of accusations, quiet?"

"I just wanted to ask if he knew anything about the school or—"

"Stop! Just shut up! We are on this and have been for quite some time."

"Well, you don't seem to be getting very far!" *Stupid, stupid, stupid, Steele!*

"Your meddling has now cost the lives of two people, not to mention nearly getting killed yourself."

"I have bodyguards."

"I don't give a friggin' shit if you have a whole army. If you go near this again, you will spend time in my cells, comprende?"

"Can I ask a quick question?"

"No. Now, get out of here!"

"Okay, fine."

"Where are you going?"

"Quick stop at my office, then home. I have a date."

"Good. Why don't you spend the whole weekend with the good doc. Keep you out of trouble."

Not even pausing to try and figure out how he knew about Charlie, I said, "I have friends coming for the weekend. I do have a life, thank you."

"Could've fooled me." Voice softer, he looked up at me. "Take care of yourself. These guys are nasty and they know where you live and work."

I nodded as a shiver went up my spine. *Thank God for Frank. Maybe he needs reinforcements?*

CHAPTER 29

When I got home, there was a note under my door. "Dinner at my place, 7 okay? C."

Right away, my pulse quickened and I felt my heart race. Still standing in the doorway, I turned and waved to Frank, then stepped in. Five thirty. I had an hour and a half to primp and then dress like it was the most casual dinner in the world. *Who am I kidding?*

I arrived at his doorstep promptly at seven. He opened the door in striped apron, a wooden cooking spoon in one hand. "Hey, welcome. Come in." He leaned forward and pecked my cheek.

"Welcome back. How was your trip?"

"The usual."

As if I know what that is in the world of international medicine? "Hey, the house is coming along."

"Yea, Vinnie and crew got a lot done."

"It's gonna be amazing."

"Yup," he said, giving me a dazzling smile. "White or red? Or would you rather have a drink drink?"

"Red would be great, thanks." I slid onto a bar stool, putting the makeshift counter between me and Mr. Gorgeous. "You know you're way overbuilding for this neighborhood."

"So everyone tells me, but what the hell? It's been a long time since I made a nest. Might as well make it a cool one."

"Nest, huh?" I said, smiling as he handed me the wine. I took a sip. "Mmm, nice."

"It's one of my favorites. A Chianti I found by chance."

"My favorite red. I mean, not this fancy one, but I do love Chianti."

"Something we have in common," he said, clinking his glass against mine. His blue eyes held mine, their message unmistakable.

I looked away, blushing. "So, what're we having? Can I help?"

"Pasta and a salad. Sorry, pretty simple. I stopped on Federal Hill on my way through Providence and picked up everything. Otherwise, we'd be eating Fruit Loops or whatever Josh left."

"Pasta's good, although I've been known to eat Fruit Loops from time to time."

"Everything's set. I can throw the pasta in anytime so let's head out to the back and enjoy our drinks for a bit, okay?" He grabbed a wooden serving dish with two sections, one mixed nuts, the other Kalamata olives.

"Sounds good." I followed him through the French doors, still covered with cardboard, and was amazed to find a beautiful terrace, furnished with new chairs, tables and a porch glider. "Wow! I had no idea this was here." Two sides of the wide terrace were five-foot-high walls made out of stone, in front of us, the river. Around its perimeter, the yard was fenced, a beautiful, artistic-looking split rail fence covered with almost invisible chicken wire. It enhanced rather than obstructed the gorgeous view.

"I built this before we started the house. Even if it looks like hell inside, I know I can come out here. It is summer, right? I've even slept out here a few nights."

"I'll bet Carter loves it. Where is he, by the way?"

"Still at Mike's. I'll collect him in the morning."

"Boy, this makes my view look pretty dinky."

"Does not."

"Well, this is spectacular."

"So are you," he said quietly. "Come, sit, relax." I took a seat and he sat opposite me with a small table in between.

"Charlie, I think we should talk about this, before the wine goes to my very tired, sex-starved head."

He smiled. "You don't look tired, and I like the sex-starved part."

"This isn't funny. I really don't think a relationship is a good idea for me, for us, right now for so many reasons."

"I think we've covered that already."

I set down my wine and waved my arms like a crazy person. "Yes, but when you say things like you just said, it puts pressure on me, you know? And, I can't… I don't."

"Hey," he said, reaching over to take one of my flailing hands. "There's no pressure here, Ricky. Promise. I'm sorry I said anything. Friends is fine with me. Okay?"

I smiled. "Okay," then turned to gaze at the boats coming in for the night.

We decided to eat on the terrace. I adore linguini with pink sauce and Charlie served it with crusty bread and a light arugula and fennel salad. "This dressing is terrific."

He smiled. "One of my specialties."

"Oh, my goodness, I'm feeling more pathetic by the minute. You've been all around the world doctoring and saving people *and* you can cook."

"In a lot of the places I've lived, you learn to cook or starve."

"No MacDonald's?"

"That stuff'll kill you, you know."

"Maybe, but what a way to die."

He grabbed the wine bottle. "More?"

"Please. Charlie, thank you for this. It's heaven after the week I've had."

"My pleasure."

"You've created an amazing space back here. So relaxing and beautiful."

"Come back in six months or a year. I've got all kinds of plans for a flowers, herbs, maybe a few vegetables. I'd also like to build a pergola."

"I've always wanted a pergola!"

"I was thinking over there," he said, pointing to the right stonewall. "Cover it with grape vines and I'll have grapes *and* privacy. It'd be a great sleeping spot."

"You've probably slept outside a lot over the years."

He nodded. "I prefer it, actually."

"What about bugs?"

"I've got a mosquito magnet. Haven't set it up yet, but soon. I also have netting. That's pretty cool and private, too."

All this talk of privacy pointed toward a direction I did not want to go. "You must be tired."

"Not especially, but if you are we can call it a night. I picked up a small fruit tart at Pastiche. It'll save if you'd rather not."

"I'd love a small slice."

"Coffee?"

"No thanks. I'm a tea drinker."

"I have some great herbal teas."

"Anything's fine. Surprise me. Can I help?"

"No, stay here. I'll bring everything out," he said, clearing the plates.

Ordinarily I'd have protested and hopped up to help, but I was relaxed from the wine and enjoying the twilight view of the river. "If you're sure?"

He returned carrying a tray with two slices of berry tart, each with a small dollop of vanilla ice cream on the side. He set them down along with steaming mugs of what smelled like a mint tea. "Comfortable?"

"Yes, I'm very jealous of your view."

"Well, it's available any time you want to stroll over."

"Wouldn't want to intrude. I'm sure you entertain lots of people here." *Women, lots of women.*

"You're the first, except for a few beers with Vinnie and the crew. Mike comes by, of course, but she doesn't count."

"She's lovely, Charlie."

"She's a keeper."

"Why isn't she doctoring? Did something happen to her?"

"Mike is a hothead, like her dad. One of the reasons she couldn't hack it in the field. She can be impatient and she exploded at too many people when diplomacy was critical. She's mellowing, but she needed a break. Mike wants to save the world and no one goes fast enough for her."

"What about you? You don't seem the hothead type."

He leaned back, smiling. "I've mellowed. My temper used to be ferocious. Almost gave me a heart attack several times. Years of therapy have helped. Starting my day with mindfulness and yoga have calmed me down, too. I teach both when I get the chance. They've made a huge difference."

"I couldn't move without my daily yoga."

"Me neither."

"Where do you teach?"

"Just the clinic at the moment, but when the new Grove community center is completed, I was asked to teach either mindfulness or yoga. We'll see."

"You have gotten around, haven't you? I'll be sure to sign up if you do teach here."

"Then it's definite. I will."

After dessert, we took our teas to sit side-by-side on the glider. The night was warm and stars blanketed the sky above. We talked about his house and travels. He asked about some of my previous cases and I gave him a quick rundown. "So, have you been back to your prep school since that first caper?" he asked, taking my empty mug and setting it on the table beside him.

"No, that week was enough. Lots of painful memories. It was a difficult time in my life. Whitley School was not a happy place for me except for the dear friends I made, who will be arriving tomorrow."

"Oh, that's right. Love to meet them."

"You will. We're going to the clambake at my dad's. I understand you are, too."

"Guilty as charged. Nice of your dad and his wife to host it."

"Hmm."

We chatted about this and that, gazing out at the water, its inky surface dancing with light from dwellings along its banks. A crescent moon in a clear sky was also reflected in the water. Next thing I remember was the breeze on my face and a strand of hair tickling my cheek. I sat up with a start and realized I'd fallen asleep on his shoulder.

"I've done it again," I said, rubbing my eyes, then smoothing my shirt, gazing over to find that he was rubbing his eyes as well.

"Some date, huh?" he said, grinning. "And I can't even use jet lag as an excuse."

"No old age jokes, okay?"

"I'm older than you."

I stood, grabbing our mugs. "Never mind. I've got to go."

"Hey, don't worry about those."

He followed me into the kitchen where I set the mugs in the sink. "I should stay and help you clean up."

"No way. Will take me five minutes. Let's go. I'll walk you home."

"Not necessary."

"I want to."

I peeked out one of the side lights at the front door, gazing out at the street. Frank's truck was there. "Okay, that'd be nice." I turned back to him. "And, because I do not want to put on a show for Frank, I'll do this here."

"Do what?"

In answer, I circled my arms round his shoulders. "I lied. I don't want to be just friends."

"Oh?"

"No."

I kissed him, open mouth, lots of tongue, hit-one-out-of-the-park kind of kiss, which I'm happy to say he returned. His strong arms drew me closer and my knees threatened to buckle under me. *Yikes, he is a great kisser!*

I stepped back before I collapsed. "Okay, better go now."

"Sure you don't want to stay over?"

"Not tonight," I said softly as my fingers traced the line of his strong jaw. "Maybe sometime soon though."

"Good."

"Now let's go. We don't want to keep Frank waiting."

"I'm sure he'd understand."

"Come on," I said, grabbing my bag and opening the door.

CHAPTER 30

I had not planned on working Friday, but then decided to head to New Bedford after ascertaining that Carolyn Winter was indeed working in the ER at St. Luke's until eleven. After calling Wilda and Mike, I grabbed a green tea and an egg white and veggie on a flatbread from Ally's, patted myself on the back for my healthy food selection, and hopped on the highway.

I parked several blocks from the hospital, waved to Frank, then headed toward the emergency room entrance. I asked at reception and they said Carolyn was with a patient, but they would tell her I was here. I took a seat in the waiting room as far from a mother and her son as possible since the boy was hacking like he had whooping cough. The only other person waiting was a twentysomething kid covered with tattoos and piercings. He was dressed in work pants and a wife-beater tee shirt and he held up his left hand, which was wrapped in a bloody towel.

Ten minutes later a short blond woman in green scrubs appeared, gazing around the room.

I stood up. "Ms. Winter?"

Her gray eyes registered puzzlement, mouth set in a frown. "Who are you?"

"Is there somewhere we can talk? I promise it will be quick. My name's Ricky Steele. I'm a private detective."

She hesitated, and I was afraid she was going to bolt back behind the double doors. Finally, with shrug, she said, "We can talk outside. It's my break anyway."

The minute we stepped outside, she pulled a cigarette from her pocket and lit up. "So, what's this about?"

"I'm investigating the disappearance of two young girls who apparently attended Meridian's school. What can you tell me about that?"

She looked genuinely surprised. "School? My husband runs an import business."

"Yes, but apparently Meridian also runs or ran a school on the premises, for young children, helping them to learn English and other basic skills."

"First I've heard of it." She took a long drag on her cigarette, half closing her eyes.

"How much do you know about your husband's business?"

"Not much. They import junk, if you ask me. Designer knockoffs and crap."

"Have you ever been to Meridian's offices?"

"Once or twice, why?"

"I just wondered if you'd seen children there."

"Never. Have you talked to Oscar or Wade?"

"I can't seem to locate either of them."

"Not surprised. Haven't seen Oscar in weeks and Wade's a spook."

"You mean you don't live together?"

She shook her head. "We've been separated for over a year. I'm living with my sister."

"Do you have kids?"

"No, thank God. If you want to know about what goes on at Meridian, ask Nancy or Kim."

"What about Betty?"

"Never heard of her."

"Who would know more about the import side of things, Nancy or Kim?"

"Neither. For that, you'd have to ask that bimbo, Fiona."

"Fiona?"

"Fiona Veruga. She does most of the buying and all the marketing for them. If you ask me, she spends most of her time marketing herself."

"Does she spend much time at the office, do you know?"

"Not unless she's boffing my husband. She's the reason my husband and I are no longer together."

"I'm sorry."

"Don't be. Oscar and I had drifted apart. Besides, he likes 'em much younger than me. Look, I've gotta get back."

"Of course. Just one more thing. Do you have any idea where could I find Ms. Veruga?"

"I'm not sure if she even has an office, but she has a condo somewhere. Dartmouth, I think, or maybe Freetown? Sorry, I gotta go."

As Ms. Winter hurried inside, I jotted a few notes, then strolled toward my car, wondering how to locate Ms. Veruga, the home wrecker. Back at the office I executed an online search for Fiona Veruga, then chatted with Mike and Wilda while I waited for the results. Correction—Mike and I chatted and Wilda occasionally contributed a monosyllable or maybe a subtle gesture. Mike was making real headway with my files and the office mess. Absently, I wondered what task I could give her once the Inner Sanctum was shipshape. There was probably a day of organizing in the outer office, but then what?

I watched her moving about, her face serious. "What're your plans for the weekend, Mike?"

"Beach. Josh invited me to come down to his parents' house. Apparently, they have some amazing beach right in front of them."

"You have no idea. So, you guys are seeing a bit of each other?"

She turned and gave me a look. "Just friends."

"Well, Wilda'll stick with you and I'll keep Frank. Is there a guy on Josh?" I asked turning to my associate.

Wilda nodded. "Spike. You won't see him. He drives a dark blue sedan that blends in with the landscape."

"Sounds miraculous—an invisible car and invisible bodyguard," I said.

Wilda grunted, no doubt having exhausted her conversational quota for the day. My computer pinged and I checked. The report on the Veruga woman had come in. I pulled out one of my burner phones and tried Fiona's number. A silky voice invited me to leave a message, which I declined to do. I printed the report, scanned its contents, then shoved it into my bag."Hey, ladies, time for me to hit the road. You both have my numbers so call if anything comes up. My friends arrive this afternoon for the weekend, but I'll continue to poke around. I seriously need to speak to this Veruga woman."

"What are you and your buddies up to?" Mike asked.

"Catching up, mostly. We're going to a charity clambake tomorrow. It's at the Bluffs, not far from Josh's parents' house. Your dad's going, apparently."

"Yeah, he told me. Wanted me to be his date, but I'm allergic to seafood."

"Yuck. All kinds?"

"Well, I know about shrimp and lobster so I've never dared try the others. Clams don't appeal too much with those squishy bodies."

"And chewy necks, yum!"

"Yuck. Isn't the bake at your dad's house?"

"Yup."

"Fancy."

"Their lifestyle, not mine. See ya." I motioned to Wilda, who rose and followed me out. At the end of the hall, out of earshot, I paused. "Take care of her. Hire another person if you have to, but don't let her out of your sight. I may have ruffled a few more feathers today."

"No worries, boss."

CHAPTER 31

I swung by the market for breakfast supplies. While there I grabbed a spinach pie from the deli and ate it while I shopped. Satisfied that I had enough snacks and breakfast items, I checked out and headed home.

I pulled into my driveway just in front of Katie.

"Hey, girl!" I cried.

I was so happy to see her I almost burst into tears. Lolly's car was parked on the street, but she was nowhere to be seen. I assumed she'd found the key and let herself in. Frank pulled up as Katie grabbed me in a bear hug that would have crushed a lesser mortal. Katie gave great hugs.

"Hey, Steele! What a place. You're in trouble for not having us here before this. You are literally on the water." Katie had several homes in various exotic locales, most on one body of water or another. All of her houses could fit ten of my little shack inside their vast interiors.

Gorgeous as ever, her hair still sandy blond, face almost wrinkle-free, she was dressed in jeans and a plaid cotton shirt, untucked, with a jaunty scarf at her neck. Despite her size, she moved with grace and agility, still the athlete of her youth. Rare was the day that she and her husband Bob didn't play a round of golf and usually a game of tennis at one of the several country clubs to which they belonged. As we tussled and tugged her bag out of her enormous SUV, a cab pulled up, back window down.

"Woo-hoo, ladies, lookin' good!" Alice Bannister waved as she pulled in behind Katie and hopped out.

It had been years since I'd seen Alice, but she hadn't changed a bit, except for her salt-and-pepper hair very like my own. The shortest of the Musketeers, Alice was just over five feet. Dressed in tan chinos, a bright coral jersey and navy sneakers, she looked as fresh as a daisy after her long trip. Hugs all round, we then hoisted her bags, only to drop them as Lolly pushed open my back door, screaming, "Yeah, yeah!"

She sported one of her signature casual pantsuits, this one canary yellow with shorts that stopped just above her knees. Slim and glamorous as always, her thick brown hair fell loosely at her shoulders. Even at midday, she wore full makeup, mascara and eyeliner accentuating her coal-black eyes. "I've been waiting for hours!" she cried, flinging herself at each of us in turn. "Come in, come in! I'm on my third iced tea and if I don't switch to something stronger soon you'll have to tape my eyes closed tonight after all this caffeine!"

"If you're drinking my tea from the fridge, it's not heavily caffeinated," I said, hugging her.

"Surely you jest? I am serious about my caffeine, sweetheart. You know this about me. I brought my own high test."

*****

After a quick bout of unpacking, iced teas in hand, we settled on my deck, the river lazy and calm in front of us.

Alice leaned back and sighed. "You are so lucky, Ricky. This is paradise."

"I hope we'll catch a glimpse of Mr. Gorgeous next door," Lolly said, taking a drag on her Benson & Hedges extra-long.

I frowned. "I see you still have that nasty habit."

She tossed a cigarette to Katie. "My one vice. I only smoke when I travel. Ron, the health nut, doesn't approve," she said, referring to her husband.

"Bob, either," Katie said, grabbing Lolly's lighter. "Oh, I feel sixteen again!"

"Me, too," Alice said.

"I'm thinking we'll switch to wine after this round," Lolly said, tipping her iced tea in my direction. "I brought a case of Chardonnay."

I smacked my forehead. "Oh, hell, I was going to stop at the fish market for our dinner and I forgot! I can run out while you guys relax."

"I vote for the Rainbow," Lolly said, "and let's invite Mr. Dreamboat."

"Mr. Dreamboat's truck is not in his driveway, so I fear he's busy."

"Let's call him, then," Alice said, sitting up, eyes sparkling. "I've never met him and I've heard so much from Loll."

Before I could reply that Mr. Dreamboat was elusive and hard to reach, Katie slammed down her drink and leaned forward. "Okay, Rick, enough about your neighbor. Let's hear it. What gives with the case? No bullshitting."

"Excuse me?"

"Something's up and I for one want to hear it!"

"I'm just a little preoccupied with one of my cases, that's all."

"So preoccupied that you tried to warn us off?"

"Oh, God," Lolly said. "Not again!"

"Yes!" Alice said, pumping both arms. "I'm in and Briarwood came armed to the teeth. Pepper spray, cuffs and who knows what else?"

"Damn straight," Katie said. "My purse is an arsenal."

What a comforting thought. "Now listen gals, I promise to fill you in, but let's please decide on dinner before we morph into the Rambettes."

"I'll get the wine," Alice said, standing. "Rainbow's great with me, too."

"It's unanimous," Katie said, clapping her hands.

At the sliding door, Alice turned. "And don't say a word until I get back!"

Alice returned in record time and I filled them in on my activities over the last week, glossing over some of the gory details. After we'd polished off an excellent bottle of Chardonnay, I suggested we head to dinner.

CHAPTER 32

Friday night, the Rainbow was packed. Not an empty table, booth or bar stool. Lolly threw up her hands. "What'dya think girls? Takeout?"

Hands on hips, Katie scanned the room. "Takeout? No way. You girls order. Get a pitcher of Coles and order me a bowl of kale soup and three chorizo rolls. I'm starving." She turned and forged her way into the crowd.

"Where are you going?" Alice called after her.

"Never mind," she said, giving us a backward wave.

As Alice and I stood slack-jawed, Lolly said, "Leave her be. She'll take care of things. Just wait and see."

The three of us inched our way to the end of the bar and gave Jack, our order. As we waited, we caught glimpses of Katie stalking from one end of the room to the other, finally settling between two tables of young adults, who appeared to be nursing their beers in a semi-coherent state. By the time Jack set the pitcher and four glasses in front of us, we looked over to see Katie waving.

"Go ahead, ladies. I'll bring the food in a few," Jack said.

"How did you do that?" I asked when we reached her. Hands on hips, Katie stood to the side supervising Eddie, one of the kitchen staff, as he wiped the now empty table.

"No prob, thanks, Eddie," she said, nodding as he headed off. "I just persuaded the kids that they should respect their elders."

"Remind me to take you along if I ever go on safari," Alice said, laughing as we took our seats. She poured us each a glass of Coles.

"Well, it's cold," Lolly said, "but I still prefer my Chardonnay."

"Doesn't go with chorizo," I said, tipping my glass. "So good to have you guys here."

"So, what's our next move?" Katie said.

"Dinner?" I said, knowing full well what she meant.

"Baloney. After the story you told us, you can't afford to be off the case all weekend."

"This is *our* time," I said.

"Listen, girl," Katie said. "After you tried to warn us off, I packed my stun gun, several cans of pepper spray and cuffs. I also brought a couple of the kids' baseball bats I found in the garage."

"Oh, Lord," Lolly said. "Kill me now."

"None of that will be necessary," I said. "Frank will always be with us. He's my bodyguard, drives black Tacoma."

"I saw him," Alice said. "Built like a brick shithouse. It must be serious if you've hired him."

At that moment, Jack and Eddie appeared with our food. I wanted to jump up and hug both of them. "Let's eat, "I said. "We can plot strategy later."

As we ate, we chatted about life, Alice's travels and day-to-day, comfortable topics that did not include murdered people and premature burials. It was wonderful and relaxing. As I started in on my second chorizo roll, feeling almost full, Vinnie strolled up. "Hey, ladies, lookin' good."

As we greeted him, I gazed over to see Lolly batting her eyelashes. *Geez!*

"Join us," Katie said, ignoring my glare. "We're plotting strategy with Ricky's case."

"Thanks, but no can do. Just getting' takeout. Got a job tonight over at Ricky's boyfriend's house. Besides, none of you pretty ladies should be mixed up in that shit, including your friend the PI."

"Ha ha," I said, as a chorus of "boyfriend?" rang out. *I will be killing Vinnie very soon.* I glared at him, but he ignored me. He even had the audacity to wink!

"She must not have gotten to that part in your catching up. Stop over on your way home. It's gonna be a spectacular house. Doc's got great taste." With a nod and a wolfish grin, he turned and headed for the bar where Jack had a large bag waiting.

Stop by, indeed. Over my dead body!

"Okay, dearest," Lolly said. "Seems you left out something major in reciting your recent activities. Hmm?"

CHAPTER 33

Saturday morning I woke at nine with a headache, no surprise. Half-asleep, I schlepped into the kitchen, where I found Katie and Alice bustling about. They had been assigned breakfast so, of course, it was amazing—fruit, eggs, bacon, bagels, lox, five flavors of cream cheese, and every kind of muffin from Katie's local bakery. Lolly sat at the table observing, head in hands. She wore sunglasses and a diaphanous robe of swirling colors that made my head spin.

"Good morning!" Katie said, grinning as if she hadn't consumed the same gallons of alcohol as the rest of us.

"Too loud!" Lolly said.

"You gals are slippin'," Katie said as she set plates and cutlery on the table. "Make yourself useful, Pruit. Push those around."

Lolly pushed everything to the middle of the table as Alice set platters and baskets beside her. "Come on, eat, gals. Make us all feel much better."

I gazed out at the river. "Looks like a great day for a beach walk."

"A very slow, silent one," Lolly said, loading up her plate.

Alice was right. The food perked us up. After stuffing ourselves, we dressed and headed out into the beautiful morning. We took a two-mile walk, returned to shower and planned our day. Katie and Lolly loved to shop so we spent the morning hitting gift emporiums and small, high-priced clothing boutiques. We then ended up at Terry's Tea Room for a late lunch. Attached to Terry's was a gift shop full of trendy jewelry, handbags, and other useless stuff. After lunch, Katie and Lolly browsed while Alice and I sat on a bench in the shade chatting. When we arrived home at two, we all decided a nap was in order.

*****

Perked up and raring to go after our power naps, we arrived at the Bluffs shortly after four and parked in the residents' lot several blocks from Dad and Rita's. Two huge green-and-white-striped tents covered their backyard and the smoky smell of the bake drew us in.

"This was a terrific idea," Alice said. "I haven't been to a clambake in years."

"Me, either," Katie said. "Some of my fondest summer memories are being here at a clambake."

Lolly groaned. She hated clams. Lobster, yes. Clams, no.

One of the first people I spied as we skirted the house and strolled across the lawn was Rita's son, Matthew. He lived in Maine and I saw little of him. At fifteen, he had fathered a son with his fourteen-year-old cousin Bella, Rita's sister's daughter. His son, Bobby, now sixteen, stood beside him.

"Hey, Matthew, Bobby. Good to see you guys." I gave them both a hug, then introduced the gang.

"Hi, Ricky. You're looking well." *Translation: you don't look bad for an almost senior citizen.*

"You, too. How's Maine?"

As we talked, I glimpsed Dad and Rita on the terrace, greeting guests. I recognized some of their neighbors from the rare summer cocktail parties I've attended in the Magic Kingdom. One of them, Lincoln Ramsay, rumored to be the wealthiest resident of the Bluffs, stood chatting with Lindsay and Bill Kickham. Venture capitalists, Lindsay and Bill were friendly with dad and Rita, but Ramsay was just a passing acquaintance as far as I knew. He and his wife, Catherine, lived at the Annex, home to the Bluffs' wealthiest residents.

As Katie regaled Matthew and Bobby with tales of her latest travels in Chile, I excused myself and headed across the lawn.

"Ricky, hi, hello!" Lindsay Kickham called.

I paused, surprised that she even remembered me. "Hi, Lindsay, great to see you."

She pulled me into the group, introducing me to Ramsay as well as Chip and Patsy Bolton, whom I'd met before. Chip Bolton owns several mills in Spindle City devoted to innovation. They are constantly inventing new variations on sewing machines and his mills also provide space for a number of designer clothing manufacturers.

"Hi, Patsy, Chip. Good to see you again," I said, shaking their hands.

"You're Ralston's daughter, aren't you?" he said.

"Guilty as charged."

"Didn't I hear you'd gone into some kind of interesting work?"

"Ricky's a private investigator," Lindsay said. "Isn't that cool?"

"Intriguing line of work at your age," Patsy Bolton said.

"Tell us about your cases," Lindsay said.

The others looked bored and ready to be rid of this raggedy interloper. "Not much to tell," I said. "Mostly insurance fraud, the odd missing person, that sort of thing."

"Where's your office?" Chip asked.

"Not far from one of your mills, actually. I'm off Quarry in the middle of outlet central." As I spoke, the Ramsays wandered off to join another group.

"Quarry, I know it well. You're in the old Sagamore Mill, right?"

"The very one. Just me, the outlets and a few other offices. The original dream of turning it into an upscale office building has faded away. So far, at least."

"The mills are a challenge, but no one builds anything that cool anymore."

"Couldn't agree more. The woodwork in mine, or what remains of it, is exquisite."

He nodded as Lolly approached. Out of the corner of my eye, I caught a glimpse of Katie barreling across the lawn toward Rita and my dad, Alice in her wake. My father loved Katie and the feeling was mutual. I wasn't sure Rita had ever met her, but that would be changing soon.

As the Kickhams strolled away, I said, "Chip, since you're in the business in Spindle City, do you know anything about a company called Meridian?"

He gave me a sharp look, then gazed upward, doing a very poor imitation of someone thinking. "Doesn't sound familiar. What do they do?"

"Imports. Clothing and other designer knockoffs."

"Not my area, sorry."

"Just thought you might've heard of them. The city's business community is pretty small, right?"

"I'm not really a part of that community," he said. "My dealings are mostly in Providence, Boston and New York."

Another lie? I nodded, but stayed silent.

"What's your interest in them, anyway?"

"Nothing special. Just heard the name the other day."

At that juncture, Lolly poked me. "The bar's free, dearie. Let's go."

We excused ourselves.

"He knows someone," Lolly whispered as we neared the bar.

"Yup," I said, looking up to see Rita waving furiously. My father had been waylaid by Katie and they were deep in conversation, thus taking him from his hosting duties. Alice caught my eye and headed toward us.

I put up my finger in a "wait a sec" gesture, eliciting a frown from my stepmother.

"Thank, God, saved!" Alice said, coming to stand beside us. "Alcohol! Any kind! Now!"

We all ordered gin and tonics and, drinks in hand, we reluctantly made our way toward the host and hostess.

"Took you long enough," Rita whispered. "Take her away, please. Your father is hopeless when it comes to extracting himself from uncomfortable social situations."

"He looks fine. It appears most people have arrived anyway."

Rita rolled her eyes. "Have you seen Matthew and Cassie?"

"Him, yes. Haven't seen Cassie yet."

"She's a wreck, thanks to your horrible client."

A change of subject is definitely in order. "You remember my friend, Lolly Pruit?"

"Yes, hello," Rita said, ignoring Lolly's outstretched hand.

"Nice to see you again," Lolly said. "It's incredibly generous of you and Ralston to host this."

"Yes, it is," Rita said, "and it won't be happening next year. Let someone else's lawn be destroyed! And those ghastly Porta Potties— yuck!"

"This is another Whitley friend, Alice Bannister. I don't believe you two have met."

"Hello, Ms. Steele," Alice said, smiling.

"Rita, please. Always lovely to meet one of Ricky's chums." She turned from Alice to me. "By the way, speaking of chums, I didn't know you knew the Ramsays?"

"I don't, except for the times I've seen them at your parties."

"Horrible people. He's a terrible snob and she's a relentless do-gooder!"

"Then why do you socialize with them?"

"Wake up, dearie. This is the Bluffs and no one leaves Lincoln Ramsay off their guest list."

"Hey, Dad," I said, deciding it was time for an extraction. "Can we steal Katie for a bit?"

"Hello, darling. Lolly, so nice to see you again. And, Alice, isn't it? It's been a while, my dear." He stepped forward and gave each of them a warm hug.

"Katie, we're needed over there," I said, waving toward the beach. "Catch you later," I said, waving to Dad and Rita.

We made our way to the edge of the crowd, pausing long enough for Katie to visit the bar. When she returned she had a small platter of appetizers in one hand, her gin and tonic in the other. We found an open table in the cocktail area, sat down and dove into the oysters, crab puffs and shrimp cocktail. Occasionally someone would pass by and we graciously shared with them.

I scanned the crowd and spotted my stepsister, Cassie, on the arm of a tall, preppy guy in rugby jersey, faded red shorts and boat shoes. *Best to steer clear of that!* Katie was going on and on about how handsome Dad was and how he never changed a bit when I heard a familiar voice nearby. I turned to find Charlie Bowen chatting with Sim and Betsy Khan, two of Rita and Dad's best friends in the area. One of the city's top orthopedic surgeons, he was originally from Iraq, but had come to the states for medical school and met Betsy at Harvard. They now lived in the city, while maintaining a second home two doors down from Dad's in the Magic Kingdom.

Charlie turned and caught my eye, then nodded to the Khans and excused himself, heading our way.

"Hey, Ricky," he said, coming to stand over me. His gorgeous smile was not lost on my companions, whose jaws had nearly hit the table. "Good to see you."

"Charlie," I said, giving in to the inevitable. "As you can see, the gang's all here." I introduced him to the girls, who were batting eyelashes spouting syrupy platitudes.

We chatted for what seemed like hours, but in reality was probably less than five minutes, when traitorous Katie said, "Sit down. Please, join us. We've heard sooo much about you, we want to hear more." My glare was lost on her.

Charlie laughed as he stole a glance at me. *If my cheeks got any redder, I'd turn into a giant beet.* "Love to, ladies, but I've got to get back to my group. I came with a bunch of people from the clinic. Don't want to be rude. Love to catch up later, though. Maybe I'll see you around the neighborhood? How long are you staying?"

"Just till tomorrow," Lolly said, hanging her head. "But we'll be around until later in the afternoon," she added, batting her long eyelashes.

Could this get any more ridiculous?

"Well, stop by my place for a drink, if you have time," he said. "I'm just around the corner from Ricky. My house is a work in progress, but I'd love to give you a tour."

I opened my mouth to make excuses, but Alice beat me to it. "It's a date, Charlie. I love restoration projects!"

"Anytime. If the truck's in the driveway, I'm there." With one more look in my direction, he turned and headed off.

I gazed at the crowd, hoping for a diversion.

"Whoa," Alice said. "He's a hottie, Rick!"

I groaned. "Oh, Lord, here goes. What happened to our girls' weekend?"

Lolly raised her now empty glass. "We're talkin' special circumstances here, girl. We will definitely be visiting Dr. Dreamy tomorrow." Katie nodded. "Top priority!" As I cringed, waiting for more, Katie's attention turned from me to the crowd. "Hey, gals, I see someone I know!"

Chapter 34

Katie stood up, leaving her empty glass and us to forge into the crowd.

"Where the hell is she going?" Lolly said.

As we watched, she descended upon a couple who looked to be in their forties, the woman's dark-hair pulled back in a tight ponytail. She was skinny as a swizzle stick, overdressed for a clambake in a pencil skirt, linen blouse and six-inch heels. Her companion wore a sport coat, no tie, khakis and boat shoes, his longish, sandy hair tousled by the breeze.

Katie flung herself first at the woman, then her escort, giving each a bear hug.

Alice asked, "Do you know them, Rick?"

"Nope."

"Well, I need another drink," Lolly said. "Let's stop by the bar, then go over and meet Mr. and Ms. Stick-up-their asses."

Alice jabbed her. "You're bad, Pruit."

Drinks in hand, including another gin and tonic for Katie, we sashayed over to Katie and her best friends. As we neared them, she turned, "Oh, great, come here, girls. I'd want you to meet dear friends of mine, Muffy and Flip Richardson."

Who names someone Flip? I thought, saying hello to the beautiful couple who looked ready to bolt at the first opportunity.

"Muffy and Flip live in our neighborhood," Katie said. "We've known them for years."

"Oh?"

"Yes, but we've lost touch with all the traveling Bob and I have been doing. We're rarely in Connecticut anymore so didn't know about their summer home here."

"So you live nearby, then?" I said.

"We're in the Annex. Built our home two years ago. We love it." she said. "And you?"

I laughed. "I live far, far away in a different universe."

"But Katie said your family is here?"

"My father and stepmother, our hosts tonight."

"Oh, we love Rita and Ral," she said. Her husband continued to stand mute. He appeared to be in a fog, occasionally doing the now-familiar crowd scan for people as important as he imagined himself to be. *Ral, indeed.* I could not imagine my father ever answering to that.

"Yeah, they're great people," I said through gritted teeth. "Do you spend much time here?"

"Most of the summer," he said, suddenly awaking from his stupor. "I work from home."

"Flip's a venture capitalist," Katie said, looking as proud as if she'd birthed him.

Of course he is, I thought. The profession was almost de rigueur for residents of the Bluffs. "How nice," I said as we were all saved by the bell.

From somewhere on the opposite side of the lawn near the tent, a gong sounded. We turned and I spied Ruth Channing as she stepped up onto a small raised platform to the left of the tent's entrance.

"Welcome everyone," she said, speaking into a handheld mike. "Thank you so much for coming! Each year this event surpasses our expectations and this year is no exception. Before we find our seats and enjoy this amazing bounty, let's all raise our glasses in thanks to our hosts, Ralston and Rita Steele. Their incredible generosity has made tonight possible. Thank you, thank you, Ralston and Rita." After the applause died down, Ruth said, "Without further ado, please check the tables beside me for your place cards with table seating. Each table has brochures listing all our wonderful benefactors as well as a complete list of auction items. Now, one and all, please enjoy the first course of chowder and fritters!"

As we made our way in, I heard someone call, "Fiona!" and turned in time to spy a short, stocky guy in his late sixties, early seventies, waving to a thirtysomething babe, medium height, long, voluminous raven hair and violet eyes. A young Liz Taylor came to mind, until one took a gander at her attire—billowy, floral clown pants, rose-colored kimono top and clunky beaded necklace that appeared to have come from Carmen Miranda's personal collection. She was heavily made up, enormous synthetic breasts visible beneath her diaphanous top. Her suitor was what I call oily, his dyed black hair slicked back with gobs of Brylcreem. His pants shone, and his shirt was unbuttoned, revealing several gold chains on a hairy chest.

"Coming Oskie!" she called as she sashayed in his direction, waving their place cards.

I had little doubt that I was looking at Oscar Winter and his home wrecker paramour, Fiona Veruga. "Find our seats and I'll be right with you," I said to my companions, sprinting forward to catch up with the couple.

"Hello," I said, flashing them my best smile. "How fortuitous. I've been trying to reach you both for days!"

He glared as she regarded me, eyes wary. "I'm sorry, what is it you want?" she said.

"I'm a private investigator trying to locate some missing children. They attended the school at Meridian."

She took hold of his arm. "Come on, Oskie."

He shrugged her off. "What are you, high on something lady?"

"No, just trying to get some answers."

"Well, I don't talk to strange dicks, so step aside."

"We have a mutual acquaintance, if that helps. The late Jimmy Chen? And, let's not forget, it was your goons who tried to bury me alive."

In vain she attempted to propel him forward. "Come on, Oscar, our table is waiting."

"Mr. Winter, if I could just have a few minutes of your time. I have no wish to disturb your business." *Liar liar, pants on fire. I want to annihilate you all!* "I'm just trying to find the missing sisters, Lin and Joy?"

"Ms. Steele, I have absolutely no idea what you're talking about."

"Oh, I thought you didn't know me."

"Excuse me?"

"I didn't introduce myself, yet you just used my name."

He leaned close to me, his voice a low growl. "Go to hell, lady."

"You first."

I stepped in front of them, barring the way to their table.

"Back off, cunt," he hissed, "or the next time you won't be so lucky."

"Is that a threat?"

"You bet your sweet ass it is. Now get the fuck out of my way." He pushed past Fiona and stalked off.

I touched her arm lightly. "Please, Ms. Veruga, five minutes of your time?"

"He's right, honey. You should back off. These guys don't fool around."

"So you know about Jimmy Chen's murder?"

"Are you serious?"

"Do I look like I'm joking?"

"I handle their marketing, period. Meridian imports all kinds of designer labels."

"What about the kids?"

"What kids?"

"Some of them are as young as four or five. How do you sleep at night, Ms. Veruga?"

"I haven't the faintest idea what you're talking about. Now, if you'll excuse me, Mr. Winter is waiting."

I stepped aside and watched as she made her way toward her table. As she sat, I scanned her tablemates, wondering who they were. Beside Winter sat a tall, patrician-looking guy, sandy hair, slender. He appeared to be roughly the same age, but somehow the two men didn't fit.

I jumped as I felt a hand on my shoulder.

CHAPTER 35

"Good evening, my dear."

I turned to find Ruth Channing behind me. "Hey, Ruth, nice party."

"Why aren't you at your table, enjoying your chowder?"

"Just headed there."

"Aren't getting into trouble, are you?"

"Who, me?"

"Stay out of it, my dear. Tonight is not the time or the place."

I hugged her. "I know, I know… Can I ask you one teeny little thing before I gorge myself on fritters?"

"What is it?"

"Do you know everyone here?"

"Hardly, but try me."

"See that table?" I said, indicating Winter's group.

She shook her head. "Don't know 'em, but Clara might. She was with your dad and Rita, taking tickets." She waved to a young woman who appeared to be counting heads as people entered. Reluctantly she abandoned her post and headed toward us.

"Clara, I told you we don't need to keep track. You already have everyone's tickets."

"But what about people who simply walk in?"

"Well, for one thing, they won't have a seat," Ruth said, smiling at the young woman, who appeared to be twentysomething. Her auburn hair was styled in an unruly bob and she had a pale complexion, but arresting green eyes. She wore a United Way tee shirt, khakis and penny loafers. *Who wears penny loafers these days?*

"Sorry, Ruth," she said, not sounding the least bit sorry.

"Clara, I don't think you've met my dear friend, Ricky Steele?"

"Are you related to Mr. Steele?"

"Daughter," I said, extending my hand, which she shook firmly. "Nice to meet you."

"Clara, Ricky was wondering about the people at table six. Do you remember their names?"

She nodded. "That's Mr. Pullman's group."

"Oh, really," I said. "Which one is Mr. Pullman?"

"He's the tall one, pink shirt, next to his business partner, Mr. Winter."

"And the woman beside Mr. Pullman?"

"His wife, Lesley. Isn't she gorgeous? Used to be some kind of model before she went to work for him."

Surprised, Ruth gazed over at her assistant. "And you know this how?"

"She told me. We chatted a little as they came in while your dad was talking with her husband."

"What about the couple across the table?" I asked.

"That's Mr. McCann, Barry McCann, and his wife Sarah, I think. They live here at the Bluffs, in the Annex section, I believe. He was Mr. Pullman's college roommate."

Now it was my turn to gaze in awe at Clara. *I need her on my team*, I thought.

She noticed my surprise and laughed. "Ms. Pullman is very chatty and they came in with the McCanns."

"Now go and eat," Ruth said. "That's an order!"

"Yes, sir," I said, giving her a mock salute. "Great to meet you, Clara." As I headed to my table, I mused how I'd hit the mother lode at this clambake. *All these elusive shadowy figures I've been trying to track down here in one place! How could a girl get so lucky? Now, how am I going to talk to them?*

"It's about time, girl," Lolly said as I slid in beside her.

"Sorry, ladies. I've been trying to find certain elusive people all week and it turns out that some are here."

"And?" Katie said, leaning over her empty chowder bowl.

"And, zip. They wouldn't give me the time of day, of course, and Winter went a little further with threats, etc."

"If you're talkin' about that greasy little guy and balloon pants woman, they're sitting with Muffy's uncle," Katie said.

"Excuse me?"

"Her uncle Barry. She introduced us earlier. Can't remember his last name."

"McCann," I said, grinning. If Katie had been sitting beside me, I'd have kissed her. *I have my in with the pack of wolves.*

"Oh, you met him, then?" Katie asked.

"No, my darling, but after dinner you are going to introduce us so I can get close to Wade Pullman."

"Oh, Lord, save us!" Lolly said, rolling her eyes. "I think Frank better bring in reinforcements. I'm sure after you rile them all up, they'll send an army of guerillas after us."

"God, this chowder's amazing," I said. "Might even be better than Francis Farm's."

Lolly made a face. "Don't change the subject. We're talking about life and limb here."

Katie patted her shoulder. "We'll be fine, Loll."

Lolly rolled her eyes. "Thank goodness I stuffed myself with appetizers since it'll be hours before the lobster arrives. By the way, Rick, Dr. McDreamy keeps stealing looks in our direction and they're always trained on *you*."

"Baloney. Now can we please focus!"

As the meal and auctions went on, Katie and I spent the time plotting a way to infiltrate the Meridian gang. By the time the last auction and raffle winner had been announced and the wait staff passed trays of watermelon and ice cream, I had amassed my usual mountain of clam shells, lobster shells at the summit. I had worn my lobster bib so as to avoid looking like Ms. Greasy Galore when I met Wade and the gang. Even so, I was covered with grease and clam juice up to my elbows. As I rummaged under and around my clam mountain, searching for wet wipes, a wet towel magically appeared attached to Charlie's arm. "Need this?"

I looked up to find him grinning. "Where did you—"

"I come prepared. After the last bake, I brought a bag of wet dish towels for my tablemates and me, but I saved one for you."

"Thank you. This is really helpful."

"What're you ladies up to now?"

"Don't ask," Lolly said rolling her eyes. "Alice and I are planning to stroll the grounds, working off our dinner, but Holmes and Watson here are on the case."

"Need any help?" he said.

I glared at Lolly. "No, thank you. And, we are not on the case. We just want to do a little mingling."

"Funny, I didn't figure you as the mingling type," he said, gazing around at the four of us, grinning.

"There's a lot you don't know about me," I said, a trifle too huffily.

"Well, I'll leave you to it. Ladies," he said, bowing slightly. "Don't get into too much trouble. I'll hope to see you tomorrow."

"Count on it!" Lolly said, batting her long, thick eyelashes.

"We'll see how the day goes," I said, giving him a smile.

As Alice and Lolly headed off for their stroll, Katie and I made a beeline for the Meridian group. Our plan was to linger nearby out of sight, then swoop when the moment seemed right. She would have some cockamamie question for Barry McCann. I would stay out of sight, then swoop in after she'd been introduced to the Pullmans, Winter and Fiona. As often happens, the best laid plans can go awry.

CHAPTER 36

Oscar Winter had not yet spotted me as I watched Katie's introductions to the Meridian group. She had just shaken Wade Pullman's hand when a voice behind me bellowed, "Why Ricky Steele, as I live and breathe! Haven't seen you for ages!"

I turned to find Sol Perkins, one of my father's oldest friends. "Sol, hi, what a surprise!" As I hugged him, I gazed over to spy the Meridian group practically running out of the tent. McCann and his wife stayed behind and were chatting with Katie, but the rest had vanished as I listened to Sol go on and on about this and that. I love Sol, but wanted to strangle him. When we parted, I headed over to Katie and she introduced me to McCann and his wife.

After a few pleasantries, I said, "Wow, your table cleared out in a hurry."

"You know these charity things. Once they're over everyone disappears quick," he said.

"Oh, I wasn't aware of the end-of-the-night charity event stampede phenomenon," I said, smiling sweetly.

McCann appeared to be three sheets to the wind, his pale blue eyes watery. His stomach strained the buttons of his plaid seersucker sport shirt, and his wrinkly, grease-sprinkled khakis sat well below his nonexistent waist. His wife, Sarah, who appeared to be about his age, was in considerably better shape. Slender, she impressed me as a stalwart Yankee-type, who looked as if she'd rather be anywhere but standing beside her red-nosed, blurry-eyed husband. She was what one would call a handsome woman, angular face, little makeup, shoulder-length salt-and-pepper hair pulled back in a thin black velvet headband. She wore a pale pink cotton sweater, a single strand of pearls, tailored gray linen slacks and espadrilles. Her outfit was immaculate, not one drop of grease or clam juice anywhere.

As he swayed back and forth, McCann's gaze took in every inch of me. "You're Ralston's daughter, aren't you?"

"Yes," I said. It could have been my imagination, but I thought I glimpsed a flicker of interest in Sarah McCann's gaze.

"He's a great guy. Wouldn't want this mess on my lawn though, I can tell you."

"Katie tells me you live nearby?" I said.

"Couple of streets over. In the Annex. We built our dream house a few years ago. Come for a tour sometime. The wife and I love it here, don't we hon?"

"I wouldn't know. I haven't spent a night here in five years," Sarah McCann said as she turned away from her husband and gazed over the crowd.

"Wife loves the city and our condo," he said. "Not much of a beach person."

"What about your kids?"

"Don't have any. Sarah and I were never blessed," he said, gripping the back of a chair to steady himself.

"Does your friend Wade Pullman live out here?" I said, hoping Wade and Fiona had not communicated to Barry the reason for his hasty departure.

Watery eyes attempted unsuccessfully to focus on me. "You know Wade, do you?"

"No, but I'd like to," I said sweetly. "For some reason, he's avoiding me."

"Would you excuse me?" Sarah McCann said. Not waiting for our reply, she turned and headed for the side of the house leading to the street.

"Don't mind her. This isn't her scene. Why don't I buy you and Kathy a drink and we can discuss why a snoopy over-the-hill PI is harassing one of my best friends."

"It's Katie," my companion said. "Why don't I get the drinks and you two sit and chat?" She winked at me and disappeared not even bothering to ask us what we wanted.

"For a big woman, she moves fast," he said as we watched Katie head off.

"So, about your dear friend Wade. Do you know much about his business, Meridian Imports?"

"Not a lot."

"Do you know about the school that was run on the premises?"

"Nope. You sure you've got your facts straight? Meridian's an import business. What'd they want with a school?"

"They were teaching English to young Asian children."

"Well, good for them."

"The children have disappeared."

"I haven't the faintest clue what you're talkin' about."

"How well do you know Wade Pullman, Mr. McCann?"

"We roomed together at Yale. He went his way, I went mine, but we get together from time to time. My wife can't stand him, never could, so we tend to do guy things. You know what I mean."

"As a matter of fact, I don't. Could you enlighten me?"

"Guy things—you know, like golf, fishing trips, and other stuff."

"Other stuff?"

"Look, Ms. Steele, I wouldn't even be talkin' to you if I weren't half in the bag. Outta courtesy to your dad, I'm playin' nice, but what I do with my buddies is none of your goddamn business. Where is porky Jean with our drinks, anyway?"

"Her name's Katie and I will find out about your friend's dirty business, one way or the other. Your roomie's not a nice guy."

"Look, I gotta go. Tell Katie thanks for nothing."

With that he staggered off toward the street. I hoped his wife had taken the car and he would be forced to walk. I turned to spy Katie talking with Lolly and Alice, no sign of the mythical drinks. Time to call it a night and hang out with my friends.

CHAPTER 37

As the last of the guests straggled out, Dad asked us to come in for a nightcap. We settled in the solarium, brandies all around.

"What a night!" Rita said, plunking beside my father on one of the wicker sofas. She did have good taste, my stepmother. The muted pastels of the fabrics covering the very comfy matching wicker set blended perfectly with the colors of the ocean views surrounding us. "The damage to the lawn doesn't look too bad, after all. As soon as they remove those dreadful Porta Johns, things will be back to normal."

"Did you girls have fun?" my father asked, gazing around at us.

"It was delicious," Alice said, "and what a gorgeous setting. I hope they made lots of money."

"The auction bidding was pretty lively," Lolly said.

"You got something, didn't you?" he asked.

"One of those beautiful carvings of the blue heron. My husband, Ron, will love it."

"And you two are going on safari. How fun," Katie said. "Bob and I have been three times. Can't get enough of it!"

"Actually," Rita said, setting down her glass, "we bid on the safari for our… my daughter, Cassie. She's going with a friend to take her mind off her recent heartache after the breakup with her boyfriend. Thank God, the Peabodys were out of town tonight. I couldn't have faced seeing them and I'm sure it would have been very upsetting for Cassie!"

"Tell me a little about the Annex," I said, deciding a change of subject was in order.

Rita rolled her eyes. "Billionaire row. Fifteen mansions that make the rest of the Bluffs look like a shantytown."

Yeah, right. What universe is she living in? "Do you guys socialize much with that crowd?"

"As I said before, they mostly keep to themselves, but we see the Ramsays once and a while. He's a bore and so is his do-gooder wife. I saw you talking to Muffy and Flip Richardson. They're the youngest residents over there."

"They're friends of Katie's from Connecticut," I said.

"We've heard good things about them, but they're new. Just built their house a year or so ago. Not my taste, too Greco-Roman. I mean, columns at the beach?"

"Rita," my dad said. "These are friends of Katherine's."

Rita waved her hand. "No offense intended. I bet it's spectacular inside."

Katie laughed. "No offense taken. You should see their house in West Hartford! And her parents' house next door is almost an exact replica of the Parthenon!"

"What about her uncle, Barry McCann, and his wife? Do you see much of them?"

My father opened his mouth to speak, but Rita beat him to it. "She's a doll. Very successful attorney. Office is in Providence. He's filthy rich, but drinks too much and is grossly out of shape. We had to call the gatekeeper to get someone to drive him home tonight. Sarah just left him here. Don't blame her, but really—what an imposition!"

"And his business is?"

"Yacht broker to the stars," Rita said.

Dad nodded. "His company, McCann and Herrington, manufacture some of the most expensive boats in the world. He's been incredibly successful."

"You name a celeb who has a giant, ostentatious boat and I guarantee it's a McCann and Herrington," Rita said. "Now, girls, if you'll excuse me, I've got a headache and I think I'll head up to bed."

"Of course," I said. "We should be going too."

We all hugged them and made our way out. As the others headed for the car, my father held me back. "Be very careful, my dear. The kinds of people you've been discussing are incredibly powerful. I have no idea what they're mixed up in, but they have the money to cover up anything. I imagine they have the means to stop anyone as well."

"Don't worry, Dad. I'll be fine." I hugged him and turned away. *Who am I kidding? In a moment's notice, any one of the jerks on Billionaires' Row could make me disappear without a trace!*

CHAPTER 38

Alice was the designated driver as we drove out of the Bluffs. The rest of us were slightly tipsy when we arrived home. Lolly suggested a nightcap on the deck, to which we all agreed. A curvaceous blonde plastered to his side, Vinnie waved as we made our way in. Frank parked in his usual spot, giving me a slight nod as I checked to see if he was there.

Once we were settled in, Alice began the inquisition. "Okay, Rick, give. We want to hear every detail about Dr. McDreamy."

Katie nodded. "Don't leave out a thing."

Lolly sat back, smiling. Our conversation at the bake had already satisfied her curiosity. She has been at me for years to find a man. She's also met many of my previous beaus and was never impressed until now.

I took a deep breath, surrendering to the inevitable. "There's not much to tell. He's just moved into the neighborhood. We're friends. Maybe more someday. I try not to get too excited since you know my dismal relationship history. His daughter, Mike, is working for me temporarily. Vinnie's working on his house. That's about it, end of story."

"End of story, my eye," Alice said. "And what is that obnoxious music?"

"Ice cream truck. Comes by three or four times a day all summer. Seems late tonight, but who knows. Katie, you haven't told us anything about Bob, your girls and the grandkids. How are they all?"

Katie sat up, pointing her finger at me. "Don't think you can change the subject that easily, missy. We have all day tomorrow to catch up on my humdrum news. Now, let's hear more about Charlie."

"Better tell 'em, Rick," Lolly said, raising her wineglass in my direction.

I glared at Lolly, who was really enjoying herself. "There's nothing to tell! Lolly's just playing with you."

Alice turned to her. "Loll, you knew about this?"

"Not till tonight."

Why does everyone derive so much pleasure in nosing into my love life? "Okay, okay, enough. Charlie's great. We've been out a couple of times, strictly first-base kind of stuff. I'm attracted to him. Maybe something will develop. He's determined to see that it does. But, as you observed tonight, he's not my type—way too nice and respectable. And, as you well know, I suck at relationships."

"Do you hear yourself? That's crazy!" Lolly said, waving her arms. "What's that weird noise? Do you hear it?"

Alice nodded. "Rick, your cat might have cornered a rat."

I was about to say that Beaky was not a ratter, when I heard scuffling sounds from inside the house. Goose bumps crept up my spine. "Put down your drinks," I whispered, "and go through the gate to Vinnie's, now!"

In a flash, Katie whipped a can of pepper spray from her jacket pocket. "Not without you, Rick. Damn, I left my purse inside."

"Me, too," I said. "Now, move it. I'm right behind you."

A glint of light and a huge gun appeared on the edge of the porch. It was attached to a dark-haired, sinewy figure, ripped tee shirt, black jeans, arms and neck covered with amateur-looking tattoos. Before I could move a muscle, three others surrounded us.

"Move," tattoo guy said, waving his gun barrel toward the house. "Inside, all of you."

Where the hell is Frank? "Let the others go," I shouted. "They have nothing to do with this!"

"Shut up, cunt, or say goodbye to your friends." He nodded to one of his associates. "Get the pepper spray from Tubby there and herd 'em inside."

"You'll be sorry," I said. "I have protection and in thirty seconds this place'll be—"

"If you mean Tacoma, he's been neutralized. Now move it!"

"If you hurt Frank, you'll be in a shitload of trouble," I screamed in the loudest voice I could muster. "The police watch this house and—"

"Shut the fuck up," were the last words I heard. Then everything went black.

*****

When I came to, I was trussed up, as were my three friends, all of us duct-taped to my dining room chairs. My head pounded as if someone was hammering on it.

"Boss, the ringleader's awake."

I gazed through a fog at my friends. Lolly's eyes were wild with fear, Alice's watchful and Katie's resolute. *Why hadn't I tried harder to persuade them not to come?* "These chairs are antiques. They were my mother's. If this duct tape mars the finish, you're paying," I said, glaring at Mr. Tattoo.

"Shut your mouth, bitch, or I'll shut it for you."

"Wanta know what I think?" I said.

"No."

"I think you wouldn't dare touch us. You're just a lackey."

With lightning speed, he was behind me, hands round my neck. As he squeezed tighter, I saw stars and wondered if this really was the end.

"Leave her alone, you bastard!" Katie said, and we all turned to stare. Katie might be resolute and strong, but she almost never swore.

"Shut your gob, Tubby, or you and the rest of the Golden Girls are history." As he spoke, he loosened his grip around my neck slightly.

A click. That's all it was and my bedroom door swung open with a bang. Vinnie stepped into the room brandishing what looked like an Uzi. Beside him, Fulty held what appeared to be a Revolutionary War musket.

"Drop 'em, assholes," Vinnie said in a low growling voice I'd never heard before. "If you don't, your buddy here dies along with the rest of you."

"Fat chance," Tattoo said. "Who's this, Gramps and the Fonz?"

Before we could blink, Vinnie knocked him down, using him as a shield as Fulty aimed his musket at one of the others' head. As another of our assailants stepped forward, gun raised, Lolly's foot, now loose from the duct tape, shot out and tripped him. As he headed toward the floor, his gun flew from his hand across the floor and under my china cupboard. The other two ran out the open door to the deck and disappeared into the night.

We watched as Vinnie tied up the other two, who lay side by side on the floor. With shaking hands, Fulty untied us one by one.

"You okay?" Vinnie said, eyeing what was no doubt a nasty welt on the side of my face.

"Fine."

I walked over to stand beside tattoo man. "Who sent you?"

"Fuck you."

Vinnie kicked him, hard. "Answer the lady, asshole, or your kneecap's history."

"Fuck off, Fonz."

Vinnie stepped closer, gun pointed at his knee. "I'm counting to three. One, two…"

"We don't know!"

"Bullshit," I said.

"It's the truth," he said. "None of us know."

"How does that work?"

"Someone calls. We take the job and do it."

"Are you the guys that buried me in Oak Grove?"

"Nope. If we did that job, you'd still be buried. In fact, that's where you and the blue-hairs were headed when we were done with you."

"Blue-hairs!" Lolly said, glaring at him.

"This blue-hair has a stun gun, buddy," Katie said, "and I know how to use it."

Calm and cool as a cucumber, Vinnie said, "Well, Fonz is gonna take you two for a ride and Gramps here will blow off your head if you move a muscle. He doesn't hear well, but his vision's fine." He held up their guns. "These'll be at the bottom of the river if you need them. Now, does the name Chaz mean anything to you dickheads?"

The two looked like they might pee in their pants.

"Thought so. Well, if either of you morons or your friends come near this house or neighborhood again, you'll answer to Chaz or me. Comprende? We can have you vaporized without a trace faster than you can say 'help.'"

I stared at him. "Why didn't you call the police?"

He waved his gun. "Well, maybe this isn't quite legal, and you can bet Fulty's musket won't pass muster. We'll get them loaded into the truck and—"

"You're not going to kill them?" I said, horrified.

"Naw, we'll dump 'em somewhere and hope the rats get 'em before they wriggle out of their restraints."

"Yuck. Wait, where's Frank? What did you do with him?" I asked.

"Sleepin' like a baby, I'd guess," Tattoo said. "Your mini-hulk out there likes ice cream."

Incredulous, I stared at him. "You shanghaied the ice cream truck?"

"Like takin' candy from a baby."

"Well, it seems your other two goons drove off without you," Vinnie said. "Lucky we're givin' you a lift."

We followed as Vinnie grabbed the two by the collar, dragged them out, and threw them in the bed of his truck. In the driveway, Fulty hugged each of us. "You gonna be okay, gals."

"Thanks, Fulty," I said, tears in my eyes.

Vinnie looked at me. "You okay?"

I nodded. "Thanks, Vin."

"Call Wilda and get another guy out here. Frank's awake, but he's really groggy."

"Will do."

I sighed as we returned to the living room. "Sorry, ladies. I did try to warn you."

Katie stared at me, jaw set, hands on hips. "Okay, I'm pissed now. What's our next move?"

"A drink, then bed," I said. "I'll lock up and wait for Spike to get here, but you guys get a drink and watch the stars."

I breathed a sigh of relief when Spike arrived. He came to the door, checked in and informed me that Josh was secured for the night and Wilda was with Mike.

What the hell am I going to do now?

CHAPTER 39

I had just settled into my deck chair, gazing upward at a blanket of stars, when one of the cell phones from my collection rang. "Ms. Steele?" The woman's voice was unfamiliar. "This is Betty Bell. I work at Meridian."

The hairs on the back of my neck stood up. *There really is there no hiding from these people.* "How did you get this number?"

"Ruth gave it to me. She suggested I call because we can't reach Danny and she thought you might have been in contact?"

"Excuse me?"

"Could I meet you somewhere? I'm not sure it's safe to speak by phone."

"Earnshaw's under the bridge. Do you know it?"

"Yes."

"Twenty minutes?"

"Yes." She clicked off.

"Are you crazy?" Lolly said, without even knowing the details.

"I picked that diner because it's always crawling with cops. Besides, I'll have Frank with me."

"We'll have Frank with us," Katie said, already up and arming herself.

"You guys can stay here. You *should* stay here," I said.

"No way, Jose," Katie said. "I hope you're bringing your gun."

Jesus Christ, what have I gotten us into? "Against my better judgment, yes."

Alice hopped up. "Count me in!"

We all looked at Lolly, who sat, arms crossed, in her chair for thirty seconds before giving in. "If you think I'm staying here alone, you're crazy!"

I phoned Wilda, then filled them in as we drove. I insisted upon taking my car. After explaining the fate of my jeep, they all agreed it might be best. Wilda and Spike had both managed to infiltrate the airtight security at the Bluffs and were watching Josh and Mike. She informed me that Mike was at the Peabodys' for the night. Apparently, she and Josh had spent the day at the beach and she had been invited for a sleepover. *How cozy.* I suggested to Wlida that she might want to join us at Earnshaw's and she clicked off.

At first I thought Betty was a no-show, but then spotted a small figure in a black hooded sweatshirt at a booth in the corner. The place was deserted except for a couple of patrol officers at the counter and two couples in booths near the front. By prior arrangement, the girls headed for the counter to order coffees and I slipped into the booth opposite Betty.

"Hey," I said, peering into the recesses of her hood. "That you, Betty?"

"Thanks for coming. I got freaked. I can't reach Danny and he was supposed to be in touch hours ago."

"What about the police?"

"He forbid me to blow his cover or mine unless I wait twenty-four hours."

It sounded like a dumb plan to me, but I kept my opinions to myself. "So I guess you're the inside person at Meridian?"

She nodded.

"Where do you think he is?"

She swallowed hard, then peered at me for several minutes.

"Listen, Betty, you got me down here. Now, what's going on?"

"He found Kim and the kids. At least, I think he had."

"Where?"

"I don't know, or believe me, I would have gone there."

"Why didn't he call the police? I thought that was the plan once the kids were located?"

"A bunch were missing. At least two or three. He was trying to find out where they'd taken them before blowing the whistle."

"By Kim, you mean Kim Smith, the other teacher from Meridian?"

"Yes, he's been getting close to her for weeks."

Hmm, he left out that little detail when talking to me. "How close?"

"You've seen him. He's hot. I think Kim was pretty into him."

"Oh?"

"They went out a couple of times when she wasn't on duty."

"What do you know about Kim?"

"She's the main person who oversees the kids. There's also a couple who feed them and stay in the houses with them, but Kim's mainly in charge."

"What houses? Where are they?"

"I'm not sure. They move 'em around pretty regularly. Last week, I found out that Meridian has a bunch of properties north of the city. I gave Danny the addresses. He's been watching them, but until today, he hadn't seen anyone around."

"And?"

"He texted me around noon today. The message said, 'Bingo,' so I knew he'd found them."

"So Meridian probably knows he's found them too. I'm sure your cell phone has been compromised."

"I don't think so. I'm using burners, just like you."

"Addresses?" She stared at me blankly. "What are the addresses you gave Danny for the houses?"

"Oh, yes, here, I wrote them down for you." She handed me a crumpled sheet of paper.

"Where are you going now?" I asked.

"Home, I guess."

"I wouldn't. Who knows if they've grabbed Danny and he's—"

"He would never betray me, Ms. Steele. Never."

"Let's hope not, but I'd feel better if you went someplace safer."

"I s'pose I could go to my parents'. They live in Mattapoisett."

"Good plan. Take care and please let me know if you hear from Danny."

"Will do." She slid out of the booth without a sound and vanished into the shadows.

CHAPTER 40

"This is a bad idea," Lolly said as we headed to the fourth and final address on Betty's list.

"We'll just check this last place. Then we're heading home, I promise. Besides, both Frank and Wilda are behind us."

"Why don't I find that comforting?" Lolly said.

We drove along a darkened road, bordered on one side by the Reservation. Once an Indian reservation, the property encompasses the county's largest reservoir as well as many miles of undeveloped land. Its lush pine woods were beautiful, but not particularly safe, especially at night when the gangs took over. Since it was inside city limits, the police patrolled, but there were dozens of dirt roads leading into the deep woods. A cat-and-mouse game could go on half the night with the rowdies still at large.

"Keep checking mailboxes. We're getting closer," I said.

"There it is," Alice cried. "Number seventy-two."

Dandy, I thought as I turned into the dirt drive. *It would have to be on the Reservation side.* As we proceeded, woods enveloped us, overhanging branches cutting off all light from the moon and stars. Finally, we reached a clearing and spied a dilapidated farmhouse. One light shone in a front window, but otherwise the house was dark, like its surroundings. If the kids were here, they must be scared to death.

A truck was parked to the side of the porch, but no one appeared to be in it. I drove as close to the house as possible and switched on my high beams. Cautiously, we stepped from the car and were deciding what to do when the front door opened and a tiny figure appeared, then another and another. "Call 911 and give them the address," I whispered to Lolly. "Ask to have Sergeant Roberts respond, if he's in."

Katie, Alice and I made our way slowly toward the porch, watching the shadows. When we neared the children, I heard a groan and noticed a lump to the side of the front door. Katie shone her flashlight on the lump and Danny Leonardo sat up, his hand over a nasty cut on his head. "Check on him," I whispered. "I'm going inside."

Alice stayed with Danny as we waved the children out and told them through words and gestures to sit near Alice. Lolly ran up to assist. "The police are on their way," she whispered, helping to herd the tiny group.

"Disgusting," Katie whispered as we stepped into a room littered with trash. The stench was overpowering. Blankets and what looked like yoga mats were thrown about, a few dirty pillows here and there. A table was piled with plastic water bottles, junk food and a few pieces of rotting fruit. There was no running water and what had once served as a bathroom was now a fetid, stinking, unspeakable mess. There was a second room. We slowly crept to the door, my gun drawn. It was furnished with two cots and several boxes. As we peered in, Danny spoke from behind us. "There's no one else here."

"How do you know?"

"They took her away."

"Who?"

"Kim Smith."

"Are you okay?"

"Yeah. I was watching them from the window, waiting for a chance to surprise them, when someone hit me from behind. I came to for a second as they dragged Kim out, then blacked out again."

"Why don't you go sit on the porch. We'll just check in here and be right out." I said, wondering how much longer I could hold my breath against the stench.

Katie and I rummaged around, finding nothing except a few adult-size clothes, and some kids' stuff in the boxes. It looked used as if they'd picked up at secondhand stores. We were about to head out when she shone the light on the walls, where a bunch of pegs held hangers and hangers of brand-new clothes in various sizes. Underneath, on the floor were piles of shoeboxes.

"This is what they dress 'em in when they're placed," I said, fighting back a wave of nausea.

"Place them where?" she asked.

"Come on, I hear sirens. Let's get out of this hellhole."

CHAPTER 41

The children were impossibly small and appeared to be malnourished. Their eyes reflected both fear and resignation. They appeared to range in age from around five or six to ten. Six were Chinese, five Indian. As the police led them to the patrol cars, one little Indian girl approached me. She reached out her tiny hand and I took it. She took a deep breath and stood very still and calm, holding tight.

"Hey, sweetie," I said, peering into luminous brown eyes. "You're going to be okay now." I picked her up, brought her to the car, and seated her next to a boy, his face streaked with dirt and tears. "I'll come see you, okay?" She gave me one last look, then turned and faced straight ahead as my heart broke.

The kids, all eleven of them, were taken to Belmont House. Ruth had volunteers standing by to clean them, feed them and settle them in. After the officers questioned him, we took Danny Leonardo to the emergency room. I drove Danny's jeep and Katie and the girls followed in my car.

As we sat waiting for him to be treated, he said, "This is bullshit. We've gotta get out of here. I'm fine, just feeling like a world-class idiot. I let 'em take her, Jesus Christ!"

"What happened? Why were you there?"

"She wanted out. The last few placements had sickened her and she couldn't do it anymore. We've been meeting and she asked for my help two days ago. We had a plan to grab all the kids and get 'em to safety. It was supposed to happen tomorrow afternoon when their caregivers went out to get food."

"Who are these caregivers?"

"It varies, but lately it's been this same grungy couple. She's a junkie so they work for Meridian to feed her habit. Anyway, Kim called a few hours ago. Said the couple had gone out and it had to be tonight and to come right away. I could tell she was scared. She gave me the address and I came right over. I had just stepped onto the porch when someone jumped me from behind and that was it. We've gotta move and find her soon."

His eyes filled. Clearly, he and Kim Smith had gotten to be more than friendly. I'd never met the woman, but I didn't like her chances. I suspected that the only reason she had been taken out alive was so they could torture any information out of her about Danny and anyone else she might have spoken to. I very much doubted we'd find her, and if we did that she'd be alive.

"That head needs stitches. Let them do their job and then we'll see."

"Sergeant Roberts said we're to bring him to the station," Lolly said. "I heard the officer tell you that."

"Yes, but that was before we knew Kim Smith was in danger. Stay with him. I'm going to call the station," I said and stepped out of the room and down the hall.

I asked for Sergeant Roberts, who must have been standing two inches from the phone. "Steele, this had better be good. Where the hell is Leonardo?"

"Now, hold on, Douglas. They told us we should take him to the hospital."

"Bullshit. Now I want him here ASAP, comprende?"

"He's sure Kim Smith is in grave danger."

"That's our concern, not yours. My people are on it. Now back off. Drop Leonardo here and you and the Golden Girls call it a night or I'll lock you all up."

"Is someone checking Water Street? They could have taken her there."

"What'dya take me for, a complete idiot? Now, get off the goddamn phone and get Leonardo over here, pronto."

He clicked off and I headed back to the examining room. Lolly, Alice and Katie were there gathering their things. "Where's Danny?"

"He left," Alice said.

"What?"

"We couldn't stop him, Rick," Katie said. "Believe me, we tried."

"But how? He has no car and I have his truck keys."

"Actually, you don't," Alice said, holding up my bag. "We tried to stop him, but he grabbed your bag, found the keys and took off."

"Did he say where he was going?"

"Not a peep."

"Christ," I said, rummaging through my bag for the notebook where I had scribbled Wade Pullman's address. Clearly the police were at Meridian's offices so if Kim Smith hadn't been taken there, the most likely people to know where she was were Winter and Pullman.

"Come on!" I said, hurrying past the ER nurse. "Sorry, patient flew the coop."

*****

Pullman lived in an exclusive condo complex bordered on one side by the river, the other the Aquinessett Country Club. With a prime location the units, which started at half a million, included the club initiation fees. *Such a deal.* Theirs was a corner unit with an unobstructed view downriver. There was a man on duty in the lobby, but he was busy on his iPad, back to us, so we tiptoed past him. When we reached the Pullmans' door, I turned to them. "You should go back to the car. This is my fight and these guys are worse than evil. Wilda and Frank pulled in right behind us so the parking lot's secure and I'm okay."

"Nothing doing," Katie said, one hand holding her stun gun, the other pepper spray. "We've come this far and we're goin' in!"

The Rambettes ride again, I thought, knocking on the door. After about five minutes and several repeat rat-ta-tats, Lesley Pullman opened the door in a silky, pink robe. It appeared she had just stepped from the shower. "Yes?" she said, staring from one to the other of us.

"May I speak to your husband, Ms. Pullman?"

"I'm sorry, he's not in and I don't know you, so please leave."

She attempted to shut the door in my face, but I stuck my foot in it.

"Listen, whoever you are, I'm going to call security now. How did you get in here, anyway? That deadbeat doorman must be sleeping again."

"It's the age of technology," I said, smiling.

"Lady, I don't know what you're selling, but this is private property and if you don't remove your foot immediately, I'm calling the police."

"You go right ahead, Ms. Pullman. Please, call the cops. They'll want to speak to your husband too. Let's see, there's kidnapping, child exploitation, probably abuse and pornography, too. And, let's not forget attempted murder."

"What the hell are you on?"

"Listen, Les, we don't have time for you to play dumb here. You worked for Wade so you know all about Meridian's dirty businesses. We have the kids, by the way, most of them. Now we're looking for the others and Kim Smith."

"I haven't a clue what you're talking about."

"But Wade does. Now, where is he?"

"Not here."

"Then where? Quick, because they're going to kill her, if they haven't already."

"He got a call about an hour ago from his partner, Oscar. He sounded upset. Wade ran out and I haven't heard from him."

"Let's go," I said, removing my foot from her threshold. She wasted no time in slamming the door in our faces.

CHAPTER 42

Winter lived in the Highlands, his home one of the older mansions, mansard roof, multiple chimneys, brick façade, perfectly landscaped grounds. The house appeared dark, but as we drove up the side street, I noticed lights in the four-car garage, which appeared to have an attached shed. I drove past and parked a block up the street. Frank and Wilda pulled ahead of me.

"Stay here," I said to the Rambettes, "and call the police if I'm not back in ten minutes. Wilda has my back."

Katie, who was riding shotgun, was already out, Alice too. "We're coming," Katie whispered.

Geez. "Okay, but keep down."

As we crept through manicured shrubs, I counted five vehicles in the drive. One was a Town Car, the others a jeep, truck and two nondescript dark sedans. *Looks like we have the whole crew,* I thought, wondering if Wilda was armed. *Pepper spray, a stun gun and my little Smith & Wesson will probably not be sufficient to subdue whoever is gathered in the potting shed!*

Just as we reached the side of the garage, I heard a click to my right. "Well, well, well, if it isn't the Golden Girls. Don't you blue-hairs ever give up?" I felt steel against my temple and winced.

"We're here to get Kim Smith, asshole," I said, shifting slightly so the gun barrel no longer touched my skin. *Tattoo guy, terrific.*

Katie and Alice were in similar straits, Tattoo's associates with them. No sign of Wilda or Frank.

"Move it, bitch," he hissed, shoving me toward the shed. As we reached the door, I spied Winter, dress shirt rolled up, flecks of blood across his middle. I suspected we were looking at Kim Smith, or what was left of her, strapped to a chair in the middle of the room, a single light bulb hanging above her. She had been severely beaten, two black eyes, face swollen, fingers intact so far. She appeared to be either unconscious or dead.

"Look who we found, boss," Tattoo said, shoving me onto the cement floor.

"Jesus Christ, why'd you bring 'em in here? Tie 'em up, throw them in the truck and we'll get rid of them with this one," he said, indicating Smith.

"You won't get away with it, Oskie. We've got the kids. The cops are searching for you right now. They're on their way here."

"Bullshit. Rico, put some duct tape over her mouth so I don't have to listen to any more of her yappin'. Hurry up."

Out of the corner of my eye, I spied two shadows just outside the door, one tall and slender, the other resembling the Hulk. I kicked back, catching Rico square in the crotch at the same time as I jabbed him with my elbow. He doubled over just as the guy holding Katie screamed and fell over. *Double whammy, stun gun and pepper spray.* The third guy held fast to Alice. "Over there," he said, indicating the inside wall, "or I shoot Granny in the head."

As he waggled his gun around, waving it in our faces, a black arm came down and I heard a loud crack! *No doubt one or more of his arm bones.* The gun clattered to the floor as Frank subdued Gun Waggler and his companions. In the melee, no one noticed Winter until the door at the far end of the shed closed behind him. I rushed out, but the Town Car was already speeding down the drive, spitting gravel in its wake.

"Damn," I cried, my head spinning.

Lolly ran up and hugged me. "Are you alright? I just phoned the police."

"Fine, but Kim Smith isn't," I said, heading back into the shed.

Katie stood over tattoo man, who was alternately swearing and groaning. "Lose the attitude, your weasel," she said, her foot now resting on his cheek.

Frank had tied up the other two and Alice and Wilda were hovered over Kim Smith, untying her. "She's alive," Wilda said, "but just barely. Call an ambulance."

Smith opened one swollen eye and looked at us in bewilderment. "Ms. Smith, I'm Ricky Steele. Danny sent us. We have the kids. They're safe. Now, where are the others?"

She shook her head.

"You don't know or you won't tell us?"

"Ask her one question at a time," Alice said, dabbing her bloodied face with a clean rag.

"Do you know where they are?" I said.

Smith shook her head.

"What about Wade Pullman?"

Another head shake. I could hear sirens coming closer. Not much time.

"Where would Winter go? Do you know?"

Through swollen lips she mouthed "Buh, buh, uf."

"Maybe she's saying Bluffs?" Alice said.

"But where? None of these guys lives there. We can't just go barging in to every house out there. We're not even sure who they're friendly with except maybe Barry McCann and he's not about to let us in. Besides, he's surely passed out by now."

The ambulance arrived and took Kim Smith away. Roberts also appeared, face beet red, looking ready to kill. "I warned you, Steele. Guy, throw her and her fellow senior citizens in the wagon and take 'em to the station. They want a sleepover? Let 'em have it on the city's dime."

"You can't do that, Douglas!"

"Watch me."

"We knew Kim Smith was in mortal danger. We couldn't just go home and do nothing!"

"That's when you call us. Now shut up and get in the wagon. At least I'll know you're safe."

"Winter got away!" I called over my shoulder. "He did this to Kim, then drove away."

My words fell on deaf ears as the four of us were dumped side by side in the city's decrepit paddy wagon. Guess who sat across from us? Rico and the gang. *How cozy.* At least they were shackled and tied so they couldn't do any damage. Wilda and Frank disappeared and I wondered why they were not crammed in with us. *Just as well. They needed to get back to Mike and Josh.*

"You're toast, bitch," Rico said, glaring at me.

"That coming from the person who's all tied up, neat and tidy."

"I'll be out by morning and I know where you live."

"And I have Chaz watching my back, or have you forgotten?"

"Fuck Chaz. He's a fuckin' myth, anyway. Everyone knows that."

"Watch your mouth," Alice said.

Unlike our fellow detainees, we had not been frisked. The cops had taken possession of my gun and my bag was in the car, but I had my keys and cell phone in my pockets. Surreptitiously, I pulled out the phone and called one of Josh's burners. He answered on the first ring. Before I could explain about a possible Bluffs connection, he said, "She's gone."

"What are you talking about, who?"

"Mike. Her car's in the driveway, but she's gone."

"How the hell did that happen?"

"We decided to stay the night here with my folks. After dinner, she went out to the car to get some things. When she wasn't back in ten minutes, I went out to find her and she was gone. The back of her car was open and stuff was thrown around, but no sign of her."

"Shit," I muttered, thinking of Kim Smith and Jimmy Chen, then Charlie. "Does her dad know?"

"Yes, I called him right away."

"And?"

"He called the cops. They came out, but there's no sign of her, Rick."

CHAPTER 43

Charlie picked us up at six a.m., the earliest Douglas agreed to release us. Lolly was almost comatose after three hours in a dark, cold cell furnished with a toilet and soiled mattress thrown on a rickety cot. Mercifully, they had put two of us together—Katie and Lolly, Alice and me.

"She's a wreck, Rick," Katie said. "In shock. Gotta get her home and warm."

I took one look at my dear friend and nodded. "Yes, let's all go home. Charlie's going to drop us at my car."

We departed the station and rode into the Highlands in silence. When everyone but me had hopped into the Subaru, I turned to him. "Charlie, I am so sorry."

"For what? Mike's a big girl. She knew what she was getting into."

"Not this! Never this. I don't even do this."

"She can take care of herself."

You don't know these people, I thought, *and you haven't seen Jimmy or Kim.* "I can't believe Wilda left her. And where the hell was Spike?"

"Knocked out. They found him in his car down the street."

"Oh Charlie, I've failed her in every way."

"Go home, take a shower, let the cops do their job." His eyes were kind, but I could see the fear in them, too. *Fear for his beloved daughter, who might be able to take care of herself in a war zone, but not against such unmitigated evil.*

I nodded. "Please let me know if you hear anything." I hugged him, wanting to hang on forever.

As I opened the door and hustled Lolly in for the first shower, I noticed an envelope on the floor. It had been slipped under the door. I tore it open to find a grainy black and white copy of a photo with the words, "Back off or she dies." Mike, tied to a chair, duct tape over her mouth. Her eyes stared straight at the camera, calm and steady.

"Bastards," I muttered.

"What is it?" Katie said as Alice took care of Lolly.

I held out the paper. "Oh, my God, Rick. Can you tell where she is? Anything?"

I studied the background, which was mostly in darkness. It looked to be a storeroom, boxes and garbage bags lying around. I shook my head. "Could be anywhere. Cops tore Meridian apart a few hours ago so it's definitely not there. Listen, I'm going to throw some water on my face, brush my teeth and change clothes, then head over to the hospital. Kim Smith knows more about all this."

"I'll come," she said. "Alice will stay with Loll. She says she's had enough."

"You should stay, too. Bob would kill me if he knew what we've been doing."

"No such thing. I've been giving him regular updates. He's keyed."

"Ready in ten, then?"

"Roger that!"

As she bustled off to change clothes, I washed up in the kitchen sink, then pulled out jeans, a clean tee shirt, socks and undies. I called Josh and told him to stay put. I also called Wilda and insisted she return to the Bluffs and take Spike's place. Frank would trail me and Vinnie agreed to come over and sit with Lolly and Alice.

When we reached the emergency room, we were told Kim Smith was with the doctor and could not be disturbed. As I paced, Katie poked around, making friends with everyone on the floor. By the time the doctor departed, her new best friend, Karla, was only too happy to usher us in to see Kim. "Only a few minutes, ladies. She's groggy and needs to rest."

Kim's face was still black and blue and even more swollen than before, but now she also had stitches on her forehead, lip and jaw. Her jaw was set and her left arm was in a wrist-to-elbow cast.

Hey, Kim," I said, approaching the bed slowly.

She eyed us warily. "Where's Danny?" she said through clenched jaws.

"We haven't been able to locate him."

"He's going after them. They'll kill him."

"Where are they, Kim? Please help us. They've taken one of my associates, a young woman."

"I don't know, truly. The sales and auctions are Fiona's business. I just looked after the kids."

"Auctions?"

"Well, only two that I know of. When you stumbled into Meridian and they killed Jimmy, they had to change the way they handled the kids. The room at the warehouse, mirror and all. That had to be dismantled."

"And?"

"And, they found a client willing to host an auction. That's how Lin and Joy were placed."

"Sold to the highest bidder?"

She nodded. "I believe whoever it was may have taken both girls as they were inseparable and refused to eat, sleep or do anything without the other."

"Who took them?"

Her head listed to one side and she looked as if she were about to fall asleep. "I'm sorry, I don't know. If I did I'd tell you. You've got to believe me."

"You said auctions."

"Last night," she said, closing her eyes. "They took a few kids for one last night."

"Leave it, Rick. She doesn't know any more and she needs to rest."

"Come on, we're going to the Bluffs," I said. I phoned and asked Wilda to grab Josh and bring him to my dad's. I doubted the Peabodys were involved in Meridian's dirty dealings, but I didn't know who to trust.

CHAPTER 44

Rita greeted Katie and me at the door. "What's with Whip Woman?" she whispered, ushering me through.

"Wilda is a woman of few words," I said. "It's a vigilance thing."

The group was assembled in Dad and Rita's living room. My father rose as we entered. "Darling, thank God you're safe." He hugged us both, then indicated empty chairs. "Can we get you something to drink or eat?"

"No thanks, we're great." Katie did not look so great. In fact, she looked like she could eat a horse, but sat down and nodded thanks as Rita handed her a bowl of peanuts, which disappeared in the blink of an eye.

"Lolly and Alice are at my house. They've had enough. Vinnie's with them."

"Not that shady neighbor of yours," Rita said.

"Vinnie saved our lives yesterday," Katie said. "He's good people."

Rita shrugged as she sat down next to Dad.

"What've you found?" Josh said. He looked ready to crawl out of his skin.

"Not much, but we think someone here may be involved with Meridian. They apparently held an auction last night."

"Really?" Rita said. "I was just up at the owner's club. I didn't see a notice."

"You wouldn't have," I said. "It was private."

"What kind of auction?" Dad said.

I hated to voice the truth about Meridian's dirty business, but took a deep breath and filled them in, summarizing what we knew.

"I can't believe it," Rita said when I finished.

"Did you see anything unusual after the clambake? Maybe a lot of cars at someone's house?"

"Now that you mention it, the Ramsays looked like they were having something," Rita said. "I saw a lot of cars when I walked Skipper. We walk on the beach, then cut through at the point and come back on the Annex road." Skipper was her terrier mix, small, white, and unlike most small dogs, very quiet and unobtrusive.

"That's not unusual, though," she continued. "Linc is always entertaining when Catherine's out of town. She left the clambake for their Providence condo cause she's leaving today for a garden tour in England with her ladies' group."

"Have you ever been to one of Linc's parties?"

Rita guffawed. "Surely you jest. We are much too lowly for that."

"Once," Dad said. "They had a lawn party a few summers ago. Hundreds of people."

"What about kids? Do you ever see any children around the Ramsays'?"

Rita waved her hand. "Hon, there are *very few* kids living out here. I feel a bit sorry for those new people with kids, the Richardsons."

We talked a while longer and then I proposed that Katie call Muffy and Flip Richardson for a pop-in. After receiving a welcoming "sure, come on over," we decided to take the beach route, which would lead us up to the side of the Ramsays' property. Their house was the most enormous on a row of gigantic monstrosities. In the style of a French chateau, it seemed to go on for miles, grabbing up as much beach frontage as possible. A high wall made peeking a challenge, except from the beach side, where the twelve-foot wall was made of Plexiglas so as not to obstruct the castle's views.

"Yikes, this must've cost a fortune," I said as all four of us stopped and stared.

"And think of the staff that must be out here every day to clean it," she said. "Salt and ocean spray must cloud it constantly. I've only seen one other wall like it."

All around us private property signs were posted, many with warnings about trespassing, but as long as we stayed below the high tide mark, even Lincoln Ramsay couldn't keep us out. A terrace ran the length of the beach side of the house, dotted with furniture and topiary. No one appeared to be out enjoying the magnificent view.

Once we turned away from the ocean, the wall was brick. At twelve feet with no peek holes, it appeared dull and lifeless, not a single vine of clump of ivy to help scale it. When we reached the road, we walked for several hundred yards until the brick was punctuated by twelve-foot-high iron gates. Just inside there was a gatehouse. We peered around, but couldn't see whether someone was manning it.

"Surely you're not thinking we can break into Fort Knox here," Katie said as we resumed our stroll.

"Who knows," I said, "maybe they'll invite us in." I gazed back at Wilda, who gave a slight shake of her head. It was weird seeing her out in broad daylight. She looked really uncomfortable.

"I don't know, Rick," Katie said. "We may have met our match."

"Nonsense. Maybe Muffy and Flip have a ladder they can lend us?"

"Ha ha," she said as we rounded the corner and headed downhill.

"I can climb this," Josh said. "Are we thinking they've got Mike in there?"

"Who knows. They use those Javelin people for their grunt work. They could have taken her anywhere, but I'm thinking close by just because she was grabbed in the Bluffs."

He started testing footholds as we neared the Richardsons' until I told him to lay off. Wilda declined to join us and remained on the street as the three of us strolled up the Richardsons' gravel drive. Half beach house half Greco Roman temple, the columned front porch was white clapboards, the rest of the house shingled with pale blue shutters. *No accounting for taste, I guess.* The grass was perfect, the gardens a work in progress, the plantings not yet filled in.

Muffy greeted us at the door. "Hey, welcome, ladies! So glad you called! It's great to have visitors! The Annex crowd are not exactly chummy types. Don't get me wrong—as a getaway, this place is great—but it doesn't have what you'd call a neighborhood vibe. Flip took the kids to Old Harbor for miniature golf and ice cream, so it's mercifully quiet."

After a house tour with lots of oohing and aahing, we sat on the back terrace, iced teas in hand. Katie and Muffy discussed their mutual friends back home and other mundane topics until she turned the conversation toward the Ramsays. I could have hugged her.

"I don't know them well," Muffy said. "I mean, look where they live. The biggest, most gorgeous property on Billionaires Row. They don't socialize much, at least with us."

"We heard they had a big party last night," I said.

"Oh? I wouldn't know. They have a driveway area that can fit fifty cars, I'm told, so you wouldn't know what they were doing unless you peeked through the gates."

Like my nosy stepmother. "Different world, I guess," I said.

She nodded. "I mean, don't get me wrong, Flip and I are very comfortable. We're just not in Lincoln Ramsay's league. Never will be. I was just saying to Flip yesterday that maybe we'd have been better off to build in the Bluffs proper. At least there's a few kids over there. Your parents live in the Bluffs, don't they, Josh?"

He nodded. "No kids, though."

"Well, we've spotted a few around."

"Oh?"

"I saw kids in uncle Barry's yard last week. In fact, I wanted to ask him about them at the clambake, and we got interrupted. They looked about our kids' age. I mean, I know they're not his, but maybe one of his other nieces and nephews, or staff kids? "

"Excuse me? You mean Barry McCann?" I said.

"Yes, why?" she said.

"What did they look like, these children?"

"Just saw 'em from afar. Two little girls."

"Can you describe them?"

Muffy stared at me as if I had two heads. "Oh…well, let me think. Dark hair, cute summer dresses like they'd just been to a party. Only saw them from the rear. Never saw their faces. I'd say one was around four, the other maybe eight or nine. Our Cassie who's seven would kill for a playmate out here."

"Had you seen them before?" I asked.

"No, that's why I wanted to ask Barry or Sarah about them last night."

We chatted a few minutes more, then made our excuses. Time to visit Lincoln Ramsay and then Barry McCann.

CHAPTER 45

"Are you thinking what I'm thinking?" Katie said as we reached the street.

"Where did Barry McCann suddenly get two little girls? "

"Exactly," she said, hands on hips. "So, what's the plan?"

"First, we check out Fort Knox. Then we pay Uncle Barry a visit."

"It could be Lin and Joy," Josh said. "I'll head down there and—"

"No one's heading anywhere alone," I said. "We are staying together. Now, come on."

We walked the perimeter of the Ramsays' great wall, searching for the least exposed section. Wilda refused to allow anyone to stay behind, so the first two over the wall were Katie, then yours truly. It was an inelegant process to say the least and involved lots of inappropriate touching and shoving. Josh stood on Wilda's shoulders and I stood on his to push and shove Katie over. She waited for me, lying flat across the top of the six-inch-wide wall. Then we contemplated our descent into what appeared to be rosebushes with five-inch thorns.

"I feel like the prince in *Sleeping Beauty*," she said.

"Except no magic sword," I said. I wondered if Ramsay had found a way to make hybrid roses with poisonous thorns.

As we contemplated our fate, Josh hopped up beside us, Wilda following in short order. It looked like she'd flown. "Come on, boss. We're sitting ducks up here," she said, pointing to a spot where the rosebushes parted slightly.

"Geez, Louise," I said, pushing off, heading for the spot. I missed it by a mile and landed on a bed of thorns that pierced every piece of clothing except my sneakers. I grimaced, but kept silent, in agony as I scrambled to my feet. Without warning, Katie followed, landing partially on top of me, ramming my side, thorns and all, into the ground.

As I fought to throw her considerable bulk to the side, Josh and Wilda flew through the air, clearing the bushes and landing on soft, cushy grass. *Damn them!*

"Hurry," Wilda said, pulling us to our feet. "Won't be long before they set the dogs on us."

"Dogs?" I said, recalling a previous caper where we'd come close to being eaten by a horse dog.

"Just a figure of speech," she said, but the perimeter was surely rigged with motion detectors.

"Terrific," I muttered, yanking out the last of the thorns sticking into my jeans. Some had left rips and tears. Fortunately ripped jeans were in this season!

Katie's khakis and linen top were shredded in several places and now dotted with blood from her thorn stabbings. Fortunately, my body had shielded her and I'd taken the brunt of it.

"Come on," I said, "let's try around back. Maybe a terrace door is open. Remember, the minute we see a kid or Kim or Mike, we call the police."

The words were barely out of my mouth when we sensed movement to our right as three enormous German shepherds rounded the corner of the house. *Of course, it had to be German shepherds, the smartest breed known to man!* As they raced toward us, Katie deployed her pepper spray on the leader, then zapped the other two with the stun gun. The stunned ones dropped like rocks with barely a whimper, but the recipient of the pepper spray rolled around on the grass, emitting a high-pitched keening sound I'd never heard a dog make.

"Better stun him, too," I said. "Put him out of his misery. Let's move. They won't be out forever and my guess is the tattooed warriors will be joining us soon."

As if on cue, three thugs came around the house, guns brandished. Wilda pushed me out of sight and Josh yanked Katie into the bushes. So focused were they on the canine patrol, they hadn't spied us yet. We sidled along the west wall of the enormous house, and had almost reached the terrace, when we came to a very fancy bulkhead, teak doors and brass handles. I grabbed a handle and was surprised to find it open. We could hear yelling as the gang approached, so we slipped in the door and descended the dozen steps to another door, Katie's flashlight lighting our way.

I opened the inner door, also teak with an even fancier set of handles, and we found ourselves in a small theater, no doubt where Lincoln and Ms. Do-Gooder enjoyed first-run movies. I stared at the darkened screen before heading for doors at the opposite end of the room. The others followed and we stepped into a hallway, the walls covered in dark red brocade. Tacky, if you ask me, but what do I know about interior decorating?

We could hear scuffling from behind us and above. It was probably a matter of seconds before they would find us. There were three closed doors in the hallway. The first led to a small office, the second to a stairway going up, an elevator beside it. The third had been painted with bright colors, rainbows and flowers. "Bingo," I said, trying the handle. Locked.

Before I could moan and groan, Katie produced a set of lock picks and had the thing opened in less than minute. Just as well, as we heard footsteps coming down the stairs and others in the theater. "Come on," I said, pushing everyone in and closing the door.

Katie shone the flashlight for just a second. We were now in a small closet-like space. A wide green plastic laundry chute appeared to be the only other exit besides the door to the hall where the footsteps were converging.

"What the hell is this?" Josh whispered.

"I don't know, but let's go!" I jumped first, careening down a twisting tube until I landed on a large circular trampoline. As usual, Katie followed and was soon on top of me. Josh and Wilda managed to descend more gracefully as the voices above told us we'd been found.

"Shit," I said, "get off this thing and let's find a light switch. They know where we are anyway."

As I spoke, we heard more scuffles and realized we were about to have company coming down the slide. Without a word, Wilda and Josh took hold of the trampoline and shoved it across the room. Fortunately, at that moment, Katie found a bank of light switches so we had a bird's-eye view of the three as they crashed to the floor, guns flying. We took advantage of their momentary disorientation to disarm them.

"Katie, stun gun two of 'em and leave this one alone," I said, pointing to a meaty little guy, whose head was under Wilda's boot.

With two of them out cold, number three subdued, we had a chance to survey our surroundings. It looked like we'd landed in Kiddy Heaven. There were climbing walls, jungle gyms, kitchen areas, and shelves of toys as well as an impressive library of children's books. At the far end of the room, there was an enormous mirror, similar to the one I'd seen at Meridian. I opened a door beside it to find a small space with tripods and camera equipment. I shook my head, a wave of nausea creeping over me. "What do you wanta bet this is connected to a projector upstairs in the theater? Jesus Christ."

"But where are the kids?" Josh asked, gazing around.

"Sold," Wilda said as she ground her foot into our captive's face.

CHAPTER 46

I was certain there were more evil ones on their way so I crossed the room and leaned over, addressing our captive. "We've got to get out of here. How?"

"Fuck you."

I waved at Katie. "Pepper spray, now."

As she stooped ready to aim at our recalcitrant captive, he waved his arm. "Wait. Take the door over there."

"Where will it lead us?"

"Just behind the kitchen."

"What's your name?"

"Fuck you."

"Katie, pepper spray, now!"

"Paco."

"Now, that's better." I said, grabbing a jump rope and throwing it to Josh. "Tie his hands. He'll be our leader. Take some of those doll clothes and gag him, too."

Josh tied his hands as Wilda held him. They then fashioned a gag out of several articles of clothing tied together, a tiny flannel nightgown shoved in his throat first. Katie grabbed a few more ropes and tied up the stunned duo. Then Wilda and I each took and elbow and dragged Paco between us up three flights of stairs. When we reached the top, I pressed my ear against a closed door. Silence.

We could be walking into a trap, but what the hell. Better than dying three stories below the ground. I opened the door a crack and realized he'd been telling the truth. It looked like a mud room, paneled with white shiplap and easily twice the size of my living room. Every conceivable type of storage lined its walls—closets, cubbies, peg racks and benches.

"Wow, wish I'd brought my camera," Katie whispered as we stepped into the empty room. "So many great ideas here."

"No time for pictures. Come on," I said, shoving Paco along. He had suddenly developed a limp and was clearly lollygagging. I eyed Wilda and she lifted him off the ground, propelling him across the room.

"Looks like a trap, boss," she said, peering out the back door.

"Can you see anyone?"

"No, that's what worries me."

"Okay, well, we could shove Paco here out and see if there's any response."

Immediately he began to moan and cry, shaking his head back and forth. "Do you know something we don't?"

His eyes registered terror. Wilda was right. It was a trap.

"Change of plans," I said, pulling him back. "We may have to take a house tour instead. Paco will be our guide."

I pushed him toward the kitchen door. This elicited yet another round moans and head shaking. Turning back to my companions, I whispered, "Any ideas, people?"

Our only other choices were a small window that I was pretty sure only two of us could fit through and a door at the end of a small hallway that appeared to lead to the garages. I handed Paco off to Wilda and crept down the hall, then opened the door a crack. Sure enough, an eight-car garage, silent as a tomb. Two of the bays were empty, the other three occupied by two Bentleys, a Mercedes coupe and SUV, a small pickup truck and a John Deere mower.

I waved to the others and they joined me, Josh and Wilda on either side of Paco, who seemed even less inclined to exit through the garage. No matter, we were sitting ducks anyway. At least we might stand a chance if we could get one of the vehicles going. I grabbed a sturdy chef's apron hanging on a hook by the door and whispered to Wilda. She slid into the garage and disappeared into the shadows. Katie and Josh held fast to Paco and I stayed in the hallway, listening. I was reasonably sure the house had a monitoring system so they knew exactly where we were and what we were doing. It would not be long before we were besieged.

Josh peered over my shoulder. "Jeez, a Bentley Mulliner and a Mulsanne. What kind of business is this guy in, anyhow?"

"Right now it's the track-down-and-kill-us business, so get ready to move," I whispered.

As I turned back to the garage, I saw a shadow pass behind the Bentley Mulsanne. In what seemed like thirty seconds, there was a low rumble as the engine purred to life. A hand shot up from the driver's window.

"Let's go," I whispered. "We'll tie his legs with this when we get him in the trunk." I handed Katie the apron as Josh and I dragged Paco down six carpeted steps toward the purring car. As we neared it, the trunk opened and we wrestled Paco in. He was kicking now and very uncooperative until Katie brought out the pepper spray and waved it in front of him. "Not a sound, asshole, or we'll neutralize you." His eyes glittered with hatred, but he stopped kicking.

We hopped into the lush leather interior just as the door from the kitchen opened and three armed assailants rushed in. "Door?" I screamed to Wilda, who sat in the driver's seat. She reached over and pressed a button. The garage door began to open just as the first man reached the back seat window.

"Go!" I screamed as he fired, missing us, the bullet, passing through the open window into the quilted leather front seat, just missing Josh, who was crouched down.

"Everybody down!" Wilda cried and the Bentley shot forward.

As we came into the drive, a phalanx of firepower assaulted the car. Bullets zinged and pinged as bits of glass rained down, but the armored doors protected us as we cowered on luxurious carpeted floors. Wilda drove blind, pedal to the metal as we raced down the gravel drive toward the gates. "Can't find the goddamn gate remote," she said, rummaging around.

"Try the dashboard. It's probably built in!" Josh said, leaning toward her. As our pursuers ran to catch up, the two of them scanned the ridiculously complicated collection of knobs, dials and gauges searching for the magic button, I held my breath. *So close, but yet so far. We'll never get all four of us over the wall in time.* Less than fifty yards from thick iron grate, he cried, "Eureka!" as we watched the gates slowly open.

"Close them," I screamed as a pickup hot on our trail rounded the drive.

As we raced out, gates half closing then opening behind us, I heard sirens. "Thank God," I said, turning to Katie, who was white as a sheet. "You okay?" I said, putting my arm around her shoulders.

"Never better," she said, leaning against me.

"Still glad you came?"

"Wouldn't have missed it for the world," she said. "Wait till I tell my cardiologist! He's always nagging me to lose weight, watch my cholesterol, blah, blah. If this didn't give me a heart attack, nothing will."

"Just take it slow," Wilda said. "Sometimes when the adrenaline wears off, that's when your body reacts."

"Just what us mature ladies need to hear at this moment," I said. As three Fall River police and two Old Harbor cruisers rounded the corner and screeched to a halt, I breathed a huge sigh of relief. "Thank God, our heroes," I said.

CHAPTER 47

Douglas Roberts stepped out of cruiser number one. Two cars behind, an old friend, Roger Demaris, originally a member of the Old Harbor police department, emerged. As they and eight officers approached, I wasn't sure whether to laugh, cry, or jump up and down. Then, I realized if I did any of those things I would surely wet my pants.

Demaris grinned as he approached us. "Ricky Steele, why am I not surprised?"

He and I had met on a previous case. He had made romantic overtures, but I was so besotted with Jay Harp at that time that I was not encouraging. Besides, he was years too young for me. He looked well, thick, dark hair longish with a few streaks of gray, trimmer, healthier.

"Hey, Detective, heard you have a new position."

He nodded. "You remember Detective Dugan? This is the third member of RHD, Detective Greta Burke." He referred to the Regional Homicide Division he now headed with his two detectives.

I shook her hand, but Dugan hung back. "Nice to meet you, Detective Burke. I heard you got a promotion too, Detective Dugan?"

He gave me a curt nod. "And, it's Lieutenant Demaris now."

Hands on hips, Roberts said, "Listen folks, I hate to break up old home week, but we've got a situation here." He stood beside the Bentley, which now resembled

Swiss cheese, its beautiful tan roof and sleek black sides dotted with dozens of bullet holes. "Jesus friggin' Christ, what the hell is this?"

You can guess to whom those words were directed. I decided talking really fast with a smile on my face was my best option. "We'll explain later. There's a bad guy tied up in the trunk, who you really need to talk to. His associates were right behind us, but I'm assuming they've now retreated beyond the iron gates of Chez Ramsay, where Linc and his cronies have been hosting secret auctions."

He motioned to two officers and they headed for the trunk as Wilda pushed the release button. "What auctions? What the hell are you talking about?"

"The kids, Douglas! This is where they've been selling the kids after Meridian's site folded up. You got to get hold of Ramsay, Pullman and Winter and find out where they've placed the kids. There were some sold off last night, we think. They're gone and we need to—"

Ignoring me, he nodded to the officers taking Paco away. When he turned back, he snapped, "You, you, you and you, in my car, now."

As officers surrounded Josh, Wilda, Katie and yours truly, I stood my ground. "Wait, Douglas, please! You can take us in, lock us up, do whatever you want, but please promise me you'll search Lincoln Ramsay's property and let me make one stop along the way?"

"Search his property, you say? Would that be at the same time I return his bullet-ridden limousine?"

"It's a Bentley," Josh said. "And we have to go somewhere. It's just a couple of streets over. They're holding two girls and—"

Roberts turned his gaze to Josh, eyes blazing. "I don't care if it's a fucking zoomobile. You four are going nowhere! Pacheco, get him in the car."

An officer ran up to Demaris, who had been quietly observing our little tête-à-tête. "Search warrant, sir." He handed him a paper and Demaris waved to his team, which included five other officers, all men. "Okay, people, vests on, then head up the hill!" He nodded to Roberts. "You guys okay here?"

"Thanks, Rodge. If it's okay, I'll send a couple of my guys with you."

Trying in vain to wriggle my arm out of Officer Pacheco's iron grasp, I said, "Please, Douglas, five minutes! Two little girls' lives are at stake, please. Can we all just head down there, take a peek and then you can haul us away? *Please!*"

"Jesus Christ, I must be crazy. Where're we going?"

"Barry McCann's."

"The boat guy? What the friggin' hell, Steele. We've got no cause, and no search warrant."

"But we have Katie, who knows him, or his niece, at least. They're real chummy. If you just let the two of us pop in, see what we can find out?"

"You've got five minutes. You, Hardy Boy, in the car."

CHAPTER 48

McCann's monstrosity was in the French chateau style. The cost of the slate roof alone would feed a small army. Unlike many of the Annex dwellings, the McCanns had no wall or gate, so we were free to cruise right up the circular drive and park to the side of the castle. The police cruisers stayed on the street with Josh and Wilda in the car, ready to spring if needed. I nodded to Katie, then rang the bell. Our plan was to pay a visit to Uncle Barry and ask for the tour he'd offered us at the clambake.

The door was opened by a short, stooped bald visage in butler livery. He was barely five feet tall and appeared to have the weight of the world on his narrow shoulders. "Hi," Katie said, giving him one of her beautiful smiles. "We're here for the tour Barry promised us yesterday."

He regarded us with a disdainful eye. We must've looked like aliens from Frumpville, I thought, with my ripped jeans and Katie's khakis in shreds, streaked with blood. Our hair looked like we'd just come from the Munsters' hair salon. I giggled maniacally. "Sorry about our clothes. We went on an early morning hike and got caught in some beach rose bushes."

"I'm sorry, Mr. McCann is not in. Was he expecting you?"

"Oh, what a shame," Katie said, dabbing imaginary tears from her eyes. "I'm leaving for California at noon and I wanted to take away memories of the home

Barry told us so much about. He was insistent that we drop in anytime this morning."

He hesitated and I prepared to stick my foot in the six-inch-thick door jamb, an action that would no doubt break all the bones in my foot and ankle should he decide to slam it in our faces. To my surprise, he gave a slight bow. "I'm Stewart. I run the house for Mr. McCann. I could give you a quick tour. Come in." He stepped aside and swung the door open.

It wasn't the Breakers, but it would certainly give some of the Newport mansions a run for their money. As Stewart led the way, we marveled at the marble floors, paintings and tapestries. Like an experienced docent, he pointed out many of the pieces and described their origin and history. The mirrored ballroom had apparently been modeled on one at Marble House in Newport. We oohed and aahed appropriately. Except for the cook, Freida, and an upstairs maid tidying up the gigantic master suite, there did not seem to be anyone else about.

As we completed the tour of the living quarters that included nine bedrooms, ten baths, and a library, music room, solarium, study and conservatory, Stewart said, "Mr. McCann is a wine connoisseur and has an extensive cellar. Would you like to see it?"

I wanted to kiss dear little Stewart. "Yes, please," I said, restraining myself. The cellar revealed nothing except a collection that included over three thousand bottles. I wasn't sure McCann would be around to drink it all. It seemed as if Stewart had skipped a few rooms so I nodded to Katie as we ascended the stairs behind the butler. "I think my glasses fell out of my pocket back there. You two go up. I'll be right there."

Sure enough, there were two locked doors down the corridor from the wine rooms. Katie had slipped me her lock picks earlier so I quickly picked my way into the first room, which appeared to be a work room with tools lined neatly, hanging from a broad expanse of peg board on one wall, benches holding saws and sanders ringing the room's perimeter. There were barrels of wood scraps and a half-carved shore bird on the middle workbench.

I stepped out and headed for the other door. After picking the lock, I switched on a light and found two little beds and small dressers with girls' clothes. A few toy bins and shelves were pushed against one wall. There was an empty feeling about the space, as if it had never been used. If Lin and Joy had been here, they were long gone. "Shit," I muttered, taking a quick peek through the dresser drawers, then hurrying out.

Katie and Stewart were chatting in the front hall about a twelve-foot-tall gilded mirror. She was telling him about a similar one at her parents' house. I couldn't remember such a piece, but I wouldn't have been surprised to learn it was there.

"Did you find them?" the butler asked, giving me a kind smile. "Your glasses?"

"Oh, yes, here they are!" I said, pulling them from my jacket pocket.

"Excellent. Well, if there's no more, I must get back to work. Mr. McCann will be sorry to have missed you. He loves visitors and he spends so little time here at Rose House, but he's very proud of it."

"Oh, we thought he loved it here. He told us he spends most of his time here."

"At the Bluffs, not at Rose House."

"I don't understand," I said.

"He built this for Mrs. McCann, but I'm afraid she detests it."

And him, I thought. "What a shame. Well where does Mr. McCann stay when he's here?"

"In his much smaller home down on Osprey Circle in the Bluffs, number thirty-two. It's more of a cottage, right on the water. He has a dock down there and his boat, of course."

"Oh? Do you manage that as well?" I asked.

"Oh, no, Mr. McCann says he's roughing it down there. He takes care of things. I believe he hires a cleaning service sometimes and Freida delivers all his meals every afternoon."

"And serves them?"

"No, they have a system where she leaves the baskets on the back terrace. He takes care of the rest."

Katie gave him a puzzled look. "Don't you think that's a little odd?"

"I've learned not to wonder about the eccentricities of my employers. I do know that Mr. McCann's business keeps him very busy. Perhaps when he comes home, he wants solitude."

I tugged Katie's sleeve. "Well, thank you so much, Stewart. You are an expert guide. I learned so much about art and architecture."

He beamed and gave another bow, "My pleasure."

I felt a little sorry for Stewart rambling around, managing his empty gilded rooms. "One more question. If Mr. McCann is not in residence, why was the maid changing his bed?"

He smiled. "Mr. McCann insists on clean sheets every day, in case the lady of the house decides to pay a visit."

That would be when hell freezes over, I thought, thanking him again and saying goodbye.

"We're going to need a search warrant and police backup down at thirty-two Osprey Circle," Katie said.

"Don't I know it," I said, rejoining Josh and Wilda in the cruiser.

CHAPTER 49

We approached thirty-two Osprey Circle, but kept the three cruisers out of sight down the street four houses away. They were still waiting on the search warrant when we stepped out of the cars. While Roberts was reluctant to do it, he agreed that perhaps the safest course for the children's sake would be for Katie and me to pretend to visit while his officers fanned out around the perimeter of the house.

"I'm breaking every rule in the book here, Steele. And if there weren't kids involved, you'd be in handcuffs," he said as a technician fitted us with wires. "First sign of trouble, you duck and we'll be right behind you with both barrels. Can you hear Tim?" he asked as Tim Cottrell spoke softly into a mike.

"Yup." I turned to Katie. "Are you sure about this?"

"Absolutely. I'm ready, girl. Already cleared it with Bob."

Geez, what a couple!

"I'd like to lend support," Wilda said, stepping forward.

"Sorry," Roberts said. "You're to stay behind with Peabody here."

"But they've got Mike," Josh said, stepping forward.

"Mr. Peabody, I know you're worried about your girlfriend, but you need to stay here. Bad enough I'm taking these two," he said, waving at Katie and me. "We're not endangering the lives of any more civilians. Now cool your heels with Willie here."

"It's Wilda," I said, receiving an icy glare from Roberts before he stepped closer, surveying our fronts for telltale signs of the wire.

"I don't care if she's Wilma Friggin' Flintstone. She and Joe Hardy are staying here. Okay, ladies, don't play Wonder Women. Demaris just called. No one at the Ramsays' except for a couple of domestics. They were locked in a walk-in closet upstairs. The hired guns were long gone."

I nodded and we began strolling Osprey Circle, past numerous McMansions, each ridiculously oversized for its lot. As we reached the driveway for thirty-two, I squeezed Katie's hand. "You okay?"

"I'm pissed."

"Me, too. No heroics, though, right? I can't lose one of my oldest friends to these assholes and I'm sure not gonna let 'em kill me."

"Roger that," she said, her voice remarkably calm.

The house reminded me of Long Island, a quintessential beach house that went on and on to the edge of its lot. Stewart's term "cottage" was an understatement. The clamshell drive was bordered by blue hydrangeas and ornamental beach grass. As we neared the huge wraparound porch lined with white rockers, I whispered, "What do you wanta bet those chairs have never had an ass in 'em?" *It always helps me to talk dirty when I'm scared shitless.*

"Gorgeous place. Too bad it's full of motherfuckers," she said.

I stared at her, grinning. *Apparently, Katie also talks dirty to buck herself up.* "Here we go, girl," I said as we climbed the stairs and knocked at the door.

We rang the bell, which echoed through the house, but no one came. I then knocked several times and Katie called, "Hello, Barry! It's Muffy's friend, Katie Briarwood! Stewart sent us down!"

After what seemed like hours, the door opened and Barry stepped out on the porch, closing the door behind him. "Hey, gals, good to see you again. Now's not the best time. Maybe you could pop by tomorrow?"

"Oh, that's so disappointing. I'm leaving tonight and was hoping to take a peek at this incredible house. My husband and I are thinking of building on the islands and this is just what we're looking for."

"My niece has all my contact info. Next time you're in town, we'll get together for sure. Bring the hubby and we'll throw something on the grill."

McCann's hands shook and his eyes darted from Katie to the bank of windows to the south. *There are probably twenty Uzis aimed at our heads. His eyes have never once looked at yours truly. Maybe they are planning to knock me off, even if they let Katie go.*

"Just a peek?" Katie said. "Love to see the water side."

"Sorry, not today. Now, I've got a business call that's scheduled in five minutes. Let me walk you out. Where's your car, anyway?"

"No need to walk us out," I said. "Just hand over Lin and Joy and we'll be out of your hair."

For the first time, he looked at me, his usual boozy, friendly demeanor gone, watery baby blues flashing fire. "Listen, bitch, you and lard-ass here better get the fuck off my porch or they're gonna open fire."

"Now, that's just plain rude," Katie said, wiping out her pepper spray and blasting him. As McCann screamed and began clawing at his eyes as he stepped inside the house. As he slammed the door, I spied movement inside and shoved Katie to the porch floor, our bodies hugging the wall. The sound of shattering glass and a hail of bullets followed. The police returned fire and I prayed.

Suddenly things went quiet and I dared raise my head. Roberts grabbed us by the collars and pulled us up. Beside him stood Tim Cottrell and another officer. "You two, go with Tim and Mac. You're in the cruiser till this ends, then you can stroll on back to Daddy's to get your car."

Clearly, there was no use arguing. As we turned to go, knocks sounded from inside the front door. Roberts cried, "Back off," but before he could react, I grabbed the door handle and pushed inward. Two little girls in flowered dresses and Mary

Janes stared up at us. Behind them, Barry McCann stood, a Glock in his right hand pointed at the older girl. "Back off or I kill them both."

There did not appear to be anyone else in the foyer. The children held hands, their expressions blank. McCann looked ready to burst into tears with the slightest provocation. Before Roberts could push us aside, I said, "Please, Barry, let them go. I know you care about them."

"Fuck you," he said, hands shaking violently.

Roberts stepped in front of Katie and me. "Mr. McCann, your house is surrounded by police. There's no point in this. Drop the gun, now."

Something does not make sense. Why is McCann standing here waving a gun when he knows it's over? One of the officers ran around from the side of the house. "They've got a boat! They're takin' off from the dock, Sarge!"

"Shit, we wasted all that time and let them get away!" I cried.

Ignoring McCann, Roberts grabbed the girls and pulled them to safety, then turned to Katie and me. "You and you, out to the cars. Take these two with you. McCann, either drop the gun or we're gonna shoot you. Take your pick."

Wide-eyed, we watched as the gun clattered to the floor and Barry McCann crumpled, grabbing the bannister as he sat on the steps leading upstairs. Head on his knees, he began sobbing. "I'm sorry, I'm sorry, I didn't mean to. I can't help it. Please, I didn't hurt them."

"Take that filth away," Roberts said. "He makes me want to puke. Then, call Old Harbor, have 'em get the boats out. They've got high-tech tracking gear and speed. Besides, it'll take too long for the city to mobilize," Roberts said. "Tell 'em where we are and give 'em a clear description of the boat. Jesus Christ, why are you four still here? Get my men to remove the wires and go home. Now, get out of my sight!"

"But?" I said.

"But nothing. It's over, Steele."

"No it isn't! They've got my assistant, Mike Bowen."

"I know. Now let my men do their job. We'll find her."

But will they? Is Mike in that boat about to be tossed off somewhere in the Atlantic?

CHAPTER 50

Josh greeted the sisters, receiving a smile from each. I noticed he did not try to touch them, but knelt down and spoke softly to them for several minutes, telling them they were safe. Wilda stood beside the group, silent and watchful. Demaris was a short distance away, by the cars, talking with Detective Burke. "Hey, you okay?" he said as we approached. "These the ones you were looking for?"

I nodded. "Lin and Joy, meet an old friend of mine. Roger, this my assistant Wilda and this is Josh Peabody, a former teacher at Meridian's school."

Demaris nodded to Wilda and Josh, then knelt in front of the girls, his kind eyes smiling. "Am I glad to see you, ladies."

As her sister watched, expression inscrutable, Joy stepped forward and placed her tiny arms around his shoulders, burying her face.

"Hey, it's okay," he said softly. "You're safe now."

"What about the others?" I asked.

"We've got some leads," he said, eyes grave as he stared up at me. "Nasty business."

"Listen, Roger, I know I have no right to ask you this, but do you suppose one of your team could drop us at my dad's down the street and then take the kids to the city? They're going to Ruth Channing at Belmont House."

With a smile at the girls, he straightened up. "No problem. Greta!" he called, waving. "She'll take 'em and drop you two at your father's, but I suspect you're gonna get into more trouble." He turned to one of the city cops. "Roberts didn't want them held, did he?"

"No, sir, just gone. He knows where to find Ms. Steele."

Demaris nodded, his eyes registering momentary amusement despite the gravity of the situation. "Hey, Greta, these two young ladies need to get to Belmont House. Ms. Steele will fill you in."

"Yes, sir."

"And Ms. Steele and her companions need to be dropped off a few blocks from here."

"Yes, sir," she said. "Car's over here. Hi," she said, directing her attention to Lin and Joy. "I'm Greta."

The children followed her, silently, still holding hands. I walked beside them, Josh on their other side. As we dropped our hands to our sides, I was surprised to feel a tiny hand grasp mine as Lin took Josh's.

"Hey, boss, I can walk," Wilda said. "Not enough room in the car."

"No problem," Greta said, waving to an officer. "Skeeter, grab the keys from Les and take these guys."

"My car's outside the Peabodys'," Wilda said to me.

"Josh," I said, "I think you should probably stay put at your parents'. Wilda can stay nearby."

"No way!" he said. "I'm coming with you."

"We'll find her."

"You know damn well she's in that boat. They're gonna toss her."

"We don't know that. Now, we've gotta get moving."

"Then I want to go with Lin and Joy."

"That's a great idea. I'm sure they'll feel better with you along."

"You four go together and pick up Wilda's car at your folks'. That way Wilda can bring you back, okay?"

"Where will you be?" he said.

"I'll be in touch, I promise."

Wilda stepped closer to me. "I don't like this, boss. I'm having Spike meet you at your dad's."

"That would be great, thanks," I said. We said our goodbyes to Joy, Lin and the others and headed off.

CHAPTER 51

"How awful to have such things going on here!" Rita said as I concluded my brief, abridged summary of events.

A snappy comment came to mind about evildoers existing everywhere, even on Billionaires Row, but I kept it to myself. "We need to get going," I said.

"To where?" Dad said, eyeing me with concern.

"We're going home to make a few calls."

"Good," he said as the front doorbell rang.

"Oh, dear, who could that be?" Rita said, disappearing.

Several minutes later, Charlie Bowen walked in, Lolly and Alice beside him. My heart sank when I spied him. He looked as if he'd aged thirty years. The certainty that Mike could take care of herself had vanished from his blue eyes, which now reflected fear and anxiety.

Alice spoke first. "We couldn't sit by and do nothing. Charlie came by and we decided to come find you."

"But the gate?"

"I called the gate," my father said. "Good to see you again, Dr. Bowen, ladies." He stepped forward and shook Charlie's hand, then hugged Lolly and Alice.

Jeez Louise, can I feel any worse? "Hey," I said, hugging all three of them.

"Have you heard anything?" he said.

"Not yet, but Sergeant Roberts has promised to call the minute he knows anything."

I recounted the events of the past few hours. The three listened, and then Charlie said, "Did they have her? Was she in the boat?"

"We couldn't tell," I said. "They slipped away from us. The police are searching right now."

Tears in his eyes, he gazed at me. "What can I do, Ricky? She's my—"

"I know," I said, hugging him again. *Of course, I don't know, being childless, but I can imagine.*

One of my burner phones rang and I grabbed it from my bag.

"Steele, it's me," Roberts said. "McCann says your friend and Leonardo were not with Pullman and Winter. He doesn't know where Ramsay is and I believe him. Any ideas?"

"No, can't you get anything else out of him?"

"Nope, he's lawyered up. Cryin' like a baby."

"Thanks, Douglas. We're at my dad's. If I think of something, I'll call."

"Pronto. The Old Harbor boats are chasing them. We'll see what we get outta Pullman and Winter when we catch 'em."

I clicked off and stared at the others. *What are we missing? Where are they? There isn't anywhere else.* We hadn't searched the Pullman condo, but I doubted that Lesley Pullman had hostages stashed in her boudoir.

Suddenly I remembered one other player unaccounted for—Fiona Veruga. *Where the hell is she?*

CHAPTER 52

There was something almost comical about our little caravan until one remembered that they had Mike and maybe Danny, too. In four cars, we pulled up, parking several blocks from Veruga's condo complex in Freetown. We now had Spike, Frank and Wilda watching our backs. Fiona's unit was one of five in a long building, hers the second one in on the left. The building was nondescript, shingled, white trim, circular gravel drive, neatly trimmed front yard, and a six-car garage to its right. The surrounding area was wooded, the neighboring houses some distance away. There appeared to be a fenced-in pool behind the building and a stretch of lawn bordered by thick woods.

As we assembled a short distance down the street, I said, "I think it's best if Wilda, Frank and I take this one, guys. Spike'll stay back with you, okay?"

"Nothing doing," Charlie said, pulling a Glock from his glove compartment. "She's my daughter and I'm coming with you."

"Charlie, we don't even know if she's here."

"I'll stay out of sight."

"Dr. Bowen, this is a bad idea," Wilda said, her voice just above a whisper.

Charlie looked at me, his eyes pleading. "I can't just stand here twiddling my thumbs."

"Come, then, but stay out of sight. I'm going to the door. Wilda and Frank will be around."

Fiona answered the door in capris and a sleeveless tee, brown hair tied in a scraggly ponytail, no makeup. She looked like she was headed to yoga class. "Oh, great, just what we need. What the hell do you want? Haven't you done enough?"

She started to close the door and I shot out my foot. "I want Mike and Danny."

"Fuck off."

"Let the bitch in," a voice said from within.

Fiona shrugged. "Suit yourself." She waved me in.

As the door closed, I felt cold steel against my temple. "Well, well," I said, spying Meridian's office manager, Nancy, out of the corner of my eye. She was dressed similarly to her partner in crime—jean capris, hot pink tee shirt and flip-flops. Her red hair was tied back with a purple bandana. The her gum snapped close to my ear. "Hardly recognized you without your red suit and high heels, Nance."

"Shut the fuck up, bitch. And you can tell your little helpers to back off or I'll spray your brains all over the place."

"My, my, my, is that any way to speak to a customer?" I said, eyes scanning the room, buying time, before my impending doom. I hoped that Wilda was getting all this. It was a nice living room, tastefully furnished in greens, beiges and blues. *A little too chichi for me, but then I'm not living here. I don't want to die here either, thank you very much.*

"Listen, ladies, I'm sorry to barge in, but I'm looking for my assistant, Mike Bowen, and wondered if you'd seen her or know where she might be?"

I felt a foot in the small of my back as I was shoved to the floor. "Oh, you're wondering, are you?" Pelton said, placing a smelly foot on the side of my head.

"That's not very sanitary, you know."

"Shut the fuck up," she said, removing her foot and kicking me in the side. I heard a crack. *Was it her toes or my rib? Judging by the shooting pains radiating up and down my chest, it was me.*

I groaned, remembering the wire. Roberts' men had removed Katie's then gotten distracted before they could take mine. I continued to groan while also mumbling softly, repeating Wilda's and Charlie's phone numbers over and over. *Please Douglas, let someone still be listening.*

"What the hell is she going on about?" Nancy said.

Fiona stooped and ripped my tee shirt down the front. "Jesus Christ, she's wearing a wire." Without hesitation, she ripped it from my chest along with a sizable hunk of flesh.

"Ow," I said, not sure where I hurt more, chest or side.

"Shut up, bitch," Nancy said, kicking me again as Fiona stamped on the mike.

Pain coursed through me and I said a silent prayer of thanks that she was not wearing stilettos.

"What the hell are we going to do now?" Fiona said, stooping, as Nancy pinned me down with a foot on my back. "You know she's got her muscle out there."

"Amateurs," Pelton said. "Granny Snooper here is our ticket. Get the other one. Leave him. He won't last the night anyway."

As Nancy duct-taped my arms behind my back and slapped a piece over my mouth, Fiona disappeared down a hall. She reappeared several minutes later, armed with what looked like a Smith & Wesson. She now wore stupid-looking gold lamé sneakers and was shoving Mike ahead of her.

Thank God, she's alive, I thought, making eye contact. Mike's gaze was steady and calm. She had an angry bruise on her left cheek, but otherwise appeared to be in pretty good shape. She was similarly trussed up, duct tape over her mouth.

"Get up, bitch," Nancy said, pulling me from my knees to stand, gun barrel pressed against the back of my neck. I winced in pain. *Please don't let me black out.*

"Move it," she said, pushing me toward the kitchen, where they grabbed their bags. Apparently, we were using the back door. I considered kicking backward, aiming for Nancy's groin, but then remembered the brain spraying comment and proceeded meekly.

The fresh air felt good as we stepped out and headed for the car park and a black Escalade.

CHAPTER 53

A shadow passed to our right and suddenly Wilda appeared, as if by magic, directly in our path. Nancy shook her head as Fiona reared back and spied Frank's movement to the left, training her gun over Mike's shoulder.

Nice work, guys, I thought. *What kinds of bodyguards were these?*

"Drop all your weapons, and I do mean all, or Granny here gets one in the head."

"She dies, you die," Wilda said, her voice a low growl.

"I'll take my chances. I can use your friend here as a shield."

After several minutes, Wilda nodded to Frank and their guns clattered to the pavement, followed by his knife. I couldn't believe what I was seeing.

Nancy dragged me along, not bothering to pick up the weapons, but kicking them well out of reach. "I should shoot you point-blank, but our beef is not with you." We had reached the Escalade and she slammed me against the front passenger door. Tears came to my eyes as pain shot through my chest. Sirens screamed in the distance. Coming nearer, by my reckoning. *Douglas heard me!*

I gazed over at Mike, giving her a slight nod. She flashed a look of understanding as I stood up straight and brought my right leg back. My heel went straight to Nancy's groin. At the same time, I elbowed her as hard as I could and ducked. I could hear scuffling beside me and I hoped Mike was doing the same. As Nancy groaned and doubled over, I spied Fiona's gun aimed straight at my head.

As I tried to duck, a gun went off and Fiona crumpled, holding the arm that had held the gun. *Geez, what a shot!*

With a unison cry of "Arrgh!" Katie and Alice rushed in from the opposite side of the carport, brandishing garden rakes. *No doubt pepper spray is sure to follow*, I thought as they rained holy hell down on Nancy Pelton.

In the melee, Charlie rushed forward and grabbed Mike, pushing her to safety behind the Escalade. The sounds of sirens close by mingled with Fiona's screams as Wilda subdued her. Before she knew what was happening, Veruga was in handcuffs, her tee shirt ripped from her body and wrapped around her arm as a tourniquet. Frank had slapped handcuffs on Nancy and now had her face down on the pavement, where she moaned and groaned.

Charlie untied Mike as Katie and Alice helped me. When the duct tape was off my mouth, I called to Wilda, "Danny, I think he's inside. I'm guessing he's in pretty rough shape."

Mike came around the car. "Yes, he is. It's pretty awful."

Katie had one of my arms, Alice the other as Spike came around the side of the complex, Lolly behind him. "How are you?" I asked Mike.

"Okay, but I wouldn't have been for long."

Charlie stood with one arm round her waist as he tucked his gun behind his back. "Mike looks better than you," he said, as I saw stars and slowly began to sink toward the ground. Just in time, he caught me. "Hey, babe, it's over," he said as blackness descended.

EPILOGUE

I regained consciousness just in time to see Danny Leonardo carried out on a stretcher. They were airlifting him to Boston with a severe concussion, two broken arms, a shattered kneecap, and a fractured femur. If I hadn't known it was him, I'd never have recognized him. Both his eyes were black and blue and swollen shut and his face was covered with cuts and abrasions.

Charlie insisted that Mike and I be seen at the hospital, so we all traipsed over. As I suspected, I had two cracked ribs. Mike was shaken, but fine. We had reached her just in time. Fiona and Nancy were cleaning house. The police found their bags packed and airline tickets to France for the following day.

Thanks to the wire, Roberts had been tracking our movements, but after my mumbling, he called Wilda and she filled him in. Barry McCann, Wade Pullman and Oscar Winter were in custody. When the police surrounded the cabin cruiser three miles out to sea, they found the two Meridian owners, one of their lackeys driving the boat and Lincoln Ramsay. As they approached the boat, Ramsay put a gun to his temple and pulled the trigger.

Charlie drove us home. As he helped me out, I leaned over and hugged him. "Thanks."

"I'm gonna put Mike to bed, but I can come back if you need me?" He traced his fingers along my jaw.

"That's okay. I'll be fine. See you soon, though?"

"Count on it."

"Take good care of Mike," I said, peering through the window at her. "You okay, partner?"

She gave me a thumbs up. Before I knew what was happening, Charlie pulled me close for one of his great kisses. As I broke away and joined the others, I found all three of them grinning.

We headed in, yours truly weak-kneed, and found Bob Briarwood and Ron Pruit sitting on the deck with Vinnie. I guess they weren't taking any chances. Alice's husband was overseas, or I was pretty sure he'd have been there too. We spent several hours recounting our adventures, after which the group dispersed. Katie and Lolly packed up. Bob and Katie were dropping Alice at her sister's until her flight the next morning.

"Hey, Rick," Vinnie said as we packed the cars. "These are good people. Next time, call me and I'll get Chaz involved."

"There will not be a next time!" Ron said.

As Lolly hugged me, she whispered, "Don't listen to him. I've found my calling now."

"Oh?" I said, smiling at her.

"Dispatcher!"

"She did an awesome job with that," Alice said, laughing as she tossed her bag into Bob's truck. "Vinnie, who is this Chaz, anyway?"

"Next time, doll," he said, giving her a wink.

We hugged. Then I found Katie. "Hey, buddy," I said, tears in my eyes. "I couldn't have done it without you. In fact, I doubt I'd be standing here without you."

She grabbed me in a bear hug, but not before I glimpsed her teary eyes. "All in a day's work, baby. I'll be standing by."

Bob opened his mouth to protest, but I beat him to it. "Not for a long time, baby. Maybe never. I'm not losin' you to the likes of Meridian."

"And let's not forget the tattoo brigade!" Alice said. "Now, keep us posted about Dr. Gorgeous. Is he coming over tonight?"

If Vinnie's neck had snapped around any faster, it would have flown off. "Dr. Gorgeous? That sounds promising!"

*****

Please read on for chapters from ***Jigsaw!***

Excerpt from Jigsaw

After their dear friend, Rosie is found dead, business partners, friends and one-time lovers, Juls Whitman and Tuck Potter, find themselves tracking a serial killer. When they realize they are in over their heads, the pair call family friend, Ricky Steele, a private investigator from the nearby city of Fall River.

Together, the trio follow a puzzling trail of evidence, getting closer and closer to a monster who preys on handicapped women, then strews jigsaw puzzle pieces over their lifeless, mutilated bodies. With Juls's limp and reconstructed knee, will she become the killer's next victim?

PROLOGUE

The gloves snapped as he slipped them off, disposing of them as he always did after an outing. A deeply satisfying sound, the snapping of latex and powdery dust feathering up into the air. Brother loved it. Just as he had loved Rosie in those final moments as she begged for her life. "Oh, sweet Rosie," he crooned, lying back on the musty cot in the darkened room. "You made me soooo happy."

Already the euphoria was ebbing away, sucked into the insatiable maw of time, eroding his pleasure, washing away his joy. Try as he might, Brother was powerless to stem the flow, the precarious happiness seeping away only hours after the outing until all that remained were powdery smudges dotting his furrowed brow.

CHAPTER 1

July 27, Thursday

"Alright ladies, take the field!"

Bobby Gagnon, coach of the Flint Flames of the greater Fall River Women's Softball League, frowned watching "his girls" take their positions. In his forties, a twice-divorced recovering alcoholic, Gagnon still looked like the triple A ballplayer he had once been. While his hair was thinning on top, his wiry, muscular frame looked much as it had in his twenties, thanks to years as a bricklayer.

"Jesus Christ, Peters! Put something into your throw—anything! I haven't seen a rag like that since—

"Souza! The catcher, Souza, the catcher, for Christ's sakes! Her mitt's where it always is, at the end of her goddamn arm!

"That's the way, Gladys—stretch for the throw.

"Wilson! Center field's that way! Atta girl!"

As Gagnon continued yelling, coaxing and browbeating, the occasional compliment thrown in, his eyes scanned the street. Finally, the person for whom he'd been waiting hopped out of a dark green pickup, "J & T Limited" lettered in black and gold on the cab's door. The pickup took off and Bobby turned back to the field, feigning indifference as the latecomer jogged onto the field.

The explosion came as she reached the bench, stooping to tie the laces of her cleats. "Whitman, it's about goddamn time you showed up! I wanta talk to you!"

"Hi, Bobby, nice to see you too." Julia "Juls" Whitman smiled, straightening to her full height, gray-blue eyes regarding him without a hint of consternation. She stood at least six inches taller.

"Where the hell's Mikawski?" Bobby resisted the urge to hop up on the bench to continue his harangue. He didn't much care for women looking down at him.

"Isn't she here?"

"No, and if she doesn't show in five minutes, you're pitching."

"But I—"

"Put a sock in it and start throwin'. I gotta date tonight and we're starting on time for a change. Belles have been warming up for forty-five goddamn minutes."

"Rosie'll be here. She'd never miss a game," Juls called over her shoulder trotting out to the mound.

Fifteen minutes later the game was underway with Juls pitching—still no sign of Rosie Mikawski.

By the third inning, Juls, agitated and distracted, allowed three runs to score, two of them on errors.

Gagnon blew up. "What the hell are you doin' out there, Whitman? Jesus Christ!"

"Watch your language Bob. There are kids watching," called Dan Powers, husband of Ruby, the Flames' second baseman.

Powers's words had little effect. After the next pitch yielded a triple, Bobby charged out to the mound, arms flailing, eyes bulging, curses punctuating the night air.

Juls endured his screaming for several minutes before exploding herself.

"Stop it Bobby! I didn't want to pitch and you knew it! How do you expect me to concentrate when I'm worried about Rosie? This isn't like her. I talked to her this morning and she was psyched for this game. Something's wrong."

"You got that right, and you're it!" Gagnon snarled, worried himself, but unwilling to show it.

"Look, you've had it," he continued, turning toward the outfield. "Mendoza—get your fanny in here, now! And you, get out there where you belong."

"Fine," she mumbled, turning toward left field.

"Juls," he called after her, his voice softer. "She's fine. Forget about it and play ball. We'll go over to her place right after the game, okay?"

He watched Juls's retreat, her long straight back knit with tension. Even in league-issue Orlon, she was just short of gorgeous with those long, thin legs and slender hips. Juls Whitman had commanded his secret admiration since the day he'd volunteered to coach the Flames. Her hair had been long then, tied back in an unruly braid that reached her waist. Shoulder-length now, the auburn hair was tied back in a ponytail that stuck out above the strap adjuster on her cap. With a smile to die for and lips that begged to be kissed, the woman had no idea of her effect on men, least of all middle-aged Bobby Gagnon.

Tuck Potter, Juls's partner in a suburban caretaking business, was a boyhood friend of Bobby's younger brothers. Tuck had coached the Flames for five years, but the business had grown to the point that it was impossible for both partners to be unavailable three or four nights a week during the summer. Tuck had described the team as a "great bunch of ladies" and he had been right. Coaching the Flames had been Bobby's salvation.

Years earlier, the J & T partners had had a brief affair, but nowadays, Tuck described Juls as "one of the guys." It was bullshit, of course, since Bobby knew damn well that Tuck still harbored more than friendly feelings for his partner. Juls had prevailed, however, and she now kept Tuck, and most men, for that matter, at arm's length.

Gagnon hadn't failed to notice the tears rimming his pitcher's eyes and she was right. It wasn't like Mikawski. The Bedford Belles were their biggest rivals and Rosie would never have missed this particular game voluntarily. All the punch knocked out of him, Bobby withdrew to the bench, glumly taking his place alongside his players.

The game dragged on, Juls's dread mounting with each inning. The Belles finally put them out of their misery, burying the Flames under a merciless barrage of hitting. The ump called the game in the seventh, Belles-12, Flames-1, as darkness descended over the Globe Corners field, the headlights of passing cars a distraction the Flames would no longer have to endure.

Juls gathered her things, scanning the crowd. "Where's Tuck?" she asked no one in particular. "He was supposed to pick me up! He should have been here hours ago. The one night I really need him!" She waved at her teammates who were heading for a beer at Archie's across the street.

"Go in and call Mikawski," Gagnon yelled, tossing the equipment bag into his trunk. "If there's no answer and Tucker isn't here by the time you're back, I'll run you over."

"You sure?" Juls asked, dropping her bag at his feet. "What about your date?"

"Screw that. Now get goin'. Give her hell so we can go in and get a goddamn beer to drown our sorrows after this fuckin' game from hell."

"Thanks, Bobby. Watch my stuff, okay? Be right back."

Gagnon threw her bag into the car, then started the engine and pulled the Impala up in front of Archie's. Knowing Rosie Mikawski as well as he did, there was no way he'd be havin' a beer in the foreseeable future.

Two minutes later Juls appeared. "No answer," she said, hopping in. "Let's go."

"You know she's probably all fucked up, three sheets to the wind at the Bluebird right now, don'cha?"

"No way."

Gagnon didn't believe it any more than she did. Softball and her teammates were Rosie's life.

Bobby had spent many evenings with Juls, Tuck and Rosie, drinking, playing cards, enjoying cookouts on the beach, going to concerts, out to dinner. Just last weekend they had all sailed to Nantucket on a friend's boat and camped on the beach, all the men in one tent and Rosie, Juls and two other women in a tent up the beach, giggling all night long.

Mutt and Jeff, he called them. When the two friends walked into a room, one was first struck by the contrasts—Juls's tall, slender beauty, alongside the handsome, but shorter, stockier Rosie. The latter's coal-black curls wild and unkempt, her dark eyes dancing with light, mirrored her personality. Rosie was gregarious, loud and physical in her affections, whereas Juls, although friendly, was quieter, more reserved. Beneath the facades, however, dwelt two kindred spirits, and together, they created a whole, distinct from their individual selves, a palpable warmth radiating from the pair that enveloped all around them in its warm, comforting embrace.

Their easy camaraderie was nearly impossible to resist and people were drawn into their circle of friendship. For Bobby Gagnon—to whom women had always been strange, elusive creatures—the friendship with Juls and Rosie had been a revelation.

The "girls," as Tuck called them, had known each other since grade school, remaining close friends through high school and college despite long periods of separation. Bobby never tired of listening to the stories of their growing-up years. The Whitmans had never approved of Rosie Mikawski from the Flint, but that hadn't mattered a whit to their daughter. During her high school years, Juls was sent away to a boarding school in the Berkshires, while Rosie stayed at home, but the friends wrote, sometimes five or six letters a week, calling as often as they could. Weekends, if Rosie could get away, she'd coerce a friend into driving her up to visit Juls, sneaking her out of the dorm.

As he started down Willett, Bobby began praying. "God make everything be okay," he thought as he pulled the Impala up to park across the street from Rosie's building.

"What?" Juls asked, looking over at him.

Not realizing he'd spoken aloud, he mumbled, "Nothing," adding hoarsely, "Come on. Let's go give her hell."

CHAPTER 2

Dan "Tuck" Potter walked into Archie's Tavern not three minutes after Bobby's Impala rounded the Globe Corner rotary, disappearing from sight. Spying the Flames clustered at their usual tables by the jukebox, he waved, grabbing a beer on his way to join them.

"How'd ya do?"

"We stunk up the field," Karen Ramos replied, her leg slowly extending, pushing an empty chair toward him. A come hither move if he'd ever seen one, and he'd seen most of 'em.

"No?"

"Yup. Lost twelve to one," Ann Greeley said, rising to fetch another round. "It's okay. We have two more shots at 'em. We were missing players. We'll get 'em next time, you wait."

"Gagnon must be a happy camper. Where is the lad anyhow, and for that matter, where's my partner?"

"They've gone to Rosie's. She didn't show for the game, Bobby's pissed and Juls is a basket case."

As Ann prattled on, Karen leaned back in her chair eyeing Potter, her eyes leaving little doubt as to her intentions. The team uniform—baggy on most of the women—fit Karen like a second skin. The top was stretched tight across her ample bosom, nipples clearly visible under the thin white Orlon. Reddish-blond curls—frisky even after three hours shoved under a baseball cap—ringed her heart-shaped face, and her dark eyes danced with mischief. Karen was pretty and she knew it.

She had always had the hots for Tuck, but her interest had never been returned. He barely knew she was alive except when he needed to locate one of his buddies, Juls, Rosie or Bobby. *Fuck him*, she thought. *Not my type anyway, too preppy with all that tousled, sandy hair and sea-blue eyes.* His tan canvas slacks were worn and ripped, but she had to admit, they looked gorgeous on his trim, athletic body. A faded blue work shirt fell loosely over the broad shoulders, and although Karen had never seen what lay beneath the shirt, she could imagine.

"Well, ladies, gotta go. See you at the next game."

He had barely sat down and now he was rushing off, as usual, trailing after Juls. It was always Juls, more like a marriage than a partnership, Karen mused, grabbing his untouched Pabst, calling "thanks" as she turned back to her teammates.

"Phew," Tuck mused as he headed toward the North End, driving at least twenty miles over the speed limit. "Cat's on the prowl tonight," he said aloud, thinking that Karen Ramos was trouble with a capital *T*. He'd just broken up with one bitch and he sure as hell didn't need another.

After Gracie had packed up and left a year and a half ago, Tuck's lady luck had taken a decidedly sour turn until Marcia came into his life. In the beginning, their relationship had been sweet indeed. She was a friend of a friend. They'd hit it off from day one and Marcia had fit right into the gang. Then she moved into the beach house he shared with J & T's office, and things had gone downhill fast. Juls didn't like Marcia, but hell, Juls hadn't liked any of his girlfriends except for crazy Annie from Boston. Juls claimed he only dated bitches, but she and Annie had hit it off from the start until Annie had fallen in love with big Jim and run off to Colorado to run a saloon. They still sent Christmas cards.

He had to admit, Juls was right. He did attract bitches, no doubt about it. As soon as Marcia moved in she started screaming, a continual screech that never let up except when Juls was in the office, which wasn't often. During Marcia's residence, Juls had avoided the office as much as possible. Too much of an effort to be pleasant.

When the whole gang got together, it was easier for his partner to keep her distance, but in the office it was impossible. From day one Marcia insinuated herself into every facet of the business and once she grabbed hold of a project, there was no wresting it away from her. Tuck had initially encouraged his live-in's involvement, but things had quickly gotten out of hand. He smiled, remembering Juls's long overdue explosion after a particularly trying day with Marcia.

"That's it, Tuck! Either she goes or I do! No… that's not right. I'm not going. Marcia is, and you're telling her as soon as she gets back!"

"Telling me what?" Marcia purred, voice smooth as silk as she sauntered in from the kitchen.

Taking in the saucy stroll, the self-satisfied grin—Marcia had a wicked smile—and the haughty flip of her silky blond hair, Juls took a deep breath and let her have it.

"Marcia, I started this business with Tuck almost twelve years ago. It's a good business, we make a decent living, we get along and our customers are happy."

"So what d'ya want, a medal?"

Tuck cringed, fearing he was about to witness a murder.

Juls ignored the sarcasm. "Then you come along and suddenly Mr. Longfield's calling saying you've insulted his wife. We've got dirty units that you were supposed to have had cleaned and we've got a phone bill that's three times what it usually is. Then there's the—"

"Can I get a word in?" Marcia interrupted, her voice squeakier than usual.

"I'm not finished."

"You're just jealous. That's it, isn't it? You can't stand it that Tuck and I are partners now and doing a great job without you!"

Tuck intervened at this juncture. "That's enough Marcia. Juls is right. It's our business, hers and mine, and you've been screwing up. It's my fault. I take the blame for encouraging you to become involved in the first place. Stupid move on my part. Sorry hon, you're gonna hafta bow out. It's not working and if Juls hadn't spoken up, I would have. The Longfields are two of our oldest customers; they've been with us since the beginning. There was no reason for you to treat Janet like that, calling her dog—"

"A fucking guinea pig! I can't believe what I'm hearing! The little rodent bit me, for crying out loud, and all you care about is the old bat and that decrepit husband of hers! What's the matter with you people?"

"What's the matter with us is that J & T is built on goodwill and friendly service, neither of which you seem able to deliver," Juls replied. Her voice had lost its fire, but her cheeks were flushed and blotchy, betraying the anger still smoldering beneath the surface. "And we don't have the money for all these hour-long phone calls to California, New York and wherever else you're always calling."

Jaw set, her face flushed and angry, Marcia glared at the partners standing side by side behind the desk. "Fine, I'm outta here. Screw the both of you and your cozy little partnership. No one could step between you two and live to tell about it anyway! I've been offered a job in New York starting next week, so good riddance!"

"What the—?" Tuck stared at her.

"That's right. I'm leaving Sunday, so you can go back to your pathetically chummy existence."

So, Marcia had departed and Tuck had heard nothing from her and didn't expect to. Something told him that Karen Ramos would make Marcia look like Pollyanna. Best keep his distance from that one. Besides, it wasn't as if he needed lady friends. A coed working for J and T this summer had already caught his eye and if he and Kerry hit it off, the last thing he needed was Karen breathing down his neck.

Marcia had been right about one thing. He and Juls did lead a chummy existence. However, he doubted that Juls had ever been jealous of Marcia or any of his girlfriends. She just didn't have it in her. He had known his partner for nearly fourteen years. She was warm, funny, stubborn, practical in business matters, athletic, compassionate, opinionated, a fiercely loyal friend, a forgiving opponent, a hard worker, a loving daughter and sister, but jealous? Not Juls.

They'd met in Laguna Beach, California, where they were both attending an advanced workshop on the craft of leaded glass construction. Amazed to find fellow Fall Riverites so far from home, they had sought each other out during the workshop, spending their free time together during the six-week course. At the workshop's conclusion, they extended their stay for four weeks, traveling up the coast to Northern California, Washington and Oregon. A brief romantic fling during that trip had ended the day they stepped off the plane in Providence.

While a fierce attraction lingered, by the time they arrived at home, they had decided to go into business together and Juls had insisted romance give way to friendship if they were to work together. By his own admission, Tuck had already dated and discarded more women than he could remember and she wasn't about to start a business only to have it fall prey to his romantic whims. Tuck reluctantly acceded to her wishes, but more than once over the years he had regretted the promise made in the parking lot of Green Airport. He was still very much in love with Juls Whitman.

The past twelve years had been prosperous ones. They'd started with the glass shop, making windows and lamp shades on commission as well as restoring old windows in local churches and the turn-of-the-century Victorian homes of Fall River, Newport and surrounding areas. While the business grew steadily, stained glass was not the booming business on the East Coast that it had been out West. After three years, J & T branched out in another direction, becoming J & T Limited in the process.

Most of their business now was caretaking the summer homes, condominiums and multimillion-dollar beach houses of Windy Harbor, a wealthy summer enclave fifteen minutes southeast of Fall River. The tiny coastal town had grown by leaps and bounds over the last twelve years as farmers sold out for millions to the affluent New Yorkers and Bostonians voraciously gobbling up the last stretches of virgin coastline. A sleepy little fishing and farming village for many generations, Windy

Harbor had finally been discovered. Like it or not, the locals had had to adapt and many did not do so graciously.

The hostility of Windy Harbor's natives had in fact been largely responsible for the initial success of J & T. Snubbed and shunned by their neighbors, the Harbor's newest residents had had nowhere to turn for help and services until Juls and Tuck appeared on the scene. With open arms and friendly smiles, the partners catered to their clients' every whim with efficiency and discretion. J & T looked after clients' properties in winter and summer, handling all rental agreements and arranging to have services—water, phone, electricity, trash collection and so forth—resumed or terminated with the changing seasons.

Having spent the better part of his adult life in the Harbor, Tuck knew the plumbers, electricians, carpenters, painters and various other service-oriented people. One room in his weathered shingled beach house served as J & T's office. Thad Potter, Tuck's father, had been left the house by a maiden aunt. Since the elder Potter refused to leave the Fall River home where Tuck and his brothers had grown up, when Tuck had approached him about starting the business, he had been only too happy to deed it over. Juls's house was ten miles away in Tiverton, Rhode Island, just outside the Fall River city limits.

The partners took excellent care of their clients, running errands, searching for missing pets, investigating petty thefts—trash barrels and mail boxes were the most frequent targets—arranging for cleaning services, planning parties—or hiring caterers—and helping to arrange for clients' memberships in the area's yacht, golf and beach clubs and Windy Harbor's Ladies Literary Society, the most exclusive and selective of the all the "clubs." While not always successful in wheedling memberships for the newcomers into the Harbor's closed societies, the partners endeavored, if unsuccessful, to soothe bruised egos by suggesting alternative activities for their wealthy clients, many of whom had never heard the word no until they moved to Windy Harbor.

Business had grown so much that J & T now had a waiting list and while there were two rival companies proffering the same type of service, J & T was still the "agency of choice" for those lucky enough to "get on the list." Not a bad way to make a living if you liked people, and both partners did. Marcia had not and it showed.

As he turned onto Rosie's street, Tuck spied the Impala and pulled up, parking behind it. Brushing thoughts of Marcia and Karen aside, he wondered what had been important enough to keep Rosie from the game. She lived and died for softball. Slamming the door, he cursed under his breath, angry at himself for missing Juls at the field. "Damn the Willises and their fucked-up lawn sprinkler!"

His heart—already in his throat after taking the front steps two at a time—nearly stopped as the first of Juls's screams pierced the stillness of the night.

CHAPTER 3

Racing up the stairs, Bobby puffing along in her wake, Juls reached the third floor in seconds. Rosie's unit was at the end of the hall, number sixteen.

The building was over eighty years old, but Gladys Kenney, the owner kept it in immaculate condition. The plaster walls had recently been whitewashed and at the far end of each hallway, window seats had been built in, green-and-white awning-striped cushions inviting passersby to linger. Despite its pristine appearance, the building was still in the heart of the roughest part of the city. In an effort to thwart thieves who continually absconded with her framed prints, Gladys had decoupaged fine arts posters along the corridor's walls. Wall sconces bolted to the walls bathed the passageway in soft light, the overall effect one of peaceful serenity.

After several minutes with her finger pressed to the buzzer, Juls went to the window seat, rummaging under the seat cushion to find the key Rosie kept hidden there. "Shit! Why won't this work?" she cried, jabbing the key in, turning to the left and right. The lock refused to budge.

Hand on her shoulder, Bobby reached from behind. "Here, let me try, babe."

"I'll get it," she said, shrugging his hand off. "It just…takes a minute to… there, finally!"

She flipped the light switch by the door as they stepped into the living room, into the warm inviting space where they had spent so many evenings drinking, watching movies, playing cards, talking and laughing together. Tonight the room smelled musty, the air close and still and she wondered why all the windows were closed on such a warm summer night.

Rosie collected Native American and Mexican textiles and favored the stark lines of the mission style in her furnishings. All of her pieces were reproductions of Gustaf Stickley designs, well-made, handsome and sturdy like the woman herself. Hanging from the cream-colored walls were three Navaho rugs in bold patterns of red, gray and black. The floor was covered in gray wall-to-wall carpeting, clean and new like the rest of the building. Another large Navaho rug lay across its center, the same reds and grays slashed through it in a chevron pattern.

The large, comfortable sofa was flanked by two matching armchairs, all three pieces covered in off-white cotton duck, a number bright woven throw pillows echoing the colors of the rugs. Rosie's pride and joy stood in front of the sofa—a massive oak coffee table, also in the mission style, built by Rosie herself in a woodworking class at the local community college.

The morning papers were scattered across the table's polished surface and Rosie's body lay at its far end. She was dead, no question about that. The body sprawled half in the living room, half in the bedroom, legs twisted back at unnatural angles, naked except for gray athletic socks, which Juls recognized as her own, loaned to her friend several weeks earlier. Black curls obscured the face and aside from a few scratches here and there, her body appeared untouched, white and smooth in its deathly pallor.

Her good arm lay at her side, the scarred left arm—burned in a childhood accident—tucked beneath her. There was quite a lot of blood pooled beside the body that appeared to have come from her underside, and pieces of a jigsaw puzzle were scattered around the floor, some floating in the blood like tiny amoebae.

Juls screamed, rushing to her friend's side. As she began to claw at the smooth white rope still wrapped around Rosie's neck, Bobby roused himself and leapt forward to yank her back. "Juls, stop it. We can't touch her!"

As he pulled her away, Juls let go and the movement caused the body to roll toward them, leaving the severed left arm on the floor behind her. Her arm had been amputated at the shoulder.

"Jesus," he whispered as Juls screamed again and began to shake.

"Oh my God, oh my God," she mumbled over and over as he dragged her toward the kitchen phone.

As she struggled, lunging toward her friend, he tightened his grip. "Cut it out, Juls. Come on now, for God's sake, we can't touch her. We've gotta call the police. They need to see her just as she is. You can't help her, babe. She's gone. Now come on."

He reached the phone just as Tuck burst through the door. Juls crumpled into her partner's arms and Bobby turned away as the police dispatcher answered at the other end of the line.

The next few hours were a blur. The three sat huddled on the sofa as the police went over the apartment, occasionally pausing to ask questions. Cameras flashing, their voices hushed and somber, a small army of men collected samples, searched through drawers and closets going over every inch of the three rooms. Occasionally neighbors peeked their heads in and were led to the window seat in the hall where an officer waited to take their statements.

"Make them stop," Juls moaned, almost incoherent as the hour approached midnight. "Rosie hated having her picture taken. Please, Tuck, please make them stop." In her Flames uniform covered with grass stains, blood and dirt, she looked like a small child inconsolable after falling off her bike and skinning her knee.

Tuck drew her to him. "Hush now, Rosie's past caring. How much longer, Officer?" he called to Jack Mederois, the homicide detective in charge.

"They'll be taking her out in about five minutes. I have just a couple of questions for Ms. Whitman. Then you folks can take off."

True to his word, not five minutes later the photographers packed up their gear and Rosie's draped body was carried out on a stretcher. As his officers began sealing the crime scene, Mederois came to sit beside them.

"Where will they take her?" Juls asked.

"City morgue first. We'll have to keep her a few days. Then we'll contact the family and see about the funeral home and all."

"There is no family, just me."

"Well then, Ms. Whitman, we'll let you know when you can have her collected and—"

"Oh God, who would do this?"

"We were kinda a hopin' you might give us a hint. Someone with a grudge? Ex-boyfriends, disgruntled coworkers, whatever? Or someone new she just recently met?"

"There's no one like that. Everyone loved Rosie. No one who knew her would hurt her."

"How 'bout someone she might've met recently? A new boyfriend, maybe?"

"None that I know of."

"Do you guys know what Ms. Mikawski was doing today, someone she might've been seeing? Mr. Gagnon says you unlocked the door and there are no signs of forced entry. No broken windows, jimmied locks, what have you. Seems like she must've known the guy. Had to have let him in."

"I don't know what she was doing today except for the game. Softball. We play on a team and we had a game tonight."

"So I see. What time was that?"

"Five."

"She was long gone by then, I'm 'fraid. Preliminary exam puts time of death around one, two, somethin' like that."

"Oh, God, the whole time we were playing, Rosie was lying here." Juls crumpled against Tuck, fresh sobs wracking her slender frame.

"Okay, baby," Tuck whispered, holding her tighter as if his grip might somehow stop the trembling.

"I know this is tough, Ms. Whitman. Just a couple more questions, please. What can you tell me about her arm? Was she able to use it? The scarred one, I mean?"

"Yes." She sniffled, regarding him. "Sometimes it stiffened up in the cold, got tingly at unexpected times, things like that, but it was only a scar. It happened when she was four. A kettle of hot water spilled on her. Her family always called it an accident, but her father was a drunk. Rosie had no memory of it. Why?"

"Just curious. She's a big woman, strong, I mean. Seems like the type who'd put up a fight, but there's no sign of a struggle and I just wondered if maybe one arm was weaker than—"

"How did she die? I mean, was she—"

"Strangled. That white rope around her neck, guy brought it with him."

"And her arm?" Tuck asked.

"Happened after she was dead. Thank God for that, at least." Mederois studied Juls, aware that she was fading fast, withdrawing into herself, unaware of her surroundings. He turned to Tuck. "How 'bout the apartment? Was your friend in the habit of leaving the door unlocked?"

"Never," Juls answered for him. "I'm sorry, but I have to know. Was she…? I mean, she was naked, so was she—"

"Raped? Doesn't look like it, but we won't know for certain until forensics gets through with her."

Juls moaned.

Tuck gripped her tighter. "Look Detective, we're gonna split, okay? She needs to get outta here."

"Sure thing. I'm sorry, Ms. Whitman, about your friend and all, and about keepin' you so late. Let's leave it for now and we'll talk in the morning."

He rose, joining his men, a few of whom were still collecting their gear. "Oh," he called back over his shoulder. "One more thing—did Ms. Mikawski like jigsaw puzzles? I mean, would she have been working on one do you s'pose?"

"Not that I'm aware of. I didn't even know she owned any jigsaw puzzles," Juls said, looking to Tuck for confirmation. He nodded at Mederois.

"I thought not."

"How's that?" Tuck asked.

"Can't be sure till we check a little further, but, well, we've seen this type of thing before."

"Jesus, a serial killer!" Bobby cried, instantly regretting his words.

Juls's face, red and blotchy from crying, froze in horror.

"We don't know that, Mr. Gagnon. There are similarities to other cases, but we'll have to look further. Let's not go spreadin' stuff like that around, okay?"

"Oh God," Juls moaned as the two men half carried, half dragged her from the apartment. They drove her home.

Several shots of brandy and two sleeping pills borrowed from a neighbor and Juls settled down on tear-soaked pillow, a drugged, fretful sleep finally overtaking her. Tuck slept beside her bed in the chaise, Bobby on the living room floor.

ABOUT THE AUTHOR

M. Lee Prescott is the author of dozens of works of fiction for adults, young adults, and children, among them *A Friend of Silence, In the Name of Silence* and *The Silence of Memory* (**Roger and Bess Mysteries**), *Jigsaw, Song of the Spirit*, her contemporary romance series, **Morgan's Run Romances,** and finally the **Ricky Steele Mysteries-- *Prepped to Kill, Gadfly,*** and *Lost in Spindle City,* of which *Poof!* is the fourth! Three of her nonfiction titles have been published by Heinemann, and she has published numerous articles in the field of literacy education. Lee is a professor of education at a small New England liberal arts college, where she teaches reading and writing pedagogy. Her current research focuses on mindfulness and connections to reading and writing. She regularly teaches abroad, most recently in Singapore.

Lee has lived in southern California (loved those Laguna nights!), Chapel Hill, North Carolina, and various spots in Massachusetts and Rhode Island. Currently she resides in Massachusetts on a beautiful river, where she canoes, swims, and watches an incredible variety of wildlife pass by. She is the mother of two grown sons and spends lots of time with them, their beautiful wives, and her amazing grandchildren. When not teaching or writing, Lee's passions revolve around family, yoga (Kripalu is a second home), swimming, sharing mindfulness with children and adults, and walking.

Lee loves to hear from readers. Email her at mleeprescott@gmail.com, and visit her website to hear the latest and sign up for her newsletters!

AUTHOR WEBPAGE AND NEWSLETTER SIGN-UP:
www.mleeprescott.com

Follow me on BookBub:
www.bookbub.com/authors/m-lee-prescott

A Note from the Author

I am thrilled to bring you Ricky's newest caper. Thank you so much for reading it. It's darker than the previous books, its content deeply disturbing. I put the manuscript down many times over the past two years, not having the stomach to continue, but finally persevered to complete the book.. The sad reality is that child trafficking is rampant in today's world. There are millions of children worldwide who suffer unspeakable horrors, robbed of their childhood and often their lives. This is one story among thousands.

If you like **Poof!** and would be willing to write an Amazon review, I would be so very grateful. If you would like to sign up for future book releases and occasional notices about my books, please visit my Author Website and sign up for my newsletter. I promise I will not share your address, nor will I flood you with emails. Do visit my website to read more about my books and to hear what's next.

Finally, this book has been revised, proofed, and edited many, many times, but my intrepid assistants and I are human, so if you spot a typo, please email me at mleeprescott@gmail.com and I will fix it. I also love to hear from readers so email me anytime! If you'd like to know more about my other books, please scroll ahead to the next section where all my books are listed.

Warm wishes,
M. Lee

OTHER TITLES BY M. LEE PRESCOTT

Contemporary romances and mysteries by M. Lee Prescott include:

The Ricky Steele Mysteries

Book 1: Prepped to Kill

Book 2: Gadfly

Book 3: Lost in Spindle City

Book 4: Poof!

Also featuring Ricky Steele:

Jigsaw

Roger and Bess Mysteries

Book 1: A Friend of Silence

Book 2: In the Name of Silence

Book 3: The Silence of Memory

Contemporary Romances
Well-Loved Romances

Widow's Island

Hestor's Way

Morgan's Run Romances

Book 1: Emma's Dream

Book 2: Lang's Return

Book 3: Jeb's Promise

Book 4: Rose's Choice

Book 5: Hope's Wonder

Book 6: Ruthie's Love

Young Adult Historical Romance

Song of the Spirit